"With complex [characters], [plenty of hot/sexy sex scenes,] a strong story arc, and fast-paced writing, Bardsley cements her position as a solid author of complex, funny, and satisfyingly relatable paranormal romance." —*Publishers Weekly*

"*Must Love Lycans* is a must read for anyone who loves sexy werewolves, spunky heroines, and hilarious situations."
—Fresh Fiction

"A fabulous, joyful, and often laugh-out-loud trip to Broken Heart." —Smexy Books Romance Reviews

"Ms. Bardsley has penned a fun novel with an emotional heart." —Love to Read for Fun

"Laugh-out-loud funny and filled with action and plenty of sensual heat, *Must Love Lycans* is a worthy addition to the series and it will be residing on my keeper shelf with the rest of the Broken Heart crew." —The Romance Dish

Cross Your Heart

"Bardsley's gift for humor and passion is a reader's delight. Her newest hero is a sexy and irreverent charmer. . . . If you're in need of a mood elevator, this is just what the doctor ordered!" —*Romantic Times*

"This story more than keeps the action flowing. Off-the-wall humor, mystery, and a touch of danger add extra zing to Bardsley's latest paranormal, and fans will be delighted."
—*Library Journal*

"Another grab-you-by-the-throat, laugh-out-loud addition to the Broken Heart series. . . . If you thought the inhabitants of Broken Heart were up against some crazy evil before, you haven't seen anything yet." —Fresh Fiction

"Bardsley never ceases to amaze us with her suspense and quick-witted humor. Add in on top of that the attention to detail and the hot, sizzling romance and you will fall in love with this series." —Night Owl Romance

continued . . .

Come Hell or High Water

"The action and humor are bountiful. Tremendous fun as always!" —*Romantic Times* (4½ stars)

"If you are new to the series or a frequent visitor to the paranormal haven in Oklahoma, this is a fun read."
—The Romance Studio

"I love paranormal novels and I believe that Michele Bardsley's Broken Heart series are some of the best there are."
—Fresh Fiction

"Bardsley has brought us another amazing story . . . [with] endless wit and humor. As always, I will add this to my ever-growing keeper shelf to read over and over again."
—Night Owl Romance

Over My Dead Body

"Combining humor with romance and a serial killer mystery, the return to the center of vampire activity . . . is a fun lighthearted tale." —The Best Reviews

"I fell into this story hook, line, and sinker. I just couldn't put it down. . . . It has everything to bring a smile to your face: vampires, werewolves, pixies, dragons, and more."
—*Publishers Weekly*

"Clever, action-packed, and sensual, *Over My Dead Body* is a helluva page turner that's not to be missed!"
— Romance Novel TV

"A great paranormal romance that I would definitely recommend to readers who enjoy a fast-paced story that will leave them guessing until the end." —Fresh Fiction

Wait Till Your Vampire Gets Home

"Has action aplenty and a free-spirited, wittily sarcastic heroine who will delight fans." —*Booklist*

"Bardsley has one of the most entertaining series on the market. The humor and wackiness keep hitting the sweet spot. Add Bardsley to your auto-buy list!"
—*Romantic Times* (top pick, 4½ stars)

"Michele Bardsley's latest installment in the Broken Heart series is just as hard to put down as the ones before."
—Bitten by Books

Because Your Vampire Said So

"Lively, sexy, out-of-this-world—as well as in it—fun! Michele Bardsley's vampire stories rock!"
—*New York Times* bestselling author Carly Phillips

"Five ribbons! I laughed nonstop from beginning to end. . . . If I could, I'd give this story a higher rating. Five ribbons just doesn't seem to be enough for this wonderful story!"
—Romance Junkies

"Another Broken Heart denizen is here in this newest, hysterically funny first-person romp. The combination of sexy humor, sarcastic wit, and paranormal trauma is unmistakably Bardsley. Grab the popcorn and settle in for a seriously good time!"
—*Romantic Times*

Don't Talk Back to Your Vampire

"Cutting-edge humor and a raw, seductive hero make *Don't Talk Back to Your Vampire* a yummylicious treat!"
—Dakota Cassidy, author of *Burning Down the Spouse*

"A fabulous combination of vampire lore, parental angst, romance, and mystery. I loved this book!"
—Jackie Kessler, author of *Hotter than Hell*

"All I can say is *wow*! I was totally immersed in this story to the point that I tuned everything and everybody out the whole entire evening. Now, that's what I call a good book. Michele can't write the next one fast enough for me!"   —The Best Reviews

"A winning follow-up to *I'm the Vampire, That's Why* filled with humor, supernatural romance, and truly evil villains."
—*Booklist*

I'm the Vampire, That's Why

"From the first sentence, Michele grabbed me and didn't let me go! A vampire mom? PTA meetings? A sulky teenager? Throw in a gorgeous, ridiculously hot hero and you've got the paranormal romance of the year. Get this one *now*."
—MaryJanice Davidson

"Hot, hilarious, one helluva ride . . . Michele Bardsley weaves a sexily delicious tale spun from the heart."   —L. A. Banks

"Michele Bardsley has penned the funniest, quirkiest, coolest vampire tale you'll ever read. It's hot and funny and sad and wonderful, the kind of story you can't put down and won't forget. Definitely one for the keeper shelf."   —Kate Douglas

Only Lycans Need Apply

A Broken Heart Novel

MICHELE BARDSLEY

A SIGNET ECLIPSE BOOK

SIGNET ECLIPSE
Published by the Penguin Group
Penguin Group (USA) Inc., 375 Hudson Street,
New York, New York 10014, USA

USA / Canada / UK / Ireland / Australia / New Zealand / India / South Africa / China

Penguin Books Ltd., Registered Offices: 80 Strand, London WC2R 0RL, England
For more information about the Penguin Group visit penguin.com.

First published by Signet Eclipse, an imprint of New American Library,
a division of Penguin Group (USA) Inc.

First Printing, April 2013

SIGNET ECLIPSE and logo are trademarks of Penguin Group (USA) Inc.

ISBN 978-0-451-23777-4

Printed in the United States of America
10 9 8 7 6 5 4 3 2 1

ALWAYS LEARNING   PEARSON

To my Viking,
I love you!

To Kerry, Jesse, and Team NAL,
thank you, thank you, thank you!

And to Stephanie Kip Rostan,
you really are Agent Awesome. I heart you so much!

And also, this is for Nia Shay (http://cheznia.com), because
she is the inspiration for Dove.

ACKNOWLEDGMENTS

All hail the Viking, who is the best hand-holding, pep-talking, hug-giving, praise-delivering man *ever*. Thank you for all that you do, babe. I love you.

Stephanie Kip Rostan, Monika Verma, and everyone at Levine Greenberg Literary Agency are worth their weights in gold. And chocolate. And awesomeness.

I owe a lifetime supply of warm, fuzzy hugs (and booze, lots of booze) to Kerry Donovan, Jesse Feldman, and all those stalwart, patient souls who work on Team NAL. Thank you, thank you, and . . . thank you!

I also wanted to mention Wendy Bocock. Because Wendy Bocock (who is not named Jennifer, in case you were wondering . . . and I called her that forever because I really did think she and Mindy Fletcher and Amanda Fenley were all named Jennifer), Mindy and Amanda and Stephanie and the real Jennifer and Kelley Hartsell and Felicia Sparks are made of awesome, especially when imbibing booze at a Greek restaurant. We tend to scare the other patrons there every time with our conversations, which inevitably turn to erotica. Heh. Oh, and I just wanted to say again . . . WENDY BOCOCK.

I heart my Minions! Thank you to everyone who is on my list and on my social networks. And thank you to all the readers who take the time to e-mail me. I read all my e-mails, every single one, and even though I cannot respond to them all, please know your stories, your comments, your criticisms, and your praise are all consumed with appreciation. I get to write because you continue to read my work . . . and I'm very grateful for the opportunity to keep telling stories!

Honestly, I think the world's going to end bloody. But it doesn't mean we shouldn't fight. We do have choices. I choose to go down swingin'.

—Dean Winchester, "Jus in Bello"

Ruadan the First

Once there was a great warrior-magician whose name was Ruadan. He was the son of magician-healer Brigid and warrior-prince Bres.

Many believed Bres would bring peace to the troubled nations of Fomhoire and Tuatha de Danann. When he became of age, he married Brigid to cement his bond with the Tuatha de Danann. In time, he was made king of Eire.

But Bres was a foolish ruler, ignorant of his people's suffering and unjust in his judgments. The sons of Tuatha de Danann rose up against him and took his crown, banishing him. In defeat, Bres returned to his father's kingdom.

Bres was too prideful to turn away from the dishonor shown to him by the Tuatha de Danann, no matter how well deserved. He vowed to take back what had been taken from him and to once again rule Eire.

Brigid wanted peace. Without her husband's knowledge, she sought her mother's counsel. The Morrigu foresaw the future and told her daughter the truth: The Tuatha de Danann would triumph over the Fomhoire, but not before Brigid lost her husband and their sons, Ruadan, Iuchar, and Uar.

The Tuatha de Danann had a magical well that instantly healed their warriors so long as they had not suffered a mortal blow. Created by a goldsmith named Goibniu, the well was safeguarded by spells and men alike. "Kill the builder of the well," said Bres to his sons, "and destroy its magic . . . and the Tuatha de Danann will fall."

So it came to pass that Ruadan's wife, Aine, bore twin boys, Padriag and Lorcan. Satisfied that his family was safe, Ruadan and his brothers sailed to the Isle of Eire to fulfill his father's plan.

The brothers used stealth and cunning to break through the defenses of their enemy. While Iuchar and Uar battled those that guarded the well, Ruadan stabbed Goibniu with the fae swords. But Goibniu, though mortally wounded, thrust his spear into Ruadan's chest and felled the warrior.

Near death, Ruadan arrived in his homeland and was taken to his mother. She used all her magic and healing arts, but could not save her son. The very same night that Ruadan breathed his last, Brigid received word of the deaths of Iuchar and Uar. She fell to her knees and wailed with such sorrow that anyone who heard the sounds knew a mother's heart had been torn from her.

Morrigu heard the keening of her daughter, so she turned into a crow and flew to the land of the Fomhoire. Though the dark queen craved chaos over tranquillity and war over peace, she felt pity for her daughter and offered one chance for Brigid to regain her son.

"Give Ruadan a cup of my blood, but be warned! When he awakes, he will not live as a man, but as a *deamhan fola*. He will never again walk in the light. He will not consume food or drink, but shall siphon the blood of the living. Neither will he have breath nor beat of heart. Never will he sire another child by his own seed."

"Is there no good to be wrought, then, Mother?"

"Where there is dark, there is also light. Ruadan will never age. He will heal from even the most grievous of wounds. He will know the thoughts of those he loves. And he will be a warrior none can defeat. He is of the Fomhoire and of the Tuatha de Danann, and those skills and magic will always be his to wield."

So blinded by grief was Brigid, so badly did she want her son to live again, that she agreed to her mother's terms. But still Morrigu was not satisfied.

"Should Ruadan drain a man and replenish him with tainted blood, he shall Turn. Your son will create others and he will rule a master race long after all the ones you know and love turn to dust and ash. Even knowing this, will you still give him my blood to drink?"

And again Brigid agreed without hesitation. Morrigu cut her wrist and bled into a silver goblet. Brigid lifted her son's head, opened his mouth, and poured every drop of her mother's blood into him.

When Ruadan awoke, he was *deamhan fola*.

Bres, devastated by the loss of his sons, went himself to the Isle of Eire to wreak vengeance on his enemy, but he, too, was killed. Finally, the Tuatha de Danann triumphed over the Fomhoire, and there came to pass an uneasy peace between their peoples.

But Aine was frightened of the creature her husband had become and she refuted him, calling him demon and eater of flesh. He wished only happiness for his family, and so he bartered with Aine. If she returned with his mother to the Isle of Eire and raised their sons as Tuatha de Danann, he would leave them alone.

For twenty-five years, Ruadan wandered the world. He made six others of his kind. And then, because he longed to see his sons, Ruadan broke his promise. He visited his twin boys—and both were killed. He turned them into *deamhan fola*, and together, they left the Isle of Eire.

Ruadan summoned his first six *deamhan fola* to a meeting, and they created the Council of Ancients. They labored to create laws for their people and bound all *deamhan fola* with magic and oath to uphold these laws. Those who broke faith with their Families faced banishment . . . or death.

And so it was that Brigid's son fulfilled her mother's prophecy.

He was the creator of the *deamhan fola*.

He was ruler over all.

He was Ruadan the First.

Legends of the Lycans

It is said that the Moon Goddess wanted children, so she took her wolf form and mated with an alpha named Tark.

She gave birth to twins. The firstborn was a wolf of black. And the second, a wolf of gray. Her older son had the ability to turn from human to wolf. However, her second-born could assume his wolf nature only on the night of the full moon.

The Moon Goddess's sons grew up, and soon they wanted wives and families. The Goddess offered her firstborn a beautiful female wolf, which she gave the ability to shift into human form. To her second-born, the Goddess gave a beautiful female human. Since her son assumed his wolf form only during the full moon, she gave his mate the same ability.

And so some lycanthropes are full-bloods, shifting whenever they need to, and others are like the Roma, shifting only on the full moon.

This is the story told for generations from father to son, mother to daughter, of the lycanthrope heritage.

It is, however, a lie.

We must also consider the unexpected branch of the lycanthrope family tree: the *loup de sang*.

In 1807 a small group of *loup-garou* emigrated from France to the town of Vincennes, the capital city in Indian Territory. Among the newest arrivals was the widow Chantelle Marchand, who was eight months pregnant. She made the long, treacherous journey to the United States to join the pack of her father, Jacques Marchand.

Not long after Chantelle arrived, a territorial dispute erupted between the *loup-garou* and the *deamhan fola*— vampires. The pregnant widow was among the casualties of a short but brutal skirmish. Unfortunately, the vampire who killed her also tried to Turn her.

As she lay dying, she delivered triplets: the first was a son, Gabriel, then a girl, Anise, and another son, Ren—all with the same strange condition. They were alive, but could gain nourishment only from blood. Gabriel was given to a lycan outcast. Anise and Ren were sent to live among the Vedere psychics.

Jacques Marchand's grandchildren were the first-ever blood-drinking lycanthropes, and it was he who coined the term *loup de sang*. However, in his diary, he wrote about only the birth of Gabriel. He never mentioned Gabriel's siblings.

So, for reasons unknown, Marchand lied, too.

Then, years ago, when renowned prophet Astria Vedere was still very young, she made a prophecy:

"A vampire queen shall come forth from the place of broken hearts. The seven powers of the Ancients will be hers to command. She shall bind with the outcast, and with this union, she will save the dual-natured. With her consort, she will rule vampires and lycanthropes as one."

Alas, this, too, is a lie.

Well . . . sorta.

None of these tales includes a whisper about the only known royal lycans—the triplet princes of all werewolves who are neither full-bloods nor Roma nor *loup de sang.*

The story of their origin is not a lie.

It's a secret.

Author's note: If you want to know the secret, then all you have to do is read *Must Love Lycans.* If you have, then please keep reading. If you haven't, you can do that now. Don't worry. I'll wait.

Prologue

From the journal of Ezra Jameson . . .
July 28, 1978

Regina has been in labor for more than thirty-six hours. My only child suffers, and refuses any medication or other comforts to help her birth the baby. She has refused to say anything about the father, or about the circumstances of her pregnancy. Three months ago, she returned from her yearlong expedition in a remote area of China—obviously pregnant. The discovery of a temple said to be the place Confucius's mother met the Ki-lin had been too much for my daughter to resist.

We could not dissuade her. Her whole life has revolved around the mythos of unicorns. She's been obsessed since she was a little girl—from the time she claimed to see one standing at the edge of our back-yard, its horn glinting in the moonlight.

We tried to convince her that she'd had a vivid dream, yet even at that young age she could not be convinced that what she had seen was anything but real. Despite my wife's concerns, I indulged Regina's requests to use money and resources for her research trips because I could not tell her the truth. And I could only hope she did not discover it.

Regina had just started teaching classes and learning the ropes of being the college's benefactor. Our family had started the institution and it would always be our duty to take care of it. Then word was sent from a colleague about the China expedition. The temple of Ki-lin had been found.

We tried to talk her out of it, but, of course, she insisted on going. And my dear wife was beside herself. In the end, we could do nothing to dissuade our daughter from her mission.

When Regina returned from China, she was . . . grieving. Listless. Depressed. As though her heart had borne some terrible tragedy. My wife and I cannot fathom this change in our daughter. It's almost as if her inner light has been extinguished. She refused to leave her room, though she at least took care of herself and ate the meals brought to her.

When the labor pains began, she requested the presence of Ruadan. Though I have been friends with him for many years—from that extraordinary moment when

we met in the deserts of the Sudan during my first expedition to find Set's temple—I have never called upon
him for help.

Now my daughter suffers and refuses to see me or
her mother.

Ruadan remains in Regina's room, helping bring my
grandchild into the world.

The screaming is bearable.

It is her weeping that breaks my heart.

Chapter 1

Moira

"**F**uck, it's hot," I complained as I slipped through the tent flap. I took off my broad-brimmed straw hat and slapped it against my hip. Dust puffed into the thick air. Whew. It was probably two degrees cooler inside, and only then because of the single wobbly electric fan running at full power.

I looked at my assistant, Dove. She sat cross-legged on her cot, making notes and sketching some of our recent finds. She was a slight young thing with a severe haircut that highlighted the kind of face that belonged on either a heroin addict or a supermodel. She was cranky as hell, unrepentant about her bad attitude, and probably the most saturnine person alive. I found her two years ago. Well, I found her scholarship application in a mountainous discard pile. She'd been slated for a rejection letter, but after I read her app and her essay, I told the scholarship committee to reconsider her application. And by "reconsider," I really meant "accept that magnificent bitch as a student or die at my hands."

I tended to get what I wanted.

I stared at Dove, who was ignoring the hell out of me. "Did I not give an inspiring lecture last night about saving our solar-powered fuel cells?"

"Absolutely riveting, Moira," she agreed in her patented monotone. Her sarcasm was so well honed you were bleeding before you knew you'd been cut. "When the sun burns out in a billion years, I'm sure we will all thank you for inspiring us to save every drop of sunshine possible."

I rolled my eyes. "Ax said you needed something. Otherwise, I need to get back to sweltering while I dust sand off three-thousand-year-old pottery."

She peeked at me through the hair angled across her face. "There's something weird about one of the *ushabtis* you found." She picked up the little clay statue lying next to her and handed it to me. "It has fangs."

I stared at the figure. She was right. The *ushabti's* face was delicately carved, an ornate, beautiful piece, and yep, those were definitely fangs jutting from the dude's mouth. "Okay. It's weird, but . . . well, you know, those crazy ancient Egyptians." I did a frenetic version of "jazz hands" to indicate super-crazy.

Dove arched one brow. "Read the glyphs," she said.

If I hadn't known any better, I'd have said that Dove sounded freaked out. Um, what? She never got freaked out.

I peered at the symbols carved around the base of the statue. " 'Whom he finds in his way, him he devours bit by bit.' "

"That's from 'The Cannibal Hymn,' " said Dove.

I shrugged. "It's not exactly uncommon to see it echoed in royal burials after Pharaoh Unis."

"And the fangs were put there to reinforce the point?"

"Maybe this is a tribute to Sekhmet. She was the known blood drinker in the ancient Egyptian pantheon."

"Then why doesn't it have a lioness head? Or the sun disk?" Dove put a finger on each side of her mouth to emulate fangs. "If it was Kali, it would make sense."

"Sure. Because finding the effigy of an Indian goddess here would be oh so logical." I handed her the *ushabti*. "It's interesting and rare, so lock it up."

"Okay, fine." Dove sucked in a breath. "I'm just gonna say it. 'Cause it has to be said."

Her serious tone gave me pause. "All right, then. Sing it, sister."

"Vampires."

I stared at her. She stared back. Dove wasn't a chickenshit, I'd give her that. Do you how many grad students quaked at the mere sight of me? Or how many members of the college administration mapped out their routes so they wouldn't chance running into me on campus? *Mwuhahahaha*. Dove could care less if I terrified lesser mortals. She had never cowered before me. Not even when I was the only person standing between her and a full ride to one of the most prestigious private colleges in the United States. Dove was Dove no matter what. She didn't allow people or rules or stupidity to dictate her behavior. She was a noble, cantankerous soul, and a rare human being—nearly as rare as a vampire *ushabti* found in a desert wasteland.

I sighed in mock disappointment. "Dove, Dove, Dove. Oh, sweet little Dove. I liked you better when you were a cynical realist."

"Don't make me kill you," she responded. "You're the only human I can actually stand to be around for more than five minutes."

"Aw. I'm all twitterpated now."

"Bambi references are a death sentence," she intoned.

I knew that. I also know that the only time Dove had ever been known to cry was when Bambi's mother bit it in the forest.

"An ancient Egyptian vampire cult," she went on stoically, as though she hadn't threatened to end my existence twice in the last sixty seconds. "Maybe they worshiped Sekhmet, but they also thought they'd come to back to this world. *Maybe* when they died, they all had little fanged *ushabtis* put in their burial chambers so that their *ka* would be undead."

Because I respected Dove, I studied the *ushabti* and thought about her theory. *Un*dead *ka*? Hmm. Well, that was certainly an out-of-the-box hypothesis. I glanced at her. "You've thought a lot about this."

"Either I think up outrageous, but possibly true theories or I stare at the sand while my sanity slips away."

"I love it when you alliterate." I handed the statue to Dove. For once, she looked like the young grad student she was, the way they all looked before mundane work, hostile environments, and hard-to-please, egomaniacal archaeologists (that would be me) stomped all over their hopes and dreams. Honestly, this version of Dove was far more disturbing than the mouthy brat who tried my patience forty-two times before breakfast. I forgot sometimes that she was vulnerable. She was broken, much like I was, and broken people viewed the world differently. Our perspective was jagged, like trying to watch a sunset in the shards of a mirror. Reflected beauty had sharp edges. "Tell you what. Go back over the *ushabti*s we've found so far. If you find any more fanged ones, or anything else that supports a Sekhmet blood-drinking cult, we'll talk about your theory again."

"Fair," she said. Then she stood up, clutching the *ushabti* like it might try to leap out of her hands. She eyed me with the hostility I'd come to know and love. "Don't you have pottery to dust?"

"Shut up."

*　　*　　*

Ax was the best campfire cook, and he was punished for it nightly by having to make delicious meals for all of us (his cooking tasted good even with the sand that got in it—sand got into everything). I enjoyed tormenting my grad students, so I made them clean up. Again. Hey, at least I didn't laugh maniacally while wielding a cat-o'-nine-tails.

I only did that on Tuesdays.

I was sitting on a canvas chair staring at the fire. Already the heat of the day was giving way to the chill of night. Ax eased down to sit next to my chair. He was a big man, well aware of his height and girth, and generally a gentle soul. But I'd seen him riled a time or two, and he definitely had the kind of mean a female archaeologist needed in the South Sudan. He looked like the leader of a biker gang, but my grandfather had seen his potential years ago and put him through college. Ax was ten years older than I was, and he'd befriended me when I was an angry fourteen-year-old, ready to tear down the world with my bare hands.

"You turning in soon?" asked Ax.

"Dawn to dusk, that's the glamorous life of an archaeologist," I said.

"Quit being so bitter about Indiana Jones."

"It's directed more at Lara Croft."

He laughed.

"Permit will be up in three days," I said with a sigh. "I need another two weeks, at least."

"You're lucky you got any sand time at all in these

parts," said Ax. He reached into his shirt pocket, the place where his cigarettes had once rested, and withdrew his stash of peppermint toothpicks. He put one of the toothpicks into the side of his mouth and chewed. "Can't believe you talked me into doing this shit again. It's not safe here."

"It's not safe anywhere," I responded automatically. Ax liked to bitch about dropping his whole life—which was running a series of successful businesses, including a very popular bar—to be my muscle. We toiled away the days in hopes of finding a grand truth about humankind's past before the season was over and we had to leave our beloved sites. It could be boring as hell, but passion for my job drove me forward relentlessly. I liked delving into the lives of long-dead cultures. Ax suggested that the reason I put so much energy into archaeological endeavors was to avoid seeking the truth about my own past. He was probably right. But even so, I loved it. No matter how mind-numbing the work got, it still held a magnificence that resonated in my soul. And hell, getting a pass to explore this part of the desert had taken a lot of money, and a lot more ego-stroking of officials—from border guards to country leaders. I'd been trying to get back here for years, to the place where my grandfather had poured out his own passion and energy. He'd been trying to save me—the granddaughter who'd imploded emotionally and returned from the brink with nothing but a fierce, pulsing rage. My grandfather probably should've left me in the loony bin, but instead he put me on a plane, dragged me halfway around the world, and gave me a purpose. He gifted me with the archaeological need to connect with our ancestors, to find the core of our truths, to embrace the past in hopes of gaining insight into the present.

No one came here. Too much desert, too much danger, too much digging. My grandfather thought there was a very important temple complex out here, one devoted to Set, the god of chaos. The killer of Osiris. Grandfather may not have found the site, but he'd never lost his belief in it. He'd known something grand was out here, something that could potentially change history, change the world.

And I wanted to find it.

Granted, trying to extract ancient history from the desert while war raged around our perimeter was certainly more dangerous than trying to cross the street in Manhattan.

But not by much.

"You going to therapy once we hit Stateside?" asked Ax.

Ugh. Ax kept asking me this question—no doubt hoping to get a different answer. He didn't like my usual response. I looked at the dancing flames of the fire and pretended he wasn't staring at me. "Nope."

"Aw, Moira. You gotta do something."

"I was thinking about a mani-pedi and a shopping spree at Louis Vuitton."

"You're too fucking stubborn," he said. "You want your brain to melt again?"

"That was twenty years ago," I said.

"So what?"

"I take my meds, all right?" I looked at him and twirled my forefinger near my temple. "Two pills a day keep the crazy away."

"You need to get off that antipsychotic bullshit. Give the head shrinkers another shot."

No, I didn't. I had yet to find a psychiatrist who didn't drive me crazy. Talking about the past didn't help. Not at all. Ever. "I'd rather sit on hot coals and eat broken glass while listening to you screech the wrong lyrics to 'Material Girl.'"

"And *that's* why I stopped serving half-price shooters on karaoke nights."

"The video got a lot of YouTube hits," I said sweetly. After all, I was the one who'd posted two full minutes of Ax's Madonna-induced shame. Actions such as those probably explained why I didn't have a lot of friends. That, and my rep for being a total nut job. Honestly, you de-pant one senator's son at the country club and you get a bad rap forever. Of course, I did shove him into the pool after yanking down his swim trunks and revealing his rather small penis to the party in progress. If he hadn't tried to stick his tongue down my throat while making an awkward grab for my breasts, he would've remained clothed and dry. I was sixteen, my reputation tainted by my stint in the wacky hut, and according to the senator, I had relapsed. Years later, that same son was arrested for soliciting a prostitute, and when they searched his car, they found a shit ton of cocaine. He went to jail, the wife went to Italy, and the senator went to hell. Who was holding the handbasket then, I ask you?

"Nightmares still bothering you?" Ax asked quietly.

The question ended our moment of levity. I could hardly begrudge him, though. Real worry weighted his tone. "Nah," I said. "The corporate pill mills also make excellent sleeping drugs, which are far better than therapy."

Ax had been there the day I'd lost my mind. I don't remember much about it, other than rage, the utter, blinding rage. Years later, when I could at least talk about that part of it, Grandfather told me that Ax was the one who got to me before—well, anyway. He got me, and in some ways he'd never really let go. And that was also why he felt it was perfectly acceptable to harangue me about psychiatric treatments.

"You're one of the most fearless people I've ever met," said Ax. He looked up and caught my gaze. "Except when you gotta look backward into your own life. Your mother—"

"Is dead. And so is this conversation," I said, getting up. "See you in the a.m."

He sighed, then shook his head. His disappointment in me stung. I was thirty-four years old, damn it. Argh! How annoying that someone still existed on the planet capable of making me feel like an errant child. I put my hands on my hips. "I hear you, okay?" I sucked in a steadying breath and held up my hand with palm out as a proper vow-making gesture. "I hereby swear that I won't go crazy again." I swiped a finger over my heart in a cross. "Promise."

"What do you mean *again*? You never stopped being cuckoo for Cocoa Puffs." He smiled at me, and I could see the shadows in his gaze. After all this time, I knew that he wondered if it would happen again. I did, too. Making a promise to keep my marbles intact wasn't exactly one I could keep. But so far, my sanity was intact. Mostly.

Ax patted my arm. "I'll make the java."

I grimaced. Ax could cook like Martha Stewart, but his coffee had driven otherwise hardened souls to attempt suicide. "Don't you dare, you miscreant. Your sludge tastes like ass-flavored gelatin."

He grinned, and the wicked gleam in his eye forced a laugh out of me. He knew I wouldn't let him make the damned coffee. "G'night, Moira."

"Yeah, yeah." I waved at him.

Dove was already tucked into her cot, snoring away. Ah, the sweet sleep of ornery bitches.

Exhaustion weighed on me like the Great Pyramid.

I considered the rucksack sitting like an accusation next to my cot. Within its leathery confines were prescription bottles, including one with the magic pills that kept nightmares from manifesting. But I was exhausted, and also feeling stubborn. I didn't want to rely on a pill. I couldn't really choose not to take the others. Me without meds was like the Hulk without Bruce Banner.

I sat on the cot, my shoulders sagging. I put my hand on the rucksack's clasp, and hesitated. I blamed Ax for this sudden need to delve into dreamland unencumbered. Ax loved me, which was why he still prodded me about going to therapy and dealing with my shit. Maybe one day I would. Probably the same day I discovered Egyptian vampires ... on the twelfth of never.

I let go of the bag, went vertical on the cot, and pulled up the scratchy blanket. I fell asleep before the discomfort of my crappy sleeping arrangements had the chance to annoy me.

Chapter 2
Dove

I'm lying in the dark, listening to Moira move rest-lessly in her sleep. I don't sleep well, either, but her nightmares are far worse than mine. I watched her wrestle with the decision not to take the sleeping pill, and when she didn't, I didn't feel particularly relieved. I know Ax stays on her ass about therapy, but what does he know? We live in an era where people can be saved by medicine.

If they have the money.

I was not always an orphan.

But I always felt alone. This fact I will never admit to a living soul because: A. It is lame. B. It is no one's business. C. Moira would Mother Earth me to death.

I do not think Moira realizes she is a born caretaker. But I have never met a lonelier soul . . . and I have been very lonely. Lest you think I pity myself, let me say this: I shall indulge in self-pity if I like. So fuck off.

In any case, I was talking about Moira. She takes care of people. And things. And situations. And matters. If you enter her orbit, and she deems you worthy, then you belong to her. This is my observation. Despite the heinous attitudes of the college administration—all of whom need those sticks surgically removed from their asses—Moira takes care of everyone at the school, from the landscapers to the president. She doesn't allow bad attitudes, or ungratefulness, to get in the way of her caretaking. She is quite admirable.

Not many people are.

Especially not I. Me? Not me. Damn the lack of Internet access and the heaviness of reference books. Lo, though I weep, for I cannot access grammar guides here in this sand-covered hell.

Why she picked out my essay, why she picked me, remains a mystery I have yet to unravel. The question I really wanted answered, however, was: What does she see in me that no one else does?

Not that I require outside validation of that which is my awesomeness (ha! take that, grammar!). I am merely curious why Moira deems me worthy. Perhaps I am . . . slightly more than curious. Perhaps I want to know what glimmer caught her eye. Certainly not my personality. I have been called caustic, dry-humored, sarcastic, coldhearted, an emotional black hole (bitter boyfriends are the worst), depressing, soul-despairing, and to quote my last date, "a ball-busting bitch." Of course, that was a literal description, given that I punched him in the genitals for sticking his hand down my pants.

Men are imbeciles.

Yes, I'm generalizing and stereotyping an entire gender, but in my head space I make the rules. It's funny how the mind works. Or maybe it's not. Maybe I'm not interested in exploring, as I too often do, the reason I'm the only biological evidence walking the planet that my family existed. My mother was pregnant with me when a car accident took her and my father's lives. Well, my mother lived long enough to be removed from the car. The firefighters extracted me right before she gave her last breath. My first name was Baby Jane Doe.

My second was given to me once my parents' identities had been established.

I don't use their name.

I never belonged to them.

I was raised by a woman named Aunt Peg, who was not my blood relation. I have no idea how I came into the care of dear Aunt Peg (whom I fondly nicknamed Peg-a-saurus Wreck). She'd fallen under the categories of "batty," and "eccentric." But eventually those quirks became full-on crazy.

No one understood Aunt Peg. I wasn't sure I understood Aunt Peg. But I loved her. And I tried to protect her. Unfortunately, the fierce resolve of a thirteen-year-old is a thin shield against reality.

My nightmares are guilt-wrapped and tied with an anger bow.

Moira's nightmares are . . . forays into memory and madness. Level Ten crazy.

I know she takes sleeping pills to avoid them. And I know there have been times, though rare, when she has not, and she has witnessed the results of my own forays into sleep's dark realms. But I do not choose to escape bad dreams. I know my sins. I will not look away from them.

Moira is very smart, but she runs from the monsters that inhabit her past. I want to tell her that the monsters will come no matter where you hide. They will crawl under your bed, slip into your closet, creep under your covers. They will find you. And destroy you . . . unless you destroy them first.

Rumors chase Moira to this day. She lost her mind when she was fourteen. She went into an asylum for months until the day her grandfather scooped her out of that place and dragged her to the desert. Everyone within a hundred-mile radius of the college knows this about her.

Ax told me a little more about what happened. Not many details, though. He's not much for talking. And I don't know why he shared anything at all about Moira. He's very protective of her. Besides, Moira doesn't hide who she is; she doesn't pretend the world doesn't know she was insane in the membrane for a while. But neither does she invite you into her space—not her home, not her head, not her heart.

But not for the same reasons.

Chapter 3

Drake

"The desert sucks. I don't think I'm ever gonna get the sand out of my underwear."

Unsurprisingly, this exclamation arrived from Jessica, the mate of Patrick O'Halloran, both vampires and both my good friends. I smiled at Jess. She had volunteered for this trip into the Sudan because her children were grown: Her daughter was in college and her son was a successful journalist who didn't spend a lot of time in the United States.

Jessica was also extremely proficient with the double swords her husband had gifted her with during their courtship, and she was a fierce warrior. I liked having her protecting my backside.

There were six of us: myself, my brother Darrius, Jessica, Patrick, Eva, and Lorcan. Lorcan and Patrick were twins, and their biological father, Ruadan, also happened to be the first vampire ever. Vampire families had different abilities depending on their Family lineage. Jessica, Patrick, and Lorcan had the ability to fly. Eva had the extraordinary gift of being able to glamour—beyond what most vampires could do. She was also very emotionally in tune with animalkind. I had witnessed many love matches, especially in the town of Broken Heart, Oklahoma, where we were headquartered. It always seemed a process that brought as much pain as it did pleasure. I did not really understand falling in love—nor why anyone would choose it. Jessica told me that sometimes love chooses you . . . and beats you into bloody submission.

My conclusion: Love is messy, contrary, and chaotic. And to be avoided.

I enjoyed passion, but love? That seemed to be far too much trouble. Look at my brother Darrius, who still pined for a woman dead many years. And our older brother, Damian, ensnared by a lovely woman who bore him a son and daughter. Tragic, really.

I am, of course, completely in love with Kelsey and my niece and nephew. If Damian were not king of the werewolves, I may have killed him for his family.

But though I am second in line to rule the werewolves, I would rather be tossed into a pit of scorpions than have his job.

Speaking of scorpions . . .

"Holy freaking crap!" squeaked Jessica, apparently

forgetting she was a vampire, deadly with swords, and wearing thick-soled boots. She jumped into her husband's arms, and Patrick laughed before foot-shooing the creature out of the cave where we all crouched. Below us was the campsite of Moira Jameson and company. We had been sent as a protection detail—at least partially.

We were here at the behest of Queen Patsy Marchand, who had her hands full with four children and the rulership of the undead and another breed of werewolves called the *loup de sang*. A vampire by the name of Karn, who had been thought dead, had recently crawled out of the earth after more than six hundred years. He'd been healed from the fire he'd been tossed into by vampires who'd punished him for being a complete douche bag, so he was also carrying around six centuries' worth of fury and vengeance.

He'd gotten wind of our ongoing project in the Sudan, and our goal to find and recover two ancient vampires who'd been lost to the world for more than three thousand years. Dr. Jameson, though she did not yet realize it, was close to uncovering the vampires' locations. Her grandfather had started the work, and she unknowingly continued it.

We had arrived several hours earlier, right after the sun had set, and crouched in this cave, watching the camp below us. Since I was a werewolf, my senses were vastly more attuned to sights, sounds, smells, and movements. I scented the remnants of the humans' meal—a thick stew of meat and potatoes—as well as the wisps of campfire that fluttered in the air like fine silver threads. Shadows moved in the camp, people in their tents turning off lanterns, restless in their efforts to get comfortable in a place that offered no comfort— not the air nor the ground nor its very being. The sand had movement, too, wind and creatures that made it shift and skitter. Above us, the sky looked like tiny diamonds that had been spilled across black velvet. I think the desert was the perfect place to hide secrets. It was very much earth's graveyard.

I leaned against the rough stone wall and scanned the area. My gaze rested on the tent where Dr. Jameson and her assistant lay sleeping. Moira was an interesting human. She was not a petite woman. She was tall, close to six feet, with lush curves that begged exploring. A strong woman—almost like a werewolf. She moved with grace and purpose, and yet when she rested, she was completely still. She had thick, waist-length red hair that she kept braided. I had not gotten close enough to see the color of her eyes, or to see the freckles that I bet were sprinkled across her nose like cinnamon.

"You like her."

I turned and looked down at Jessica.

"Who?" I asked.

Jess rolled her eyes. "The redhead with the killer ass, that's who."

"Ah." I tapped my chin. "I vaguely recall someone in the camp matching that description."

"You are full of shit," she said. "You've been watching her ever since we got here."

"Everyone's been watching the camp," I said. I wasn't feeling particularly defensive about getting caught in my viewing of Dr. Jameson's assets. I don't apologize for being a man. Or a werewolf. I just liked riling Jessica. "I'm only doing my duty."

"Yeah, right. If by 'doing your duty,' you mean ogling archaeologists."

I put my hand against my heart as though wounded by her accusation. "I do not ogle, Jessica." I waited a beat. "I *leer*."

She laughed and slapped my shoulder.

"Drake."

The sharp tone of my brother, Darrius, had Jessica and me straightening instantly. We looked down into the campsite and quickly saw what had alerted him: shadows slinking between tents. My gaze was riveted on Dr. Jameson's tent, and I saw the low light of their lantern flicker, as though something had crossed it.

"We should get to sparkling," said Jessica. Ancient vampires, as well as some other paranormal creatures, had the ability to appear and reappear in locations. Jessica called it "sparkling," much to the chagrin of her husband.

"We have speed," said Patrick. "And stealth. I suggest we use it. We'll be better able to control where we enter the camp."

"I will see to Dr. Jameson," I said. I looked at my brother. "Shift?"

He nodded.

The vampires took off toward the camp, mere blurs gliding over the sand.

Darrius and I had to take precious seconds to remove our clothes. Otherwise, shifting would rip them to shreds and we would have to stay in wolf form, or walk around as naked men. Darrius was already shifting by the time I got my jeans off. He raised his snout in the air and sniffed, then turned toward me and barked.

"I'm hurrying," I said. "Go on. I'll catch up."

He barked again and then raced out of the cave, across the moonlight sands of the Sudan desert.

I got down on all fours . . . and I let my inner werewolf out.

Chapter 4
Moira

"Moira!"

"Earthquake," I mumbled as my body was flung back and forth. I opened my eyes. A distraught Dove was inches from my face. Despite the fact that I was looking right at her, she continued to shake me by the shoulders. "Ugh! If you keep doing that, I'm gonna need a Dramamine."

She let go of me and dropped to her knees next to my cot. Her skeletal fingers dug into my arm. "Something just whooshed by our tent."

"Like 'death on swift wings'? You're not gonna throw quotes from *The Mummy* at me, are you? I told you to knock that shit off." I leaned up on one elbow and attempted to give her the evil eye. Unfortunately, I was too tired to be effective, so my eyes just crossed and my lids started to droop. There was a metallic taste on the back of my tongue, and my skin felt clammy. These were typical aftereffects of the nightmares . . . but I didn't remember the terror-filled dreamscape. Maybe Dove had inadvertently saved me from the worst of it.

"Gah! You are the worst waker-upper ever," she whispered harshly. She gave my shoulder a hard squeeze. "I'm telling you someone is out there."

"Okay, okay. For the record, you're the waker-upper. And I'm the waker-uppee."

"I'm so glad you're focused on the important issue," she hissed. Her voice held a catch. The real fear in her tone was almost like a cold dash of water to my face. Almost. I really was a bad waker-uppee. I rolled off the cot on the other side, then reached under my pillow and took out my sub-compact Beretta. It was loaded with thirteen 9 mm rounds. If you're wondering how someone on psychiatric medication is allowed weaponry, well, I have lot of money and I know a lot of the right people. Learning to shoot guns was actually part of my grandfather's therapy, and knowing how to protect myself freed another part of my soul from that sea of rage.

"Sleeping with a loaded gun under your pillow?" she asked, sounding more like the smart-ass I knew and loved. "Really?"

"Relax. It has a manual safety and a decocker."

She snorted. "A what?"

"Decocker," I repeated. "It's a lever that lets the hammer—"

"I don't care." She smirked. "I just wanted to see if you'd say it again."

"I hate you," I said. And then because I was a heartless bitch, I demanded, "Go get Tikka."

"Or not." Dove imperiously pointed a finger at me. "You shouldn't name weaponry, you know that?"

"She already had the name."

"Nor should guns have gender. Personalizing the—"

"Shut up," I snapped. Her sense of urgency had wormed through me, and now I was feeling surly. "Giving someone a dirty look doesn't exactly have stopping power—not even one of your patented I-wish-you-were-dead specialties. If you want to be protected from whooshing things . . . then get the fucking rifle."

"Whatever," she hissed at me. Then she flopped onto her belly and crawled toward the footlocker that housed the rifle and other gear. Obviously she was too rattled to access the gun like a normal person. As she pulled out the weapon and the box of bullets, I glanced around. A single lantern cast a muted glow in our tent. Dove wouldn't admit it, but she was scared of the dark. Why she was studying to be an archaeologist, a profession where exploring dark, cramped, and airless spaces was the norm, was beyond me.

While Miss Quiet as a Raging Storm rattled around trying to get the rifle loaded, I crept to the tent flap and peeked outside. If the grad students had gotten stupid enough to play a prank, or to sneak out of camp to go party in the desert, I would stake them all out in the sand and leave them to burn. And then I would fail them in every single class . . . and put big, red F's on all their dissertations. And their graves. For failing life.

It took only a few seconds for my eyesight to adjust. The campfire had been doused and the supplies put away. No one was prowling around. All the other tents were dark, so it was difficult to tell if they were occupied. I glanced up into the obsidian sky, my gaze skittering across the moon and the thousands of stars, and wondered why I felt so uneasy.

It was ungodly quiet.

The hair rose on the nape of my neck. What had startled Dove out of a sound sleep? Maybe she had a bad dream, too, and had woken up so suddenly that it felt real. We were both tormented by nightmares, although Dove would never talk about hers. And neither did I. Those lingering wisps of terror were my burden to bear.

"Dove, what exactly did you—" I turned around as I spoke, and what I saw made my words tumble to a halt.

A tall, lean man held Dove by the neck in one of his hands, and the rifle in his other. How the hell had he gotten into the tent? He could've easily passed for one of my grad students, except he was dressed like fucking Indiana Jones, right down to the fedora and faded leather duster. Seriously? We were getting jacked by a Harrison Ford wannabe?

He was too lithe to have the strength to hold my terrified assistant a foot off the ground, but he was doing it. He wasn't even breaking a sweat. What the—? I nearly pissed myself. *He wasn't even breathing.* He was unnaturally pale, his eyes as dark as midnight. When he smiled, he revealed a set of sharp, ugly fangs.

"Vampire," said Dove, her voice choked and her eyes wide. Fear emanated from her in waves. Or maybe that was me, because I was more terrified than I'd ever been in my life. See: confinement to nuthouse. Although scarier still was the time I'd thrown down with a Kardashian for a Bottega Veneta leather handbag (in butterscotch cream, if you were wondering), and won.

From my crouched position, I kept the Beretta pointed at his face. Sweat slicked my palms, but my aim didn't waver and the gun didn't move a millimeter. "Put her down."

"Or what?" he asked, his voice thick with an accent I couldn't place. "She's merely the appetizer. You, my fine Amazon, are the meal."

"Wow. Really?" I said, my voice filled with disgust. "That's the worse pickup line I've ever heard."

He grinned, and then he opened his mouth, showing off those terrible, sharp fangs, and jerked Dove downward, aiming for her neck. She tried to struggle, but it was like watching a ribbon wrestle with the wind.

My focus sharpened, and I felt myself go utterly cold and still. I lowered the gun and shot out his knees. The sharp crack of the pistol firing echoed in the tent as the bullets thudded into his patellas. I was not being altruistic, mind you. It wasn't about saving his life. I wanted him to suffer.

And suffer he did. He screamed in pain and outrage as he buckled, dropping Dove and the rifle. She grabbed Tikka and hauled ass toward me.

"You have to remove his head," she cried. "Sever it! Sever it!"

"These are bullets, not hacksaws," I said as she scrambled behind me. Tikka smacked me in the shoulder as Dove maneuvered around, finally taking up position next to me. I looked at her, at the fear etched on her sharp features. "He's down, all right?"

"Not for long. He's the undead!" She brought Tikka upright, clutching the barrel. "I couldn't get the bullets before that stupid asshole grabbed me."

"I will rend your muscles from your bones," said the stupid asshole, his gaze vitriolic. He bared his fangs. "You will die slowly as I feast upon you."

"And you thought me quoting *The Mummy* was bad?" murmured Dove.

I wished we could call Ax, but cell phone service was nonexistent out here, and the walkie-talkies were over by Fang Boy. Shit. "Get Ax," I told Dove.

"The hell," she said. "We have to find something that will cut through an undead neck."

"I'm not saying he's *not* a vampire," I said. Sweat dripped down my temple, but the gun, which I had re-trained on No Knees, didn't waver. He was down, yes, but definitely not out. In fact, he was looking a little too perky for someone with shredded patellas. "Is decapitation really the way to go here?"

"The only way to kill a vampire is to take his head off or expose him to intense light. It says so in *Vampires Are Real!*"

"Oh, my God. That Theodora Monroe book? Really? That's like taking advice from the Winchester brothers."

"And you know exactly what about supernatural creatures?"

"Silence!" bellowed the vampire as he wobbled to his feet. His pants were torn and bloody, but his knees were nearly knitted back together. He eyed us with the kind of malevolence I usually witnessed only when it came time for me to approve departmental budgets. "You are both imbeciles. And you talk too much."

"Holy shit!" screamed Dove. "Holy fucking shit!"

I shot at him again, but he swooped toward us, a blur of furious motion. I shoved Dove to the side and started shooting randomly. Yeah. That worked out well.

Then *I* was shoved to the side, and I flew backward, landing next to an outraged Dove. We both watched, openmouthed, as a huge black wolf leapt into the air, howling in triumph.

We looked at each other, and then we both scrambled forward. We stayed on our knees, crouching at the edge of my flimsy cot. The vampire (yes, I said "vampire," all right?) was moving fast, very fast. Hell, I couldn't really pinpoint his location, but it was obvious the wolf could. He howled, and then leapt—seemingly at random—landing on the bastard's chest. The fanged Indiana Jones squirmed on the ground, unable to dislodge the big black-furred brute.

The fight was short and violent, ending when the wolf clamped its jaws onto the vampire's neck and tore out his throat.

"Oh, crap," whispered Dove.

We huddled closer together, creating fearful solidarity against our so-called rescuer. Was he merely dealing with the biggest threat in the room before he turned his attention to the shivering girly girls? My philosophy was that the glass was always half foe. I sat up and leveled my gun at the wolf.

Dove clutched the Tikka T3 rifle. She wouldn't shoot it, even if she'd taken me up on my invitation for lessons. She had a thing about guns—as in, she hated them. But if push came to shove, she could use the rifle to whack the shit out of the wolf. For some reason she had no problem with bludgeoning.

Both of us were on high alert. I couldn't take my gaze off the dead vampire, and I noticed that Dove was also riveted to the spectacle. Black blood pooled in the sand around the ravaged neck.

It was a gruesome scene that seemed right out of a horror movie. Except horror movies didn't have smell-o-vision, and dead vampires smelled like feces wrapped in burnt cheese. As in, they smelled like deep-fried death. You know, like corn dogs at the state fair. A vampire showing up in my tent was fantastical enough—not to mention a supersized undead-killing wolf. (Weren't vampires supposed to take wolf form, or something? I was rusty on preternatural mythology.) But oh, no, my night was about to get weirder. Our furry pal padded to a nearby space and morphed into a man.

It wasn't like a transformation you might see on a late-night werewolf flick, with snorting and snarling and breaking and sprouting. It was sorta . . . magical, I suppose. His fur rippled into skin, his limbs stretched and plumped into human arms and legs. And long, silky black hair fell over his shoulders. He didn't seem stressed out or in pain from the experience, but I would think that shifting from one being into another wasn't exactly a pleasant sensation.

"I'm dreaming, right?" I asked Dove.

"Well, if you are, you have some fucked-up dreams." Dove blinked, then said, "Whoa."

"Whoa" was an understatement.

Werewolf man was naked.

Very, very naked.

He walked over to the guy bleeding in my tent and knelt down. He grabbed the guy's head and twisted.

An ugly snap echoed in the tent as he wrenched the head off. The fedora fell off and rolled toward Dove's cot. The man tossed the head next to its body.

The vampire—body, head, and blood—turned to ash. All that remained were the fedora and the duster.

Dove and I shared a *holy-shit-did-that-just-really-happen* look.

While my heart tried to claw its way out of my chest, I watched the wolf—er, the man—claim one of my discarded T-shirts lying near the foot locker and rub his face. I realized he was wiping off the vampire's blood.

"I call the duster," said Dove in a strangled voice.

"Fuck you," I said, my voice hoarse with disbelief. "That baby's mine."

"Then I want the hat."

"Whatever, Indiana," I muttered. Like either of us would even deign to wear the duster or hat. How was one supposed to get vampire ash out of those clothes anyway? I mean . . . OxiClean can do only so much.

"Are you all right?" The naked man walked toward us, then stopped on the other side of the cot, his expression a mask of concern as he studied our faces. He had the most amazing jade green eyes. I didn't even know eyes could be that color.

He was gorgeous.

I probably should've mentioned that before, but I was distracted by all the morphing and the vampire killing. But now that he was less than a foot away, look-ing at us with a mixture of curiosity and empathy . . . well, I could focus on him.

He was huge, well over six feet tall. And muscled. And beautiful. Blood that streaked him from neck to. . . .

I gasped, and Dove followed my line of sight, and gasped, too.

"Is that real?" asked Dove in a reverent voice. "Be-cause that's the biggest dick I've ever seen."

"He can hear you," I whispered harshly. Then in a lower voice, I added, "Don't you even think about tak-ing dibs, you bitch."

"Riiiiight," she whispered back. "You want me to call ahead to the hospital, tell them to expect you and your injured vagina?"

"Then you are okay," he said dryly. He grabbed the blanket from my cot and wrapped it around his waist. "My name is Drake."

"Moira Jameson," I said. "This is Dove."

"*Just* Dove," she said severely, as she always did to forestall any questions about a last name. Like last names were even relevant. Werewolf man didn't seem to have one—or he hadn't offered one.

He inclined his head, his green eyes flashing with humor. "You handle yourselves very well. Not many humans are so . . . accepting of parakind."

"Parakind?" I asked.

"A general term. But in this case, I speak of the *droch*

fola," he said, pointing at the pile of ash that was currently messing up my new duster. "And me, of course. The werewolf."

"I didn't read about werewolves," said Dove. "Damn."

Drake cocked an eyebrow at her. "Perhaps having a conversation with a werewolf is better than reading about him, hmm?"

"Depends on how the conversation ends," she said.

"Wow. Awesome. Just another day in the desert," I said. I was starting to get the shakes. See, I was great at crisis-in-the-moment. But the aftershocks got me every time.

"Ah." He tilted his head and offered a wicked grin. "It's really too bad."

"What is?" I asked.

"You will not remember anything that happened tonight." He gave me a long look, one that gleamed with regret. "And you will not remember me."

Chapter 5

"Vampires," I said flatly. Dove and I sat on my cot looking up at six people who should not have existed.

"It's weird, right?" said the brunette, who'd been introduced as Jessica. Frankly, Jessica was not a good vampire name. It made the whole undead thing highly suspect. The other vampires were Patrick, Lorcan, Eva, and then, of course, the two werewolves, Drake and Darrius, were also there.

My gaze strayed (ha, *stray*) to Drake. Unfortunately, he had left our tent and returned fully dressed, in jeans, T-shirt, and snakeskin boots. His long hair was tied back into a ponytail. His hair was longer than mine. I couldn't help myself. I felt drawn to him, magnetized almost. Was that a werewolf thing? Or was it because I had no dating life and it was finally catching up with me? Or had I finally flipped my lid and descended into a paranormal psychotic episode?

"Those are vampires," said Dove, waving her hand toward the four undead ones. Then she pointed at Drake and Darrius. "And those are werewolves," she added helpfully. My impulse to pinch her was delayed by the dazed look on her face. She was trying to process the situation, same as I was, and I wasn't sure who was doing the better job. Neither of us, it seemed.

Dove leaned near my ear and said, "You're not crazy. This is really happening." She bumped my shoulder. "You might want look less freaked out."

"Hey, you're just *meeting* us. The first time I met a vampire was after I woke up dead," said Jessica. "Which isn't as easy as you might think."

"I wouldn't think it was easy at all," said Dove.

"Well, it's not completely horrible," said Jessica. "Just unnerving. Especially when the vampire's naked and you're facefirst between his thighs." She flashed a grin at Patrick. "Well, anyway. You're not dead. Bonus, right?"

Wait. What? Talking to a vampire was making me feel twitchy, so I assessed the people standing around the cot. Patrick and Lorcan were twins. So were Drake and Darrius. It was like having double paranormal vision. Okay. Yeah. I was crazy. Certified and everything. And even I didn't believe this shit.

"The other intruders retreated after Drake killed the *droch fola*," said Darrius.

Yeah, I remembered the part where the vampire was beheaded and then turned to ash.

"What's the difference between that asshole and you guys?" Dove asked the vampires. "Other than the part where you haven't tried to kill us?"

Yet. They hadn't tried to kill us yet.

"*Droch fola* are vampires who no longer have their humanity," said Patrick in his Irish brogue. "Soulless, if you will."

"Ah," said Dove. "I don't think that was in the book."

Patrick lifted a black eyebrow.

"Don't go there," I advised him. I looked at Drake. And he was looking at me. Electric pulses zapped the pit of my stomach. I felt drawn to him, but though Darrius had the same appearance . . . no tummy wiggles occurred when I looked at him. They looked very much alike, too.

"What about the rest of my team?" I asked him. My voice turned hoarse halfway through the sentence, and I cleared my throat.

"We saw his penis," said Dove. "She's still in awe."

Jessica burst out laughing.

Drake offered Dove a wicked grin. "And you are not?"

"Since I've only seen one werewolf penis, it's difficult to say," she said.

"Oh, my God! Can we keep her? Please?" Jessica slapped the werewolf brothers on the shoulders. "Contest!"

"Maybe later," I said. As in, never. I didn't think my

brain could handle the image of two naked werewolves. Two naked twin werewolves. Wait. What I was thinking? "Never mind. Now's good."

"You asked about your team," said Eva hastily. She was also a brunette, and seemed a little more reserved than Jessica. "Everyone's okay. And their memories have been adjusted."

"Adjusted?" I asked.

"Glamoured. Well, damn. You're going to glamour us," said Dove. Her mouth drooped into a frown.

"What the hell does that mean?" I asked.

"'Glamour' is the term we use when we remove or change a human's memory," said Eva. She offered a gentle smile. "It protects you. And us."

I really didn't need anyone messing around in my brain. It was fucked up enough in there. Before I could voice a protest, Patrick spoke.

"The temple you're lookin' for," he said. I squinted at him. Hmm. Maybe he was Lorcan. "You any closer to findin' it?"

"Why on earth would you care about a temple devoted to Set?" I asked.

"Because he was king of the vampires, right?" Dove perked up. "I knew it!"

"No," said Patrick. "The temple is a resting place for some friends of ours."

I absorbed that information. "More vampires?"

Drake knelt down, that jade green gaze assessing me in a way that made me tingle.

And I am not a tingler.

"You found something, *ja*?"

"*Ushabtis* with fangs," said Dove. She glanced at me. "I found two more in the items I was logging in for the day."

"What's a u-thingie?" asked Jessica.

"Little statues," I said. "Made by ancient Egyptians to accompany them into the afterlife as servants."

Drake reached out and put a hand on my knee. "Perhaps you can show us where these statues were uncovered."

"Now?"

"It's a few hours before dawn," he said. "If there's a chance you're close to discovering the pyramid, then we need to know."

"Yes," said Eva in a soothing voice that reminded me of all things Zen. I looked at her, and her eyes were glowing red. But I wasn't afraid. I felt more . . . floaty. "Show us the site, Moira. You feel it's the right thing to do, don't you? And you, Dove? You think so, too."

"Absolutely," said Dove in a dreamy voice.

Traipsing out to the dig site at two a.m. was the least weird thing to happen tonight. I wasn't sure why I was feeling more cooperative than freaked out, though. In fact, I felt awesome. Huh. But apparently not as awesome as Dove. She had a goofy smile on her face and looked like she'd been given Thorazine. I eyed Eva. "Did you glamour us?"

She offered another gentle smile. "We need your co-operation, Moira."

Patrick put a hand on her shoulder. "You may need to push her a little harder. She seems better able to resist than most humans."

Eva nodded, and then she looked at me, her eyes going redder, and I felt my mind fog. "Show us where you found the statues, Moira."

"Of course," I said. Even though I felt good, like I was flying almost, a sense of urgency wound through me. We needed to get to the location right away. It seemed imperative that we do so . . . now. Right now.

I got up from the cot, and Dove rose, too.

It took us twenty minutes to hike to the dig site. By the time we reached it, I was feeling less strung out on vampire mind juju. That glamour was powerful stuff.

We had cordoned off squares with ropes and stakes, and in these squares grad students would toil away trying to find evidence of our temple.

"I've been working there," I said, pointing to the northernmost corner. "That's where I found the statues."

"Was anything else uncovered?" asked Drake.

I looked at him over my shoulder. "Bits of pottery. It's nice to find items intact, but mostly we spend our days gathering pieces and playing puzzle makers."

We continued to the square where I had been spent nearly two weeks culling through sand to find evidence of Set's temple. I still had hope of realizing my grandfather's dream to make a find equivalent to King Tut's tomb.

"Here," said Darrius. He had gone to a depression in the corner of the lot and put his hand on it. "Patrick?"

The vampire joined the werewolf, thrust his hands into the sand, and began to shovel sand away incredibly fast. Jessica knelt beside him to help. Sand flew everywhere, as though the ground had exploded. I was impressed . . . until I realized they were screwing up my dig site.

That was when I fully emerged from Eva's attempt at mind control.

"Hey!" I leapt forward, arms out to push the vampires away from destroying potential evidence.

Drake grabbed my shoulders and pulled me tight against his chest. "Now, now," he murmured in my ear, "you must not get upset."

"He's ruining it!" Panic roared through me. All that work, all that time, all that effort, and they didn't care. "You don't understand! We have to be careful. It took years to get this far. My grandfather gave his entire life to this place. Please, Drake. Make them stop!"

"I am sorry, my treasure," he said. His voice was liquid warmth, and my panic began to dissipate. He had me trapped, but it didn't actually feel like I was imprisoned. Maybe because his face was pressed against the side of my head and he was whispering soothing sounds. With his arms around me, it felt more like . . .

being held. Being comforted. The feeling was so foreign, so nice, it completely disarmed me.

"Dr. Jameson?"

Patrick's use of my honorific snapped me to attention. Drake released me, but stayed close as I joined the vampires, who'd uncovered two steps into . . . somewhere.

"The temple," I said. My heart skipped a beat. I looked at Dove, and she grinned. I grinned back, and then I turned an imperious smile toward Patrick. "Well?" I said in my best kill-the-grad-student voice. "What are you waiting for?"

What would've taken us days to uncover took the vampires and werewolves less than an hour. I wasn't as upset at their methods now, given that they'd found the entrance to a building long hidden by the sand. A building that I hoped was either the temple of Set or at least one of the outer buildings that led to the main complex.

We gathered around the staircase and stared down into the darkness. Lorcan whispered something in Gaelic, and several orbs of yellow light appeared. They drifted down and bobbed in the air, revealing a stone door.

Darrius made a move to go down the stairs, but Drake grabbed his shoulder. "It is Dr. Jameson's right. She should go first."

The werewolf gave a sharp nod and moved back. Drake made a sweeping gesture, and I stepped down. Sweet heaven. *I'm here, Grandfather. We did it.*

Drake followed me, and I was so excited about reading the hieroglyphs and confirming that we had found Set's temple that I didn't even mind how cramped his presence made the tiny space before the stone door.

"What does it say?" he asked.

"'No werewolves allowed,'" I muttered. I looked over the images, and noted the circular hole in the door. Disappointment edged through me as I noted the lack of references to Set. In fact, the glyphs were sparse and basically held one command: "Stick your hand here, and let your heart be judged." There was a hole in the center of the door. Basically, the discoverer of this place was supposed to stick a hand into that hole, which would, I hoped, open the door.

Then again, the hole might hold myriad awful things. I could be hurt or trapped. But I wasn't afraid.

I lifted my hand, and Drake batted it away. "What are you doing?"

"Opening the door."

"Moira, I don't—"

I inserted my hand into the hole and his eyebrows snapped down at my impetuous gesture. I felt something wickedly sharp prick my wrist.

"Ow!"

Drake grabbed my arm. "What happened? Are you okay?"

The earth began to shake.

Sand shimmered onto us from above, and the sounds of stones grinding together echoed in the stillness of night. Drake grabbed my shoulders and tried to yank me away from the door, but whatever had clamped onto my wrist held fast.

I heard a voice whisper inside my head. *"Love will lead you. Be worthy."*

My wrist was suddenly freed, blood dripping from scratches of whatever had grabbed it, and Drake grabbed me, hauling me up the staircase and away from the groaning, trembling earth.

We joined the others, who'd moved away from the site. Our gazes were riveted to the shifting sands, and to the object rising from them.

A huge pyramid rose and rose and rose from its sandy grave. I was awed by its massive beauty. Most people were used to the look of the pyramids in the modern era—crumbling yellow stones. But if we could look at the pyramids in the time they were built, we would see them just as this one was—smooth white limestone, topped with gleaming gold.

"Holy shit," whispered Dove. She looked at me, and then over my shoulder, and her eyes widened.

Before I could follow her line of sight, Drake yelled, "Watch out!" and shoved me hard. I stumbled to the right and fell, rolling across the sand. When I stopped, I found myself lying next to an equally stunned Dove. We stared at the starry sky above, and tried to catch our breath.

"Other than that time in Guatemala, this is the strangest night I've ever had," she said.

"Guatemala? When we fell into that pit, and no one noticed until the next day?"

"No. When Ax pissed off those guys in the bar, and you and I had to sing Abba songs in exchange for his life."

"Oh," I said. "Yeah. That was a strange night." I glanced at her. "We really nailed 'Waterloo.' "

"Totally."

We rolled onto our stomachs and took a view of the chaos surrounding us. Our new paranormal friends were engaged in fierce battles.

"More vampires," said Dove. "I guess those are the bad guys."

"How do you know?"

"Ah. Good point."

"Moira." Drake suddenly loomed over us, and we scrambled to our feet. "We must go."

"Where?" asked Dove.

Drake opened his mouth to answer, but a big white blur plowed into him and shoved him to the ground. The vampire was huge, as brawny and square-faced as a boxer, and he had Drake pinned to the sand. His fangs elongated and he bent down, presumably to ravage the werewolf's throat.

"I call bad guy," yelled Dove.

"I concur!" I hurtled toward the vampire, using my whole body to ram into him. I knocked him off Drake, and we went tumbling into the sand. Dove ran up next to the vampire's head and kicked him in the temple with her steel-toed boot.

That really pissed him off.

He leapt to his feet, fanged and furious, and Drake dove between us, hitting the vampire in the face. They stumbled back, exchanging quick, brutal punches.

"Excuse me." Jessica appeared in a shower of gold sparkles. She held two magnificent short swords that she swung in deadly arcs. Oh, I recognized ancient when I saw it. And though they gleamed bright and deadly gold, they were not modern blades.

"Drake!" yelled Jessica.

He moved out of the way instantly, and she lifted the swords, stabbing one into the vampire's chest while using the other to cleanly slice off his head.

I followed the progress of the head as it rolled along the sand. Then it, and the body, burst into ash. I looked at Jessica, and she offered a grim smile. "Unfortunately, I'm really good at that move."

Her eyes widened, and she raised her swords at me.

"What are you—" The words stalled in my throat as I felt the grip of cold, steely fingers around my wrist. I was jerked backward, and felt something sharp prick my neck.

"Enough!" screamed my captor.

Drake, Dove, and Jessica had all been stalking forward, but now they stopped, their gazes on the vampire who held me. His skin was cold and dry, and as he pressed close to me, I could feel no heave of his chest to indicate breath or heartbeat. So, yeah . . . vampire.

"I will let her live," said the Italian-spiked voice, "if you do not attempt to stop me."

Drake's hands clenched into fists, and he emitted a fierce growl. "Karn! Damn you!"

I was dragged backward several feet and then yanked into an awkward turn. In front of me was the pyramid. I glanced over my shoulder, and he pointed the blade at my left eye. The sharp tip was so close that it brushed the edge of my eyelashes. "Move."

I walked forward, because I liked having two eyes and his undead grip was fierce. I got the impression that he was only slightly resisting the urge to snap my wrist. We stopped at the left corner, and that's when I saw another gold circle like the one in the door that had unlocked the pyramid. There was no inscription on the gold, or the wall surrounding it. Hell, there wasn't even an arrow pointing toward the gaping hole.

"Open it."

"You open it."

He yanked me close, placing his lips on my ear. "I will kill you, Dr. Jameson. If you value your life, then you will do what I say."

Why did psychos believe that making empty promises would grant them compliance? He meant to kill me the moment he got what he wanted.

As Dove would say: *Screw that noise.*

"No time for games," he hissed. He moved to my

side and jerked me around, grabbing my chin. "I want the ambrosia."

I stared at him, openmouthed. "Ambrosia? Seriously?"

His gaze narrowed and his grip tightened. Okay. So he was serious.

"Get away from her, Karn." This edict was issued by Drake.

My captor was surrounded by vampires and werewolves. Apparently all the bad guys had been dispatched—save this one. I took a step back, but Karn followed, keeping the knife severely close to my eye. "Back, mongrel! Or I will kill her."

Everyone believed the surety in his tone and honored the request. They didn't go too far, but I was betting no one could get to me before he buried the knife in my face. Fear beat with wings of dread in my stomach. My heart pounded so hard I could hear the rush of the blood in my ears.

"Open it." He grabbed my shoulder and spun me around.

I didn't know how to open the pyramid. Okay, so maybe sticking my hand in the circle might work again. But I wasn't going to do it. Not for that undead asshole.

"Look," I said, "just stick your hand inside the circle."

Karn squeezed my arm, and pain shot down my elbow. "Do you think I'm a fool?"

No. I thought he was crazy, and believe me, I know

crazy. I pointed at the hole. "There was another one on the door we found. I stuck my hand inside, and boom! We have a pyramid."

Karn moved the knife to my throat, pressing it against my carotid artery. "If you're lying, you'll gasp your last breath before they can get to you."

Keeping the blade pressed into my flesh and his gaze on mine, he lifted his arm and shoved his hand into the gold circle.

"Your fate does not lie within," said a male and a female voice blended together. "Seven days hence, only the chosen may enter."

Then the pyramid disappeared.

No sound. No movement. No nothing. The damned thing just . . . vanished.

Karn released a string of violent Italian, and then I felt a swish of cold.

"He's gone," said Drake. He reached me first, and put his hands on my shoulders, studying my face. "Are you okay?"

"Are you kidding?"

"What did that mean?" asked Jessica. "Seven days *hence* . . . Jesus. Who are the chosen? Where the hell did it go?"

"The pyramid is coming back in a week . . . I think," said Patrick as he joined his wife. "We'll have to leave someone here to keep a watch out for its return. And as for the chosen . . . we know it's not Karn."

"I kinda have dibs on that pyramid," I said.

"Sorry," said Patrick, and he actually did seem to be sincerely apologetic, "but the vampires had dibs first. We appreciate all that you've done, Dr. Jameson."

"But our services are no longer required?" asked Dove.

Drake offered us a grim smile. "At least you won't remember anything when we're through here."

"Hard to forget this night," I said.

I felt a hand on my shoulder, and turned. Eva's kind gaze met mine. "You'll forget most of it, if that's any comfort."

"Um, not really."

I looked at Drake, saw that same regret gleaming in his eyes. "Till we meet again, Moira," he said. Then he winked.

Chapter 6

Six days hence . . .

Dove leaned over my desk and dropped the book with a dramatic flourish. The hardback landed with a resounding thump and rattled the papers that littered the shiny wood surface. I looked at the title and sighed. *"Vampires Are Real!* by Theodora Monroe. Oh, Dove. You're killing me."

"The *ushabtis* had fangs."

"Unfortunately, the crypt we found was empty." I put my fingers near my mouth and mimicked fangs. "We'll never know if the mummies came back to life . . . and sucked all the blood of the last archaeology team to discover their secret burial chambers."

Dove ignored my sarcasm. "That crypt had a completely weird vibe. And what about the lack of wall reliefs?"

"Empty," I repeated. "No sarcophagi. No mummies. We found no ritual offerings. No canopic jars. It's likely that the crypt was never used."

"Or it was cleared out to protect the mummies and their burial treasures." She lifted a finger. "And that's why we found *ushabtis* outside."

"So the thieves and/or priests who cleared out the crypt—in theory—dropped some stuff on the way out?" I shrugged. "Anything's possible."

"Even vampires?"

"I'm skeptical," I said. "But I won't rule out the possibility of an unknown"—I waved my hand—"something. There are surprises in archaeology all the time." The likelihood of a vampiric royal was about . . . oh, nil. But the idea of a blood-drinking cult that worshiped Sekhmet was intriguing. I looked down at the book. The cover was black and the title a bold red that appeared to be dripping blood. Classy.

Dove sat down on the stiletto-shaped crushed-velvet chaise that I kept as my "visitor" chair. I was a professor at a small, stuffy private college in upper New York State. Anyone who came in to harangue me had to sit on that chair to do it. Most declined. Okay, yeah. I was known as being "difficult." I'm sure it frustrated the hell out of officials, staff, and other professors, but there wasn't a lot they could do about it. Y'see, my family founded the college nearly a hundred years ago. I was the reason the school and its various programs got funded. I was the kind of wealthy that put me on the Christmas card list of Bill Gates. I'd also been raised by a go-your-own-way-damn-the-consequences grandfather who inspired me to be brave, to be creative, and to be stubborn as hell. He challenged me, encouraged me to be strong and persistent, and celebrated my quirks. He hadn't been afraid of my mental instability. He'd loved me fiercely, and I found my way out of the dark because of him. He instilled in me the virtues and stalwart attitude that carried me through all the difficulties of life, including the old curmudgeon's death last year.

I still hadn't forgiven him for dying.

"It's almost four o'clock," said Dove. "Don't you have a gala to attend in three hours?"

"Shut up."

Dove offered me one of her patented sneers. "Dress, right? High heels. Makeup. Fancy hairdo. All your favorites."

"I hate you." Every so often I had to play nice with the regents, especially when they were glad-handing the alumni (who also weren't particularly fond of me). We didn't have fund-raisers, since the college was generously funded through the Jameson Foundation. I think sometimes the regents wanted to host fundraisers because they harbored hope that they could raise the millions needed to run the school and wouldn't need Jameson money to operate. They didn't like asking me for checks. I was very circumspect about spending money—and no one got away with abusing the privileges of their position. We paid everyone well, but misuse of school money for personal expenditures would get your ass fired. Just ask the last college president, who thought taking his mistress to Fiji for a week of fun and frolicking was a "research" trip. There wasn't a whole lot of red tape when it came to getting rid of assholes. I had ultimate say, and power, when it came to administration. Ah. Just another reason I was so popular with everyone. They sometimes blamed my eccentricities, along the lines of "that bitch is still crazy," but no one was brave enough to say such things to my face. No, they followed college protocol and talked about me behind my back. Then they put on big, bright smiles that never reached their eyes to ask me for money.

This particular gala was a charity event put on by people I actually liked, the Heart of Darkness Literary Society, which was a student-run organization. The funds were distributed among literacy programs throughout the United States. Everyone attended not only because it was a popular event, but also because it was well covered by the media. And regents, alumni, and assorted other bores liked to remind the public how altruistic they were.

Sigh.

"You're going with me," I said.

Dove stared at me for a full thirty seconds. One of the more effective weapons in her snark-casm arsenal was utter silence accompanied by her *you-are-stupid-and-wrong* expression.

But I was immune to Dove's sneers, slights, silence, and all eighteen forms of her sarcasm.

I said nothing, and we sat in my office staring daggers at each other. Finally, she gave a low, dramatic sigh and said, "I'm wearing a corset."

"And those ballerina boots? Those shiny red ones with the crazy toes?"

She rolled her eyes. "Yes. Your pet will be on display."

"You're not my pet," I said. Then I opened one of the lower drawers in my desk and withdrew a rectangular gold box. "Wanna treat?"

Dove stood up and held out her hand. "I'm not settling for one truffle. The whole box, or I dress like my maiden aunt."

She had me. Seeing Dove show up in one of her outrageous outfits designed to inspire both awe and horror was probably the only entertainment I'd have tonight.

"You don't have a maiden aunt," I said as I handed over the box of Godiva chocolates.

"Thank you for reminding me that my entire family is dead. And that I have no one on this earth who loves me." She delivered these lines deadpan, but unfortunately these were also her truths. Dove didn't have family. Except for me. Not that I would ever admit to the little shit that she was like my sister. I understood the loneliness that lived inside her because it lived in me, too. When my grandfather died, I had no one left, either.

Dove and I were orphans. It was one of the aspects of our lives that bonded us.

Not that we'd ever gone on *Dr. Phil* and discussed it, or anything.

Dove lifted the lid to the box to ensure that no chocolates had been pilfered. She sniffed. "I am appeased. You will have your show."

"Excellent."

She leaned down and tapped the atrocious vampire book. "Chapter twelve," she said. "Read it."

"Sure. Right after I finish *War and Peace*."

"You are an idiot." She clutched the chocolates to her chest and spun on her heel. Then she paused and looked over her shoulder. "I'll see you later. Don't wear that black lace thing. It's awful."

"I love that dress."

"Which is why you wear it to every function. Burn it, and then explore all those designer clothes in your closet. You're a fucking billionaire. Act like it." She swept out of the office and shut the door behind her.

Well, shit. I leaned back in my chair and rubbed my temples. I wasn't really looking forward to getting dolled up and prancing around at this party. Despite my grumbling about the politics involved with running of a college, I had a deep respect for the institution. I had always enjoyed learning, and teaching as well. But what I really loved was getting hip-deep in sand and uncovering the past one tiny piece at a time. Archaeology required devotion, passion, and infinite patience. I didn't want to seek treasure; I wanted to seek truth. I wanted to understand the past, to find a window into the lives of people who'd lived three thousand years ago, those stalwart souls who had loved, and fought, and cleaned houses, raised children, written stories, built pyramids. Yes, answering the questions about those lives lived so long ago was what I sought. Connections, I supposed.

I glanced at the clock on my desk, and heaved a tormented sigh. The countdown to gala time had begun, and I didn't want to go home and sort through my closet. After Dove's crack about my black lace dress—which was modest and pretty, FYI—the hell if I would wear it now.

I looked down at the book. A pink Post-it note stuck out of the top. No doubt Dove had marked the location of chapter 12. Well, it was either explore the theory of ancient Egyptian vampires or start Operation Beautify. Winner: procrastinating with the undead.

When I opened the book, I noticed that Dove had made notations in the margins and had even highlighted portions of text. Say what you wanted about her attitude and style, the girl was smart and studious. And had no respect for the sanctity of the printed page.

As I started to read the chapter's introductory paragraph, my academic arrogance deflated. The tone was crisp, informative, and wry with humor. Theodora Monroe wrote seriously about her topic while also acknowledging the absurdity associated with it.

I was three pages in, fascinated despite my initial reluctance, when I stumbled across another of Dove's highlighted portions:

From what I've pieced together, there were seven original Ancient vampires. The lines, and powers, of our fanged friends rely heavily on their original maker. The theory is, of course, that if the originator of the vampire line is killed, then so, too, are all the vampires associated with the Family. I believe this may be because the magic of the first vampire connects him, or her, to all their—for lack of a better term—children. Magical strings, as it were, and if those lines are instantly cut . . . ah, I suppose you understand.

The greatest mystery associated with the Ancients is the loss of Amahté. Some three thousand years ago, he disappeared. Some vampires "go to ground," which means they go into hiding in an underground location for an unspecified time. Some do it to heal from grievous wounds, others to sleep through time, or to mourn quietly the loss of their mortal friends and lovers. I speculate that Amahté has gone to ground the longest. And he must still live if his vampiric children still walk the earth. But who is to know for certain?

Alas, I have not met any vampires who can give me answers to my many questions. My research has been

*pieced together through numerous source materials
(listed at the back of this book), eyewitness accounts,
and laborious field research. Evidence is always difficult to gain, no doubt because vampires prefer to re-
main in the dark (for obvious reasons).*

I stopped reading and let the thought of an ancient
Egyptian vampire roll around in my mind. It would be
unwise to eject my scholarly insight, years of archaeological experience, and jaded mentality for a theory
that was ridiculous. And yet . . . exciting. Not that I believed in the bloodsucking undead. Theodora Monroe
obviously had an agenda in writing her book, and I
knew full well that research could often be skewed to
support a particular viewpoint. But what if there really
was an Amahté? A king, perhaps. A blood drinker who
created a Sekhmet cult. What if Amahté ruled along the
same lines of Akhenaten, who brought monotheism to
a very reluctant people?

I couldn't get rid of the idea of a blood-drinking
Egyptian pharaoh. The fanged *ushabtis* offered slight
evidence for this outlandish theory. We'd found a very
strange crypt. And I hadn't looked at it from this viewpoint at all. I'd been disappointed to find it empty, sure,
but given our time limitation we'd been as meticulous
as we could have been in collecting information.

I glanced at the clock and cursed.

I'd spent a few minutes too long with the book and
my thoughts. I grabbed the copy of *Vampires Are Real!*

and my tote and left the office. I locked the door behind me and headed out to my car.

All the while I wondered . . . what if there was a pharaoh known as a vampire king? What if he had begun the traditions of modern-day mythology about the undead? Had my grandfather been wrong about Set's temple? He'd done so much research, and gone to the Sudan every year since forever for the chance to find something wonderful. Something that could rewrite history.

Ancient Egyptian vampires could rewrite everyone's history

In one teeny tiny corner of my mind, I wondered, too . . . were vampires real?

I grinned. What a ridiculous thought. Vampires. *Real.* Ha! Stupid Dove and her stupid book. I didn't believe in the undead.

I had a front parking spot, so it wasn't too much of a walk to my car. But it was dark out, and the wind had kicked up, rattling the dying leaves on the plentiful trees. August was sliding toward September, and students who'd spent the summer partying or working were still in serious mode. The later it got in the semester, the less attentive the classes and the more plentiful the on-campus parties.

I put the key into the door of my 1956 Mercedes 190SL. It had belonged to my grandfather, who'd purchased it as an anniversary gift for my grandmother in 1956. Mint condition, baby. It was silver with a red leather interior and a stick shift, and it drove like a dream. It was one of the many items I inherited when Grandfather died. But I would've given the car, and everything else, for just one more day with him.

I started to open the door . . . then paused, my fingers resting underneath the handle.

I couldn't quite figure out what made me hesitate. Then I realized the wind had abruptly stopped.

I heard an electric crackle, and felt my heart skip a beat.

The parking lot lights nearest to my car went out.

And in the sudden, awful darkness . . . something waited for me.

Chapter 7
Drake

I hid in the shadows of the building, waiting. Moira hadn't left her office yet. As soon as she did, I would follow her home and ensure that she arrived safely. For close to a week I had slept near wherever she was, in case she needed me at a moment's notice. When she left the university, getting into her beautiful vintage Mercedes, I would turn into wolf form and run through the forest that bordered the road to her home.

After a week of this, I felt like her stalker instead of her protector. I found myself doing foolish things, like wandering past her table in the coffee shop just to get a whiff of her perfume. I was capable of tracking scents for miles, but the werewolf in me was not satisfied with drawing out that faint scent of dewed flowers from among all the others worn by humans.

The man in me wanted to be closer, too.

Much closer.

The naked kind of closer.

Just yesterday, I stood behind her in the line to get a very expensive latte, and couldn't resist a swipe of my fingers against her hair. She'd worn it loose, and it was a curtain of silky red. She smelled like she'd bathed in flower petals—a light, crisp scent that made me think of sheets and sighs and . . . well, enough of that.

She did not turn around, and I left right then before I could do something else that would draw her attention to me. Like kiss her until those cherry lips were swollen and those green, green eyes were glazed, and that . . . Down, boy.

This was my last night of keeping an eye on Moira Jameson.

Patsy, queen of the vampires—those who recognized her authority, at least—had called me earlier and said that with Karn apparently in hiding, it was probably best to withdraw our resources to Broken Heart, Oklahoma, our headquarters, and figure out our next strategies for dealing with him. We expected the pyramid to reappear in the desert tomorrow—the "seven days hence"—and others had gathered at Moira's dig site in preparation.

Karn would no doubt try for the pyramid again. We all knew that he would make his presence known eventually. He'd been popping up and wreaking havoc for the last couple of months. Pain in the ass. Some *droch fola*—the vampires who were soulless—were relentless in their stupidity. But if Karn was in Egypt . . . then he wasn't anywhere near New York State.

The most recent Vedere prophecy revealed that the return of the missing vampire ancients, Shamhat and Amahté, would herald a new chapter for the vampires. The prophecy was not particularly secret . . . but the location of the Ancients had been closely guarded. How Karn had learned of their whereabouts remained a mystery. His goal was to get to those long-slumbering Ancients and kill them. He wanted to take their power—and give himself true immortality with the ambrosia that was buried with them.

World-domination plots were so last century.

My thoughts returned to Moira. She was a fascinating woman in many respects. However, she was not very well liked around these parts, though the bits of gossip I gleaned while sitting at the coffee shop and in the library (where she loved to go ravage the sections on ancient Egypt) seemed tinged with bitterness. People who whispered their grievances and spread poison with innuendos were cowards.

Moira was not a coward.

She faced people every day who either hated her or feared her, and she acted as though their sneers and the obvious way they crossed streets to avoid her didn't bother her at all. She ignored, too, people clustering together and laughing behind their hands. Perhaps these actions did not bother Moira. Constant derision and scorn often built the most durable of shields.

All the same, I wanted to rip off their faces.

I had come to admire Moira. She had grace. Purpose. Beauty.

If I hadn't known better, I would have said she was a werewolf.

I was the only one dispatched to the college to watch over Moira. Dove did not need protection. She vibrated with the kind of energy that encouraged people to move out of her way or die.

I liked her.

The other humans Eva had glamoured were also students here, but we had no cause to concern ourselves with their memories. Their minds had been far more malleable than Moira's and Dove's . . . and most had been asleep when Karn sent his minions to the campsite. The one called Ax had presented a somewhat larger challenge, but eventually he remembered just as Moira and Dove did: They had found an empty crypt and had returned to the States hopeful that next year's dig would bear fruit.

Eva had thought the false memories of an archaeological find would better hide the real memories of uncovering the pyramid and being attacked by Karn.

I felt a growl low in my throat. *Karn.* The way he had taken Moira, threatened her. He deserved to die for laying his filthy hands on her. My sense of dread had been building all week.

Or maybe it was my attraction to Moira that coiled like a snake in my belly and caused my foreboding. I could not have her.

But I wanted her.

I heard the clip of boots on the sidewalk and straightened. I knew the beat of Moira's shoes on concrete. She strode around the corner, confident and beautiful, her red hair pulled into a casual ponytail. She wore a short-sleeved T-shirt with the college logo on it, tight jeans, and an old pair of cowboy boots. She carried a monstrous tote, and as always, her expression suggested she was deep in her own thoughts.

She seemed unaware of her surroundings, and as far as I could tell from my weeklong observations, she never seemed to show interest in detecting potential danger. Being on home turf made her complacent, even though she was surrounded by enemies. If I had the opportunity, I would show her how to protect herself better. She seemed quite capable with guns, but did not carry one on campus. Perhaps she would feel too tempted to use it on the college personnel.

But a gun would not help Moira against a vampire, a fact she would know if she remembered what had happened in the desert. A paranormal being such as Karn would not find a gun much of a deterrent. Vampires were by and large derisive of weapons that were incapable of chopping off their heads. A bullet was a mere nuisance.

I silently tracked Moira, pausing as I caught the

scent of . . . parchment. Vampires smelled like old books in a library to werewolves. It was not unpleasant, but it was distinctive. I scanned the area.

There, in the trees that lined the right side of the main parking lot, was a vampire. The red glow of his eyes gave him and his intentions away. Moira headed to her Mercedes. Just as she reached the driver's-side door, the vampire sent out a wave of power that sizzled the parking lot lights.

Moira paused and stiffened, obviously aware now that something was wrong.

I moved toward the trees as swiftly as possible without giving myself away, but the vampire had scented me, too. The moment I knew he was waiting for me to come at him, I gave up stealth and went for speed.

"Sorry, mate," he said as I entered the trees, "the girl's already mine."

"I found her first," I said. Then I punched him in the throat.

Chapter 8

Moira

The hairs rose on the back of my neck. I could hear the hushed sound of my own shallow breathing, and my heart went from erratic to spastic.

For an odd moment, I had the terrible feeling that if I moved even the *slightest* bit, something big and scary would attack me. Fear was a stupid, irrational thing, and I knew it. But still I was frozen, my fingers trembling on the car door handle, my other hand clutching my tote.

I heard a big, quick *swoosh* . . . then . . . nothing.

Silence enveloped me, and it felt thick and strange, like wet cotton had been stuffed into my ears.

I took a breath and then whirled around, ready to swing my bag at an intruder—and let me tell you, that Theodora Monroe book added substantial heft.

I was alone.

The wind tickled at my hair, sudden and playful, as if it hadn't abandoned me. Then the parking lot lights flickered back on.

My heart rate, however, remained at a steady one thousand rpm.

Because I was stubborn, I took a minute to study the area, to try and determine what had been behind me. I glanced up at the steady blue hue of the light, and made a mental note to get those damned things checked.

Then I slid into my car, eased the tote onto the passenger seat, and carefully started the motor.

By the time I reached the street that led to my house, my heart rate was normal and I could breathe again.

I had no idea what had happened. Maybe reading about vampires before venturing out into the dark had messed with my mind.

In any case, I had more important matters to worry about.

Like what to wear.

I stood near the table laden with mini quiches, puff pastries, and prosciutto-wrapped melon. I held a champagne flute while I mulled over the selections, even though I'd already filled my plate four times. What? They were *tiny* plates. Every so often I would look at the open double doors that led into the ballroom.

Where was Dove?

She was never on time, but being late always made her arrival spectacular. Still, we were nearly two hours into the gala and Dove hadn't showed. That wasn't like her. Half an hour, yes. An hour, maybe. Two hours? Never. Sheesh. Had she tripped on those outrageous shoes and broken her neck?

I slipped into a corner, pulled the cell out of my beaded wristlet, and called Dove. The phone rang and rang, and finally voice mail came on. "Apparently I didn't want to talk to you," she intoned. "Leave a message. If. You. Dare."

Oh, I dared.

"Where are you? Are you okay?" I hissed into the receiver. Then I realized I sounded like worried Mama Bear. "I'm bored! I've eaten my weight in quiches, and you're supposed to prevent me from doing that. If you don't call me in the next five minutes, I'm going to the dessert table without you. I will eat all the cheesecake, Dove. *All* of it."

I ended the call and slipped the phone back into the little purse. Worry nibbled at me like vicious hamsters. Surely Dove was fine . . . just being extra Dove-y, or something. And I really wanted her to see my dress. I suspected it might actually rate Dove approval.

I looked down at said dress and sighed. I'd un-earthed the purple sheath and matching heels from the closet. With my hair pulled into a topknot, and the am-ethyst jewelry I wore, I looked good. And with all the lotion and powder and spritz I'd put on after my

shower, I smelled good, too. Considering I spent a lot
of time in the same clothes, sweating daily, showering . . .
um, weekly, and ignoring stench and beauty in the
name of archaeology, dressing up in this kind of finery
was unusual. And uncomfortable. Why couldn't some
designer make T-shirts and khakis the next big trend?

I looked at my wristlet, debating whether to call
Dove again. Maybe I should go to her apartment and
make sure she hadn't suffocated after putting on her
corset.

Dove was an irreverent bitch, but she was responsible. And she didn't lie. If she said she was going to do
something, she did it. I was giving her fifteen minutes.
If she didn't show by then, I would track her down.
And if she was alive . . . I would kill her.

I sipped my champagne. The college orchestra
played lovely eighteenth-century music, and performers from our dance and theater programs were show-
casing Baroque dances, such as the minuet and the
gavotte.

Then the tempo changed to an upbeat tune, and the
performers dispersed, grabbing partners from the
watching crowd and dancing with sweet abandon.

"Good evening, Dr. Jameson."

I turned my gaze to the gentleman who'd approached me. He was taller than I was by several
inches, and I was six feet. He was also nicely filled out,
muscled in a non-brutish way, with sandy brown hair
and eyes so blue they looked gray . . . and cold. Like

fog rolling over a fresh grave. I had no idea where that imagery was coming from, but that's the feeling he gave me. He was handsomely dressed in an old-fashioned tailored tuxedo. I had pictures of my grandfather from his youth in the same style of formal wear.

"Good evening," I said. I felt electrified in his presence, as though I were standing near a live wire and should tread very, very carefully. "I'm sorry. Do I know you?"

"Ah, now there's a question." He studied me closely. "You don't remember, do you?" He bent his arm under his waist and swept into a graceful half bow. "My name is Karn."

His name was Karn? Last? First? Or was he more like Cher or Madonna? "I'm Dr. Moira Jameson," I said, even though he apparently knew my name.

He extended his hand. "Dance with me."

"It's kind of you to ask, Mr. Karn," I said, as though he had politely queried instead of quietly demanded. I resisted the urge to bat his hand away, "but I'm leaving."

"Just Karn," he said, in nearly the same severe way that Dove often introduced herself. He dropped his hand and offered a thin-edged smile. "A dance, Dr. Jameson." He leaned close, the smile growing sharper still. "I'm afraid I must insist. Especially if you hope to see your darling little Dove again."

"*What?*"

He kept a polite, distant expression while he took the

champagne flute out of my hand and set it onto the tray of a passing waiter. "I'm quite sure you don't have problems with your hearing, Dr. Jameson." He once again extended his hand. "Shall we?"

This man had kidnapped Dove? Why would anyone take her? I gripped his hand, resisting the urge to twist his fingers enough to break them. For a moment his eyes gleamed with challenge, almost as though he'd guessed my thoughts and welcomed my defiance. I gritted my teeth, ignored my impulse to hurt him.

He led me to the dance floor.

He placed a hand at my waist and I reluctantly put my hand on his shoulder. Then he lifted my other hand in his and whirled me around.

"What do you want?" I asked.

"The world," he said, flashing that awful sharp smile. "And everything in it."

The world? *Really?* "Well, you can't have Dove." I felt chilled to my core. Was she okay? Had they hurt her? Why, why, why would someone take an orphaned, smart-mouthed college undergrad?

"I already have her." He executed a turn. I twirled away, and then returned to the slimeball's arms. "If you want her back, Dr. Jameson, then you'll come with me and do what I ask."

Oh, was that all? Grrr! I wanted to kick him in the shins. Hard. But terror, not retribution, crawled through me like a thousand marching spiders. I pressed my lips together to keep them from trembling. If something happened to Dove . . . oh, God.

"If you hurt her," I said, "and I mean, if she even stubs her little toe in your care, then I'll—"

"You'll *what*?" He pushed his face close to mine, daring me to threaten him. Aggression rolled off him in waves. He wasn't a gentleman at all. He was a beast hiding in a fancy suit. Fear slicked my spine, and I got the distinct impression he wanted to tear out my throat with those sharp white teeth of his.

"I will kill you," I said.

He drew back, and sighed. "How clichéd. I was hoping for a far more clever response—especially from you, Dr. Jameson. You're very much known around here for your . . . hmm . . . I suppose some might call it wit."

"Occasionally it's best to stick with the classics," I said between clenched teeth. "Is it money, then? Ransom?"

"You really do like her, don't you?" He looked at me blankly, as though he didn't fathom the concept of friendship. "It's useful—this connection you humans have to one another."

"Us *humans*?" I asked, unable to keep the horror out of my tone. Great, Karn was crazy. I mean, I'd figured out he was ruthless, mean, and greedy . . . and those qualities, though heinous, did denote a villain who was at least purposeful in his nefariousness. But a man who was driven by the demons of insanity? And hel-lo, I understood emotional demons. And being mentally cracked. But not evil. Not like this man.

"You have so much to learn. And I promise that the world I will reveal to you is worth the price you must pay." He twirled me again, and when I came back to the starting point, he whisked me off the dance floor.

He grasped my elbow and led me across the ballroom, past the food-laden tables, and toward the doors that led to the kitchens. My heart started to hammer in my chest. Where did he plan on taking me? What tasks did he want me to perform? And was Dove okay?

"*Doctor* Jameson." Doriana Zimmerman stepped into our path, effectively blocking our exit. "I need to speak to you about the program funding for our sea urchin research."

Doriana was the head of our marine biology department. She was 102 years old (okay, maybe just fifty or something) with wiry gray hair that always looked electrified. She had high cheekbones that she always rouged a terrible orange color, and she loved the color blue, which manifested in the glittery eyeshadow she wore— possibly to match the dress that hung loosely on her bony frame. Dove had nicknamed her Bride of Frankenstein, which was wrong, I know, but also a fair assessment of Doriana's looks. Doriana was very good at her job, but absolutely manic about save-the-sea activities. I usually preferred entering a scorpion-infested pit over dealing with the woman's barrage of funding requests, but today, oh, today, she was an angel from heaven.

"Sea urchins?" I inquired. My captor squeezed my arm in warning. He couldn't yank me away without being obvious, and I knew he didn't want to draw attention to us. It occurred to me, sadly, that I didn't really have any allies here. I couldn't think of a single person who would know me well enough to assess the situation and see that something was wrong.

No one could help me. And several people here probably wouldn't help me even if given the opportunity.

"I sent a *memo*," said Doriana, pursing her lips. She glanced at Karn. "Who are you?"

Oh, my God. I so loved Doriana right now. She had no patience for propriety, and tended to be blunt to the point of rudeness. That was actually one of the few things I liked about her.

"I am Dr. Jameson's escort this evening," he said. He tugged me closer and kept a death grip on my elbow. "I hope you will excuse us."

"No," said Doriana. She turned her attention away from Karn, dismissing him as unimportant. Wow. I bet that pissed him off. World-dominating assholes liked to be taken seriously. At least, that's what I'd gleaned from marathon sessions of the *Harry Potter* movies.

Karn squeezed my arm even harder, and I bit my lower lip to keep from yelping. I swallowed hard. "Perhaps we could discuss the sea urchin question later." I tried to convey *Help me* with my gaze and the panicked edge of my smile, but she rolled her eyes.

"You don't return phone calls or e-mails. I have to hunt you down like a . . . a seal hunter," she said. Her expression grew sterner. "And that is another area of concern we need to discuss. Seals are—"

"Fascinating," interrupted Karn. "Excuse us."

He attempted to guide me around Doriana, but she stepped into his path. "Escort, my ass," she said in a loud voice. "You're a . . . a gigolo!" She pointed an accusing finger at me. "She doesn't date. She doesn't even know how to date. She bought you. And if she can buy man meat, she can fund sea urchin research!"

Doriana's voice had risen several octaves by now, drawing the attention of the people around us. Karn was so stunned by her accusation that his mouth dropped open and his grip loosened. I had to resist the urge to dissolve into hysterical giggles.

And I am not a giggler.

People sidled closer, pretending to be interested in their champagne and canapés, but really they were waiting for the drama to unfold.

Doriana did not disappoint.

She slapped at Karn's arm, the one that still held my elbow, and my arm popped free. "Man meat!" she cried. "That's all you are!"

"Madam," said Karn, "you are mistaken."

In a quicksilver moment, I saw Doriana's eyes go black . . . and I mean completely black . . . and she hissed in a low, snarly voice, "Vampire."

Karn's face twisted in hatred, and he hissed back, "Mermaid."

What. The. Hell?

Doriana's hand curled into a fist. Then she hauled back her arm and punched the man in the jaw. He sailed backward, into a knot of partygoers who fell down like a rack of bowling pins. Doriana looked at me and yelled, "Run, you idiot!"

I hitched up my dress, toed off the heels, and ran. I stopped at the door, my heart pounding, sweat beading my neck, and took a last look over my shoulder. Doriana marched forward, fists clenched, while my wannabe kidnapper extracted himself from the groaning group of people who'd broken his fall.

I didn't wait to see what happened next.

When I got outside, I wasn't sure what to do. I went down the steps, the feet of my hosiery snagging on the stone. The well-lit courtyard in front of the building was empty, which made me wary. I didn't want to go past the circle of lights and into the evening darkness. It was just past nine p.m., hardly the witching hour, but everything seemed creepy to me now. I had the terrible feeling that Karn would burst through the doors any second to chase me. And he'd probably catch me.

I thought about earlier, about the strange feeling of being stalked in the parking lot . . . and wondered if that experience had occurred because Karn was waiting in the shadows for me. Why hadn't he just taken me then? Why go through the trouble of kidnapping Dove if he wanted me for . . . well, whatever?

Ack! What to do? What to freaking do? Call the police? And tell them some stranger claimed to have one of my students, who was also my best friend—er, my only friend?

And what was the deal with Doriana calling Karn a vampire? And him calling her a mermaid? I couldn't quite wrap my brain around it. Didn't mermaids live in the sea and trap sailors and command Krakens? I had no idea. I really needed to brush up on my sea mythologies.

Being outside in the dark made me antsy, so I hurried toward the parking lot. Somehow, the Mercedes represented safety. I would get into my car, drive to Dove's, and tell her about my evening. We would laugh, and then break out the vodka.

Lots and lots of vodka.

I ran down the sidewalk, grateful once again for having parking lot privileges. The Mercedes was within sight when a very large man stepped out of the shadows. He was well dressed, and for some reason, I noted the Italian leather loafers that he wore to complement what was obviously a tailored suit. The man flashed a not-so-nice smile.

I skidded, and whirled, only to find my path blocked by another large man. He also wore a very nice suit, a burnt orange that complemented his dark skin. His scalp was shaved, but he had a narrow goatee. He wore mirrored sunglasses, and the smile he offered was just as nasty as his friend's.

I shot off to the side, and my feet had barely touched the grass when I felt myself yanked upward into a pair of steel-banded arms. I batted at him, but it was like smacking marble.

"Karn requests the pleasure of your company," said the man in a pleasant English accent. My struggles didn't seem to bother him in the slightest.

"I should've known he had minions!" I cried. I continued to slap at the arms holding me.

"Not minions," said the other man, who came closer. I noted the scar that bisected his left cheek, and the fact that he had one blue eye and one brown eye. His brunet hair was short and spiky, and he was clean-shaven. And very, very pale. "Partners."

He was American, and if I wasn't mistaken, had the light twang of the South in his voice. Partners? Hah! If these two thought Karn was the type of guy who had partners, they were morons.

"Let me go!" I yelled.

They both laughed, not in a diabolical, evil way, but in a way that suggested I'd just told a hilarious joke. And actually? That kind of laughter seemed a lot scarier in this situation. I continued to kick shins and punch arms, but really it was useless. He was a statue. He didn't even have the courtesy to pretend I was doing any damage. And did I mention I wasn't a delicate flower?

"I see you've detained our guest." Karn walked out of the shadows, dabbing at his bloodied lip with a linen handkerchief. "Your friend is lucky, Dr. Jameson. I let her live . . . although she may be limping for a while." He flashed a cold smile, and I noted that his split lip was healing even as I watched. I couldn't help but think of Theodora Monroe's book, and what Doriana had hissed at him.

Vampire.

Karn folded the cloth and slid it into his pants pocket. "Merfolk are notoriously vicious. It's why I avoid the sea."

I said nothing. I couldn't begin to comment on his strange assertions. Besides, my captor was squeezing my middle, and it was difficult to draw enough breath to talk.

"Now. Where were we? Oh, yes." Karn strode forward, eyed me with a relish that made my heart stutter. Then he raised his fist and hit me in the jaw.

My head snapped back, and pain exploded. I saw a burst of tiny white stars.

And I fell into the deep dark of nothingness.

Chapter 9
Dove

Sadly, it was not my first time to be locked in the trunk of a car.

It was my third.

The first time, I'd been a child exploring Aunt Peg's 1967 Chevy Impala. She discovered me curled in the corner asleep about an hour after I shut the lid on myself. I was quite surprised that she remembered she had a six-year-old in her care, much less that she thought to look for me. She patted my head and gave me cake, and then we watched George Romero's *Dawn of the Dead* until her Xanax kicked in.

The second time, I was fifteen. I ran away from my third foster home, determined to live on my own terms, even if that meant being homeless on the streets. My foster father—I believe his name was Milt—tracked me down right after the school called and said I wasn't there. When I pitched the mother of all fits right there on the street corner, he tossed me into the trunk of his Ford and drove me straight to my social worker's office.

Now I was twenty-two and stuffed into yet another trunk. My jaw hurt where my kidnapper had hit me. I guess my screaming had irritated him. I'd blacked out long enough to be trussed up with duct tape and for whoever to shut the lid and start driving.

The car moved sedately, occasionally slowing down for speed bumps. I could only assume we were still on the college grounds, which made no sense. Neither did my kidnapping. I couldn't begin to fathom why anyone would bother to kidnap me. I had no fortune. No fame.

But I did have a friend who had both of those. Moira.

The tape on my wrists was haphazard and my persistence and flexibility allowed me to get free. They hadn't bothered to bind my feet because my shoes were trap enough.

The car was an older model, and had no seat or trunk pulls. I couldn't get the taillights to wiggle even a little. After I'd exhausted all my efforts to get free of my wretched moving coffin, I stared up at the lid.

It was the damned shoes that literally tripped me up. I'd been running late to Moira's shindig. Getting into a corset wasn't easy, especially when I had to rely on Marvin, my pothead next-door neighbor, to tighten and tie the cords for me. Then I'd laced myself up into the red knee-high ballet boots and tottered out of my two-story apartment building to find Dumb and Dumber waiting for me.

Oh, and they were undead.

Which was slightly unnerving.

Trying to run resulted in my subsequent falling, wherein I was caught by Huge Dumb-Ass Number One and whisked away to the waiting car. I used my lungs to their full capacity as he threw me into the trunk.

He hit me.

My purse was lost, and so was my cell phone. I had no way to get hold of Moira or call for any sort of help.

What a crappy way to spend a Friday night.

Chapter 10

Drake

Leaving a werewolf for dead without checking to make sure you had killed him was a sign of arrogance—or stupidity. It didn't hurt that my parents were immortals, which meant I was not just a werewolf. I was a demigod. It was nearly impossible to kill me. But most of parakind didn't know the royal triplets had immortal blood.

Waking up in the sewer did not improve my mood.

If the vampire I'd tracked hadn't been joined by three other friends, I would not have been taken. The number of vampires attacking and one lucky fucking punch had been enough to drop me.

I suppose I should have been grateful that the bastards didn't try to eat me. Vampires who lived outside of Queen Patsy's rule or who refused friendship with the Consortium had no compunction about feasting on other paranormals.

Apparently they just didn't have the time to enjoy werewolf blood.

The stench was awful. I suppose I also should have been grateful I had landed on the wide concrete slab next to the brackish river of human waste instead of actually in the sewer water.

I sat up, cursing my throbbing head and my still healing body.

I knew Moira was in trouble. Or would be. I didn't know how much time had been lost. I felt my pockets and realized the vampires had relieved me of my wallet and my cell phone. Damn it. I was still playing *Bejeweled* and had just gotten my playlists organized.

As I got to my feet, I felt a sharp pain rip through my side. I looked down at my ragged T-shirt and saw that a slash of bloody skin was still knitting together.

Oh, great. I'd been stabbed.

And I really liked this shirt.

A few feet above me, I saw the manhole cover. I eyed the ladder leading up to it, took a deep breath, and went for it. Moving up the rungs hurt like a bitch, but I knew from experience that I would heal and the pain would recede.

But I couldn't run around the human world looking like I'd just been killed and tossed into the sewer. I was near the academic parking lot, and I noted that Moira's red Mercedes was gone. So, she had gotten away while I got my ass handed to me. Good.

I needed to change clothes and get to a phone.

It was time to call in the paranormal cavalry.

Chapter 11

Moira

I woke up to a throbbing headache, an aching jaw, and a numb ass.

It took me a minute to realize I was tied to a very uncomfortable chair. My arms were pinned behind the plastic contraption, my wrists chafed by thick rope.

How long had I been out?

And where the hell was I?

My jaw hurt. *A lot.* Pain zigzagged across my cheek and down my neck. Jeez. Even my eyelashes hurt. An electric lantern emitted a creepy green glow from a nearby table. The light didn't do much to dispel the darkness around me, but the room felt large. I could practically taste the dust that indicated years of disuse, and smell the staleness of the air. The atmosphere reminded me of how it felt to enter a newly discovered tomb that had lain unopened for millennia.

Not a good analogy.

"So much for getting rescued," said a familiar voice.

I looked to my left. Dove was about three feet away, also tied to a chair. Relief flooded through me. Despite her apparent bravado, I saw the terror lurking in her gaze. She wore a corset and those horrible shoes. Her hair was ratty, and a bruise shadowed her jaw. It seemed Karn and his minions liked to hit women. Assholes.

On the upside, Dove was alive.

"I'm here, aren't I? Happy rescue!" I pulled against the ropes, but realized very quickly that wiggling free was not an option. I stopped struggling, deciding it was wiser to conserve my energy. I glanced at Dove. "I'm ready to reconsider your theory about vampires."

"It only took meeting one to change your mind." She blew out a breath. "Any ideas about getting out of here?"

"Not really," I said. Why had we been kidnapped? What did Karn want with us? Panic started to edge through the pain. My jaw throbbed endlessly. Oh, what I wouldn't give for some ibuprofen and a tequila shooter. "Do you know where 'here' is?"

"I think we might still be on the college grounds," she said. "They snatched me outside the dorm rooms and tossed me into the trunk of a car. I was screaming at the top of my lungs, and Scarface hit me. I blacked out." She paused, then continued. "I managed to get my wrists free and when he opened the trunk, I went right for his undead eyes. So he popped me again.

"When I came to they were carrying me toward the building. It's the same brickwork as all the campus buildings, but I didn't recognize the location. I heard them say there wasn't any electricity . . . and it smells like a tomb in here."

Dove had reached the same conclusions I had. If we were still on campus . . . oh, crap. There was only one building at the college that was never used, had no reason to be hooked up to the power grid, and would have the dust of the ages in it.

"Shit." My eyes were starting to adjust to the darkness. "We're in Building A."

Dove's eyes went wide. She looked around, as though she might see the rumored ghost. "Some teacher was killed here, right? And people hear her screams." She frowned.

"I've heard her screams," I said softly.

"You heard . . ." Dove trailed off and stared at me. "You believe in ghosts?"

"Maybe. I've recently had to adjust my skepticism scale."

"When did you hear these screams?"

Almost thirty years ago. I was five at the time . . . only I think I was the one screaming. I shrugged. "I avoid this building like it's stacked with plague-filled mummies."

"What's going on, Moira? What do you know about this ghost?"

"Not the ghost," I said. "The woman who was killed. The teacher." I blew out a breath, and felt chills zip down my spine. "Regina Noreen Jameson." I looked at Dove. "My mother."

"Your *mother*?" Dove's mouth dropped open. "What about the whole story about your mom dying in a car accident?"

"My grandfather used his influence and money to cover up the situation, okay? It was 1978. There wasn't *CSI* or DNA or even *TMZ*. The college was even smaller then, and only my grandparents and the groundskeeper who found us knew what happened."

"Us? You were there when your mom was killed?"

A red wave of anguish and fury washed over me, momentarily robbing me of speech and sight. The meds were doing their work, obviously. Because I was still coherent and could control those waves of twisted emotion. But damn! Leave it to Dove to catch such a small slip of the tongue. Amid our current drama, being snatched, tied up, and left to mull about our fates . . . it hardly seemed the place and time to let my past suffocate me. Still. A familiar ache clutched my chest and made my lungs squeeze. I had been five, old enough to remember her. That she liked blue and strawberries and laughing. She smelled liked roses. She liked to sing, even though she was horrible at it. And getting a hug from her was like being wrapped in cashmere.

"What happened, Moira?"

"Yes," said the smarmy voice of Karn. "Do tell."

"Fuck you," I said.

"Such language from a lady." His minions had followed him into the room. They stayed behind him, on either side, forming a triangle of vampiric evil. "Do you miss your mummy, Dr. Jameson?"

"Are you going to miss your balls?" I asked. "Because I have every intention of removing them."

"You're delightful," he said in a tone that suggested I was the exact opposite. His gaze flickered over Dove. "I really don't see the point to having you around anymore."

"Don't touch her," I said in a low voice. "If you hope to get even an ounce of cooperation from me, you'll leave her alone."

Karn's gaze swung toward me, and he studied me for a long, quiet moment. "I believe you, Dr. Jameson. Your stubbornness is well known. And I also believe that if I killed your darling Dove, you'd find a way to escape, or die, rather than help me." He cocked his head, his gaze filled with the same kind of excited fascination a scientist might have for a particularly successful experiment. "If you give me any trouble, I will hurt her. And I know a lot about pain. I spent a lifetime mastering the art of torture."

Fear pulsed within me, so much so that it nearly negated the pain. Sweat dripped down my temples and slicked my throat. "When this whole thing is over, and you have whatever it is . . . then what?"

"I'll let you go."

"Liar," said Miss I Have No Decorum.

"We're vampires," he said, flashing his fangs at us. "We can make you forget you ever saw us. There's no reason to kill you."

"If you have glamour," said Dove, staring daggers at Karn because, apparently, she didn't enjoy breathing. "Why aren't you using it? You could *make* us help you."

"You know everything about vampires, do you?" he asked. He looked like he might be reconsidering his decision to let Dove live. "Glamour is overrated. It's better to gain cooperation the old-fashioned way."

Something about his tone set off my bullshit radar. No one did things the hard way unless they had to . . . so why didn't Karn use glamour? Wouldn't you use a valuable tool such as the ability to make people do as you wished? I was an archaeologist. If I had a tool that could help me uncover the historical treasures on a site faster, without any harm to the location or the objects . . . why would I get out the brushes and tweezers?

Dove opened her mouth again, probably to comment on Karn's IQ or perhaps just say something snarky about his fangs—and I hissed, "Shut up!"

She pressed her lips together, and her eyebrows

dipped into one of her patented frowns, but the girl stopped talking.

Karn offered me one of his thin-bladed smiles. "I don't know how you put up with her."

I said nothing, offering only a half shrug. He didn't seem to care that I didn't want to engage with him. He was the coldest man I'd ever met. Were all vampires like him?

"We only have a few hours before dawn," said Mr. English Vampire.

"I only need a few minutes. But you are correct. Getting off the campus is wise," said Karn. "If that bitch mermaid alerted anyone to our presence, we may have to deal with unwanted visitors."

"Mermaid?" asked Dove.

"Oh, yeah," I said. "Doriana is apparently a creature of the sea."

Dove stared at me to gauge my seriousness, and then she nodded. "That actually explains a lot."

"You two do natter on," said Karn. "Gag them, and then make sure their bonds are secure."

A god-awful shriek filled the room. The sound was so sudden, so horrific, we were all startled by it . . . even the vampires. My skin prickled with unease, and even stoic Dove looked unnerved.

The vampires' expressions turned wary, and they spread out, apparently looking around for the source of the tortured wails. I couldn't see well beyond the creepy green glow of the electric lantern, but I wondered how well vampires could see. One of their supposed powers was excellent vision. *The better to hunt you with, my pretty.*

The screams were loud and endless.

As one faded, another would rise.

The shrieks made my skin crawl. I didn't have the luxury of putting my hands over my ears, and I could see that Dove might have been wishing for the same ability. Instead, we endured the tormented cries because we had no choice.

The temperature plummeted. Jeez! It felt like someone had turned the air-conditioning to an Arctic setting. I could see little clouds form as I puffed out panicked breaths. I glanced at Dove; she looked like she was struggling to maintain her composure.

I swallowed the knot in my throat. I could no longer dismiss the idea of ghosts as ludicrous. I'd met three vampires and a mermaid tonight. And hey, what was a visit from the spirit world on top of that three-layer hell cake? Still . . . I couldn't fathom the idea of hearing—much less seeing—the ethereal form of my murdered mother.

A memory flickered. It was so rare for me to think about those times, about what had happened. My grandfather had been the buoy in a raging, bloody sea. I remembered him, and all that he did for me, but before that . . . it was a dull gray area. The color bled away and all that remained was the dark.

And yet, I remembered her. Snippets, really. Just

enough to remember the shadows of grief, and just enough to miss her. Only her. I had never known my father.

I didn't want to remember now. I'd spent nearly three decades not thinking about my mother.

But the memory was insistent, and it unfurled like a sail propelled by the wind. I could not stop it. Dodge it. Brush it away. I had to ride it out, all the way. And damn it all, I could only watch . . .

I'm lying in a bed, cowering under a thick comforter. The lights are on in the room, because the darkness scares me. I am in my grandparents' bedroom. I do not feel safe. I will never feel safe again.

My gaze is riveted on the open door, on the shadows on the wall that echo the people standing in the hallway.

Two shadows.

Grandfather. And the nice man with eyes like shiny nickels.

"What did she see?" asked Grandfather. His voice was rough, but in a comfortable way, like leather worn soft by time.

"Everything. I'm sorry, my old friend. Even if I had got-ten here in time . . ." The man spoke in a way that reminded me of music. Now I recognized that it was an Irish accent.

"You couldn't have saved Regina. I know that. She could not receive your gifts. And she would not have wanted them."

"Moira is the last," said the man, "and the only one left

who can unlock what her ancestors' blood bound all those years ago."

"It seems a terrible burden for a child. She will not have an easy path, Ruadan. How can you expect her to keep such a promise when she cannot know what she is?"

"You know the Vedere pyschics are rarely wrong." He paused. " 'When only one remains, then she shall restore to the vampires those who have been lost to time.' "

"I know the prophecy, damn it. It's been the burden carried by Camille's family for three millennia. Damn it, Ruadan. I've lost my wife. My daughter," said Grandfather. "Please. I don't want to lose my granddaughter, too."

"Her fate belongs to her, and to her alone."

"Please, Ruadan."

The man named Ruadan sighed. "Glamour is not a permanent solution. Time can unravel even the tightest of memory knots, especially among parakind."

"Maybe if we hadn't hidden the truth from our daughter . . . maybe she would have . . ." My grandfather trailed off. "I'll do a better job of protecting Moira. I'll train her, Ruadan. I'll help her as much as I can, and when the time arrives, she will no doubt fulfill what the Fates have in store for her. But until then, I want her to be as normal as possible. You can give us that at least."

Silence filled the room, and my heart beat so loud I could hear it drumming in my ears. What was wrong with me? What was fate . . . and why did I have to have it?

"Very well, Ezra," said Ruadan. "I will do as you ask."

*   *   *

The memory snapped shut, and I jerked back, as though it had somehow tried to bite me.

What the hell was that all about?

Had being in the same building where my mother had been killed somehow unlocked a memory from my childhood?

I really did not want any more treats from that part of my life.

And all the wailing wasn't exactly helping my frame of mind, either. Hel-*lo*. Crazy woman here. No one wanted to set me off.

"Didn't you say we needed to get out of here?" I called out to Karn. He'd migrated toward the middle of the room, while his friends had gone left and right. They were shadows moving beyond the green glow of the light.

The wails ebbed and flowed like an ocean of pain. I wasn't even sure that Karn had heard my desperate query. I much preferred being carted out of the building by vampires than seeing Mom's ghostly form. Or remembering one sliver more about my five-year-old self.

Close your eyes!

The command came from inside my head, and it wasn't exactly choice-driven. I closed my eyes only because my eyelids insisted on it.

The shrieks ceased.

I heard Mr. English Vampire say, "What the fuck is—"

I heard a pop . . . boom . . . and then felt a quick flash of intense heat.

The vampires screeched.

I heard Karn yell, "No! Damn you!"

The silence stretched on and on. Finally, I said, "Dove?"

"Yeah?"

"Are your eyes closed?"

"Hell, yes."

"Well, do you want to open them?"

"Sure. Because I like the idea of burning out my corneas."

"The light bomb only lasts for a few seconds, but it does the job," said a male voice with a German accent. "And *ja*, it is okay for you to open your eyes."

Dove and I both screamed. I had to admit, she was better at it. I opened my eyes, ready to . . . well, scream some more.

A man stood in the space between Dove and me, and he filled it out nicely, too. He was tall, broad-shouldered, and muscled . . . oh, so muscled. His silky black hair was drawn into a leather strap. He wore a long-sleeved black T-shirt tucked into a pair of denims that looked painted on. He had on black cowboy boots, too. He had the kind of looks you found in TV commercials touting designer cologne. Chiseled jaw. High cheekbones. Cleft chin. A mouth that demanded nibbling. But it was his eyes that drew me the most . . . a beautiful jade green. I'd never seen eyes that color before.

"What the hell are you?" asked Dove crankily.

I noticed that she asked *what* instead of *who*. When he turned to look at Dove, the length of his ponytail was revealed. That gorgeous hair hit him right above a very fine ass.

"My name is Drake," he said, not addressing that whole question of *what*. He turned back to me. "I'm afraid you and your lovely assistant will be in our care until Karn has been caught."

"Caught?" sputtered Dove. "Aren't light bombs supposed to kill vampires?"

"Unless they escape," he said. "Unfortunately, Karn excels at saving his own hide."

"Awesome," I said. "Let's go back to the part where you said we would be in your care. What does that mean, exactly?"

"We will take you to a safe location and protect you from Karn." He offered a killer smile. "I represent the Consortium. It's an organization that protects certain types of artifacts and information."

"Gawd. Why do I feel like we're stuck in a *Men in Black* movie?" asked Dove. She sighed dramatically. "Do you plan to leave us gift-wrapped so you can transport us to your serial killer van?"

Drake blinked. "Of course I will release you from your bonds. So long as you understand that coming with us is non-negotiable. We must insist on offering our protection."

"What kind of artifacts?" I asked because I couldn't help myself.

"Really, Moira? *Really?* That's the important issue here?" Dove's voice cut through my curiosity and reminded me that maybe that whole artifact question could wait.

Drake offered a grin, and I nearly melted right out of my bonds. Cute or not, it had been a helluva night, and I wasn't riding off into the dark with this guy because he was mind-numbingly handsome. Or because he supposedly had access to artifacts. I mean, what we were talking about here? "Where are the artifacts from? How old are they? Do you have items from Egypt?"

"*Moira!*"

I flinched at Dove's outraged tone.

"You'll forgive us for being cynical, given that we were just kidnapped, punched, and terrorized," she said. "But we need credentials. References."

"Yeah," I said. My jaw throbbed. "And maybe an ice pack."

"I have something better," he offered.

"No," said Dove. "We're not in *Men in Black*. We're in *Terminator*."

"What's taking so long?" A beautiful blonde dressed in a blue frock that highlighted her pregnant belly marched into our circle. She eyed us. "Why are they still tied up?"

"I was hoping to gain their cooperation before releasing their bonds."

"Oh, for shit's sake! My name is Patsy. I'm . . . uh . . . well, screw it. I'm the vampire queen. I'm seven months pregnant, in a really bad mood, and mad as hell that Karn got away again. I want some ice cream, to put my feet up, and to watch *Desperate Housewives*. I will glamour you if I have to. I don't want to, though, because it makes me dizzy." She put her hands on her very round belly. "Everything makes me fucking dizzy."

Not even Dove had a response for the woman. She just stared at the blonde openmouthed with something like respect gleaming in her brown eyes. It took a lot to impress Dove, and a whole lot more to earn even a smidgen of her respect.

"Aren't vampires dead?" I asked. Obviously, *that* was the most important question. It was nice to know I knew how to order conversational priorities. Usually I was more organized.

"True," said Dove. "That should nullify the ability to breed, right?" She huffed out a breath. "Now you've got me doing it, too."

"I'm a different sort of vampire," the blonde said. "Also, I'm Preg. *Nant.* You might want to keep that in mind."

"You really do," said Drake. He shuddered, and then winked.

Something poked at my memories. Something . . . well, I didn't know. It was similar to the feeling of going to the grocery store without a list and trying to remember what I was supposed to buy. Was it strange that Drake's wink was somehow familiar?

Patsy punched him in the arm. "Shut up." She

looked at me. "Karn wants you for the same reason that we do."

"Which is what?" I asked.

"I'm losing circulation in my arms," interjected Dove. "In case anyone cares."

Actually, I was getting the tingles in my arms, too. I bet I looked like a hit-and-run victim. Dove didn't look any better, either.

Patsy waddled toward Dove. Drake leaned over my chair to untie the ropes around my wrists, which he did by breaking them with his bare hands. Wow. Also, he smelled really, really good.

And his hair was damp, as though he'd just taken a shower.

"You are a what, aren't you?" I asked when he straightened.

"I'm a werewolf," he said. He crouched next to me, took my arms and rubbed gently, probably trying to get the circulation going again while offering comfort. But his touch was far from comforting . . . it was electrifying.

"You are a remarkable woman, Dr. Jameson." His thumbs brushed the crooks of my arms, and I huffed out a little breath of shock. Who knew the bends of my arms were such sensitive spots? He offered me a smoky smile, one that sent my stomach into a mambo dance. "I look forward to knowing you better."

"I haven't agreed to accept your protection," I said, even though they'd made it clear that Dove and I didn't have a choice. But I could bluster if I wanted to, damn it.

Drake's grin only widened. He rose and offered his hand. I took it and managed to get to my feet without tipping over. He held my hand until I felt steady enough—and then he held it a moment longer, his fingers squeezing mine right before he let go.

"Well, you might agree to that, and more, when you hear this," said Patsy. She paused as Dove tiptoed up next to her. We all looked at her red calf-length lace-up ballet boots. In order to wear them, you had to walk on your toes.

"Those are some fucked-up shoes," said Patsy. "Are you trying to cripple yourself?"

"Yes," said Dove deadpan. "That's my plan exactly."

Patsy snorted. Then she turned toward me again. "You found a crypt in the desert recently. Empty, but maybe some strange stuff on the walls?"

"And we found vampire *ushabtis*," said Dove.

Patsy stared at her blankly.

"Little bitty statues," said Dove.

"Oh."

"So?" Hey, why not cooperate? I was crazy, dreaming, or had fallen down a rabbit hole. Vampires. Werewolves. Mermaids. Ghosts. I was trapped in a world that shouldn't exist.

"It's not exactly what happened, but we have to wait for Eva to undo her work. Only the vampire who glamoured you can . . . er, un-glamour you.

"You glamoured us?" accused Dove. "When?"

"Last week," said Patsy distractedly. "Drake said you stuck your hand in some kind of lock in the door?"

"I did what?" I asked.

"Oh, right. The glamour thing. Shit." She tapped her lip, pondering me. "Your blood opened it. And we've been in touch with various sources, including the Vedere psychics. They do *not* know how to give a straight answer. Anyway, we think you're the chosen. And you'll open the pyramid when it reappears tomorrow."

"What?" I asked blankly.

Patsy shared a look with Drake, then turned her gaze to me. "You're the key to opening a magical pyramid," she said. "And saving the vampire race."

Chapter 12

"Are you high?" asked Dove suspiciously. She squinted at Patsy. "Because that's cray-cray."

"What the fuck is cray-cray?" asked Patsy. She returned Dove's narrow-eyed look. "Are *you* high?"

"Patsy."

The tone indicated exasperation of a spousal nature. A man as tall and broad and gorgeous as Drake entered our conversational circle. He was the opposite of Drake in coloring, though, his hair just as long, but moon white and worn loose.

"If you give me the wait-where-it's-safe speech, I will hurt you," she said.

"Why would I do that?" He leaned down and kissed her head, then drew her into his embrace. "No sign of

Karn. However, his friends did not survive our light bomb."

"Those two assholes are dust?" asked Dove.

The man's golden gaze dropped down to Dove, and he studied her shoes for a moment before looking at her. "Yes."

"Good. They were jerks."

"Unfortunately, they are two of many jerks that Karn has enlisted to his cause," said the man. "You are Dove. And you"—he turned to me—"are Dr. Moira Jameson."

"Believe it or not, I know who I am," I said. "It's the only thing I do know right now."

"Being introduced to parakind can be disconcerting," he offered. "I am Patsy's husband, Gabriel."

"Is it a rule that all of you must be beautiful?" asked Dove. "I mean, if someone fat and ugly and old wanted to get into the paranormal club, are they even considered for membership?"

Patsy laughed. "Oh, hell. She's a hoot." She smiled at Dove. "Wait'll you see the vampire nudist colony, honey. You have to die at the age of fifty or older to even get in." She looked at me. "It's just another perk of visiting our little haven in Oklahoma. It's getting close to dawn, and we need to rest during the day before traipsing to the desert. Ugh."

Dove turned to me, her expression serious. "I cannot live another day without seeing naked vampire senior citizens."

"You are so easy." I crossed my arms and eyed the non-humans. "I'm going to be a harder sell."

"Didn't we mention the booby-trapped pyramid that will magically appear tomorrow night?" asked Patsy.

"You forgot the booby-trapped part," I said, which honestly made traversing the pyramid an even greater incentive. "How are we going to get to Egypt? I guess I could get the private plane ready, but that takes a little bit of planning, and I don't know if my pilot—"

"We have transportation handled," said Patsy. "But it's safer if you hole up in Broken Heart until we know the pyramid will show up again. Our town is invisible to the outside world and probably the most protected spot on earth right now. We're of a mind to protect parakind. Karn wants to introduce us all to the world, and then take it over from the humans. We think that's a dumb-ass move."

"Karn didn't strike me as a dumb-ass," I said.

"He's not, and that's why he's even more dangerous." This statement came from Drake. "We need your help, Dr. Jameson. Please . . . come with us."

Oh, man. That German accent, and those gorgeous gem eyes . . . I wanted to say yes just so I could stay in proximity to that man. Er. Werewolf. Okay. I had to be a little flattered that big, bad supernatural creatures needed my little ol' human help. Except maybe, just maybe, they considered me expendable. If I got hurt or dead . . . what was it to them?

"I can't disappear from the college," I said, knowing full well I could, and it was almost expected (and, might I mention, welcomed) by most of the staff and all of the administration.

Drake lifted his brows, and Patsy rolled her eyes. "You think we don't know about you, Dr. Jameson?" she asked. "We know all about you. You're eccentric, tough, honest, and persistent as hell. You as much as own this college and can take off whenever you like. If you were to tell people you're going away on another dig, no one would think twice about it."

"You'll make us go whether we want to or not," I accused.

"To protect you," said Drake. "Karn obviously wants you to get him into the pyramid."

"I'm not the only archaeologist in the world."

"You are the one who opened it. And you are the only granddaughter of Ezra Jameson," said Drake. "He was a friend to parakind."

I stared at him as I processed his words. "My grandfather knew about supernatural creatures?"

Not everyone can receive your gifts.

On that night so long ago, had my grandfather been talking to a vampire or a werewolf? And had he known that we employed a mermaid as a teacher? Who else on staff wasn't human? I really needed to rethink our vetting process.

"Yes," said Drake. "You've been under the watchful eyes of some parakind already . . . You just haven't known it. Just like you haven't realized that you've been carrying on your grandfather's work for the Consortium."

My mind raced. "Wait. That's why he digging around in the Sudan? To find that crypt?"

"To find what was supposed to be in the crypt," said Gabriel.

"We didn't know it was a whole pyramid and that getting our Ancients out of it would require so much drama. Ugh," said Patsy. She paused, her gaze drifting over my shoulder. I looked, but saw nothing.

"No, Dottie," she said, "we can't take the banshee home. Because he's on loan, that's why. I don't care if he has a cute accent." Patsy rolled her eyes. "Why don't you just go home with him? I'm sure he'd love a smart-ass dead girl hanging around his castle."

I glanced at Damian. "Um . . . does she hear voices? You know, inside her head?"

"She can see and talk to spirits," he explained.

"Yeah," offered Patsy in a grumpy voice, "and they won't leave me alone."

"Can you see . . . er, the ghost who haunts here?" asked Dove. Her gaze skittered toward mine.

Patsy looked around. "I only see Dottie and Camdon—he's the banshee. He's not technically a ghost . . . more like a creature who screams like a pre-teen at a One Direction concert. Although he was human once. Or something. I have a hard time keeping all this paranormal shit straight."

"Are you sure?" asked Dove. "Because this building is supposed to be haunted. Screaming is reported all the time."

Patsy paused, took a breath, and then closed her eyes. After a moment, her eyes popped open and she said, "No one's answering. So, no spirits are here, or they're ignoring me—and it's really hard to ignore me."

"My mother was murdered in this building," I said faintly. My mother's spirit wasn't here after all. I couldn't bear the thought of her trapped here, in the place where she died, unable to move on. I wobbled, or maybe the world tilted on its axis, and I felt the steady hand of Drake slide under my arm to keep me standing upright.

"Oh, shit," said Patsy. "I'm sorry. Some spirits just move on. She probably didn't stick around after . . . well, after."

My stomach clenched. I sure as hell didn't want anyone, much less people who weren't exactly people, to know more about my past than I did. I kept a tight lid on my past, which was necessary. It's why I took meds. Why I had to refuse to open the door to my mother's unsolved murder. Well, at least I didn't have to do a powwow with my murdered mother. That felt far too much like I was going to therapy and dealing with my issues.

Still, my heart did a slow, painful turn.

Oh, Mom.

"We should go."

It wasn't like Dove and I had agreed to go, but . . . all the same, I knew we would. Gabriel led the way, holding his wife's hand and guiding her through the chaos of desks, chairs, and tables. Dove followed, and I went after her, and Drake was the caboose on our strange train.

A long, low moan drifted down the hallway, and lights began to flash.

"Gah!" cried Dove. She tottered on her shoes, and Gabriel reached back and grabbed her arm.

"It's the banshee," said Patsy. "He's making sure he's expelled all the vampire energy. And I think he's digging the idea of haunting a new place for a while."

It didn't take long to traverse the darkened hall. Thank God for that, because the noise and strange lights were getting louder and brighter. We finally made it out of the main doors of the building. I was glad, too, because being in that building gave me the shivers. I hadn't wanted to believe that my mother was a ghost. That she'd been trapped in that building or, worse, chosen to stay on the earthly plane. I wasn't sure how the afterlife worked. I knew what the ancient Egyptians believed, but I'd never quite figured out my own beliefs about the soul.

But why not, right? I was standing in the company of vampires listening to a banshee wail.

You know, it's no wonder I'm a little nuts.

Dove looked over her shoulder at the building where the moans echoed and shuddered. Her gaze was torn between terror and awe.

I had avoided Building A, ignored the whispered tales of the screaming woman, and generally tried to pretend my past wasn't sitting inside it labeled, "This Is the Moment Moira's Life Changed Forever." Yes, my life changed, but my mother's had ended.

I couldn't bear it, and I felt a touch on my arm.

"Are you all right?" asked Drake in hushed concern.

"Not really," I said. "But that's okay."

"I'm very sorry about your mother," he said softly.

"Thanks," I said.

He nodded, his gaze on mine, and I felt something there, hovering between us like silence and hope and desire. It was an odd moment, which was broken when Drake squeezed my shoulder and then headed down the stairs.

A man who looked exactly like Gabriel waited at the bottom of the concrete steps. I jolted. Twins? After all the events of the evening, discovering that Gabriel had an identical twin shouldn't have been a big surprise.

"Ren, this is Dr. Moira Jameson, and that's Dove." Patsy waved toward the man. "This is Ren Marchand."

He inclined his head. Then he took in Dove's shoes. One white eyebrow rose, but he said nothing. Instead, he turned to Patsy and asked, "Everyone else has returned to Broken Heart. Are you ready?"

"Yeah," said Patsy. "You take Dr. Jameson. I'll get Drake."

"Dove," said Gabriel, opening his arms.

"Wait. What?" I asked as I watched Drake stepped

into the embrace of Patsy. Now, how was that fair? I'd
sorta claimed him in my mind, and the married pregnant woman shouldn't get dibs. Plus, her belly made
the whole thing a little awkward.

"Dr. Jameson," said Ren. He wiggled his fingers in a
"c'mere" gesture.

"Is this really the time for a hugging circle?" I asked.
"I thought we were in a hurry."

"We are. Get into the man's arms," demanded Patsy.
"We're taking the shortcut home."

Dove shrugged, and tiptoed her traitorous grad-
student body into Gabriel's arms.

I was the only holdout, and I decided I'd gone along
with the madness so far, what was a supernatural
squeeze? I walked into Ren's waiting arms. He was
muscled and warm and smelled nice. But I couldn't
help but wish that Drake was my hugger. No offense to
Ren. I'm sure he was a very nice whatever-he-was.

"Welcome to travel by vampire," he said with a
quicksilver smile.

Then I imploded.

"It's always weird the first time," said Patsy.

"*Gurg,*" I managed.

When my molecules had melded back together and
we appeared in a room that looked like a white blur to
my abused eyes, I had oozed out of Ren's arms and
onto the floor. A circle of concerned faces looked down
at me, including Dove's—and some gorgeous red-

headed lady who wore a filmy green dress and no shoes. She had tattoos on her visible skin, except on her face. The tattoos sparkled and moved. Well, my bar for "weird" was really high now, so glowing gold tattoos weren't too far into the freak zone.

"I never, and I mean *never*, want to do that again." I lifted a hand to my tender jaw. "I think I'll stop talking now."

"I'll take care of that," said the redheaded woman in an Irish lilt. She glanced at Dove. "You, too. Let's go into the kitchen."

All the faces disappeared as people straightened and wandered away—to the kitchen presumably.

I groaned.

Drake crouched beside me. "Do you need help?" he asked.

"Yes," I said.

He put his arms underneath me and in one smooth motion lifted me and stood up. It wasn't lost on me that he picked up my six-foot frame and generously curvy body with the same effort he might put into carting around a bag of feathers. I wrapped my arms around his neck, and saw his eyes flare with something electric and hungry.

"I think I'm feeling better," I murmured. I resisted the urge to touch that square jaw of his. He had some scruff, and I wanted to trail my fingers over it.

He grinned.

Butterflies danced in my belly.

"Are you really a werewolf?" I asked.

"Oh, yes," he said, his grin widening to show far too many sharp white teeth. "I'll show you one day, my beauty." He leaned close to my ear and whispered, "You are not afraid, are you?"

"It's against the archaeologist's code," I said. I held up two fingers. "Brave, true, and strong." I offered him a half smile. "So, no, I'm not afraid."

"We shall see," he said in a low, growly voice. My pulse jumped, and I saw his eyes dilate. I realized he could use his animal senses to detect things about me . . . such as arousal. And I was there, all right. Drake managed to turn the rusty crank on my libido, and it was going full spin right now.

He carried me into the kitchen. It was large, open, and rustic-looking, with a huge stone hearth that had— I kid you not—a black cauldron hovering over the fire. Something bubbled inside it. Bat eyeballs? Dead man's bones? Laundry?

"Welcome to the Three Sisters Bed-and-Breakfast."

I craned my neck and saw another redhead near a table with a spread of food that made my stomach growl. It had been a long time since I'd eaten those tiny quiches.

"Healin' first, then feastin'," ordered the other redhead. "Put her in this chair, Drake."

Drake did has he was told, gently depositing me into a hard-backed chair that had been pulled out from a rectangular oak table. He stepped back.

"I'm Brigid," she said in that lovely Irish voice. "You'll be feelin' right as rain in no time."

"Dove first," I said. "You might want check her feet, too, and see if she has any toes left."

"Har, har," said Dove, who was seated catty-corner to me.

"Very well," Brigid said with a smile. She moved to Dove and lightly cupped the girl's chin. After a moment of examining the bruise, she placed her fingertips along Dove's jawline. The tattoos sparkling on her arms shifted into different symbols and then gold— well, "magic" was the only word I could use—flowed from her fingers to Dove's face and down her neck. Dove closed her eyes and sighed deeply.

Brigid stepped back and studied her handiwork. "How do you feel, then?"

"Awesome." Dove's eyes fluttered open. "Thank you."

"An' you're welcome." Brigid turned to me. "They hit you harder, seems like."

"Well, I really pissed them off."

She laughed. Then she placed her fingertips on my jaw, the tattoos swirled once again, the gold light drifted from her fingers. I closed my eyes as the tingling sensation of warmth penetrated my sore jaw and my aching head and neck. After a while the sensations faded, and when my eyes opened, I felt perfectly fine.

"There now," said Brigid. "All better."

"What kind of paranormal are you?" asked Dove.

"Oh, not a paranormal like you'll find in Broken Heart," said Brigid. "I'm a goddess."

Dove blinked. "You're *the* Brigid? The Celtic goddess of healing?"

"Among many other things," said Brigid. "All you need now is some food and sleep."

"I'm already asleep," I muttered. Seriously, it had to be a dream. Brigid the goddess of healing, wisdom, poetry, keening, and metalsmithing had just healed me. I could not be awake. I'd been bored senseless at the gala and was no doubt collapsed in a corner of the room, snoring away while people stepped over my prone form.

"It's a lot, isn't it?" The other redhead set a cup of tea on the table next to me. "Chamomile," she said. "To soothe your nerves."

"I might require something stronger than tea," I said.

"Trust me. It'll do the trick." She offered a hand, and said, "I'm Lenette."

"Moira. And Dove," I replied, nodding toward my friend. I shook Lenette's hand, and then I peered at her. "You don't seem to be dead or among the furred ones."

"Oh, no," she said, "I'm a witch."

"Of course you are."

"Welcome to Broken Heart." She placed a cup of tea next to Dove, who picked it up by the delicate handle and sipped.

"This is wonderful," she said. "Thank you."

I took Dove's lead and pretended that everything was normal, even though I was currently taking tea in a room with a witch, a goddess, a werewolf, and some vampires. The tea was very good indeed, and I did feel my tension loosen as I sipped the fragrant liquid.

"You'll need these," said Drake. He placed something warm and sticky on my shoulder. I looked down and saw a heart with a sword through it. The tattoo glittered briefly before disappearing into my skin.

He did the same to Dove's shoulder.

"The Invisi-shield requires that all within the town's borders have these emblems," said Drake.

"The Invisi-shield?" asked Dove. "That sounds like the brand name of tampons."

Patsy, who was currently getting her feet rubbed by her husband, snorted a laugh. "Well, it was that or Maxi-shield." She grinned. "You've been issued temporary invitations to Broken Heart. Then you spend tomorrow evening solving the mystery of the pyramid."

"And if I don't?" I asked.

Patsy looked at me, her expression grave. "Then it's the end of the world."

Chapter 13

"No pressure there," said Dove. She glanced at me, and I could see then she wasn't as cool a customer as she appeared. Her eyes were shadowed with a combination of fear and excitement. So far, I hadn't run screaming into the night, either. Go, Team!

"The end of the world?" I sputtered. I eyed Drake and found him studying my generous cleavage. He glanced up, saw that he'd been caught, and offered me a wicked grin. Talk about waking up the ol' hormones. I'd never wanted anyone like I wanted him, not in my whole life. Whew.

"The *world* world? As in the planet we're currently on?" asked Dove.

"Well, the world as we know it," said Patsy. She yawned, as if apocalyptic talk was more boring than discussing weather patterns. Her expression was like that of a purring kitten. Well, if I had a handsome man rubbing my feet and calves, I'd be purring, too. And there was Drake just inches away, standing like a senti-nel with his crossed arms and legs spread apart. Oh, if only he would get down on bended knee and take those big ol' hands and . . . my imagination went awry. I shut down the erotic images. Wow. Who knew my imagination was so vivid?

"If Karn has his way," said Drake, "then the world will know that parakind really exists."

"Yeah, that's been mentioned." I resisted the urge to fan myself. It seemed really, really hot in here. "If you need this tech patch to get past the Invisi-shield, is it impossible to sneak inside Broken Heart?"

"Unfortunately, no protection is foolproof and Karn's persistent."

Patsy yawned again. "I think y'all need to eat and then head on to bed. Tomorrow we'll reboot those memories of yours, take you to the pyramid, and get you started on your awesome adventure." Her husband helped her to stand and then gathered her close, resting his head against hers. It was such a natural thing to do, and I was fascinated by their relationship harmony. They seemed to fit together so well, like they'd been carved from the same piece of marble. Mates. Like bookends. Or gibbons.

"Sure. Because I can sleep. No problem." I eyed the pastries closest to my saucer. "Maybe a sugar coma is in order."

"We'll start with protein," said Lenette, sliding a huge chicken salad sandwich in front of me. The bread was thickly sliced, and I could see the grapes and walnuts among the chunks of mayo-ed chicken. I loved food. Maybe a little too much, but given my job, I tended to burn a lot of calories in sweat and effort. The sandwich seemed to weigh as much as a gold brick and it tasted like sweet, sweet ambrosia.

"Oh, my gawd," said Dove after she swallowed a mouthful.

I didn't want words to interrupt my inhalation of delicious food, so I offered wholehearted agreement through nodding.

Everyone except for Lenette and Drake wished us a good night, and I gurgled back at them through mouthfuls of warm blueberry scone. By the time we were done eating sandwiches and pastries, and drinking more tea, I was so stuffed I felt like someone would have to roll me barrel-like to wherever the bed was located.

"I think you accidentally ate a plate," said Dove, who'd been my companion in behavior most glutton. She followed up her accusation with a huge burp. "Whoa. Excuse me."

"It was a delicious plate," I said primly. I dabbed my lips with a napkin. "That was the best food we ever ate."

"Emphasis on *ever*," agreed Dove. She yawned, stretching her arms out. Then she looked down tiredly at her monster shoes. "Shit." She glared at me. "This is your fault. I honored your shoe request and now I can't feel my feet."

"Next time I'll ask for notification of our kidnapping so we can choose appropriate footwear." A full belly, an evening of stressful events, and uncertainty about the future were more than my body could take. I was the kind of tired I got after traipsing around a dig site all day. I'd slept in a lot of weird, uncomfortable places (ask me about the sarcophagus—go on . . . ask me), so settling back into the chair for a snooze would be no big deal.

"Perhaps it is time for you lovely ladies to retire?" Drake aimed a smoky bedroom-eyed gaze at me, and something hot and sizzling burst through my exhaustion.

"Va-va-voom," muttered Dove.

"Drake, why don't you show Moira to her room?" asked Lenette. "I'll help pry Dove out of her boots."

He stood, and offered a formal half bow, much in the same way Karn had, and extended his hand. My dress was filthy, my ponytail limp, and my makeup smeared. I must have looked like I'd crawled out from a sand dune in evening wear. Yikes. Still, I took his hand and wobbled to my bare feet. Wow. I hadn't even noticed my lack of shoes. I vaguely wondered if anyone had picked up my high heels. Then the thought of Doriana and the gala entered my tired mind. What had happened after the brawl?

I stared down at Drake's hand, which encompassed mine easily. That light touch was keeping me upright. I glanced up at him. "Thank you."

"You are most welcome." He kept my hand cupped in his. "Good night, Dove."

"G'night," she oofed. "Could you kill me on your way past? Ugh!"

"Maybe on the way back," he said with a laugh. "If you are still suicidal."

"Only the suicidal would wear these shoes," said Lenette as she struggled with pulling at the heel.

"I'll see you tomorrow," I said to Dove. "Probably."

"Yeah. Good knowing you." She waved halfheartedly, her focus on extracting her calves from the red leather.

Drake led me from the kitchen into the common area, which had a cozy jumble of furniture, some near the fireplace, other pieces set in an arrangement to encourage intimate conversation, and yet others near windows or alone. Those chairs were by bookshelves, so were no doubt meant for the solitary reader. The pastel colors, casually draped doilies, and plentitude of quirky trinkets made the room feel like you were visiting your eccentric great-aunt.

I liked it.

Drake led me to a staircase and gestured for me to go ahead of him. He let go of my hand, and I have to admit, for a second I felt bereft. Holding hands was such a nice, normal sign of affection. I'd never given it much merit before.

I walked up the stairs and Drake followed. At the top, I looked down the narrow hallway. "Are they all occupied?"

"Just you and Dove tonight," he said. "Lenette gave you the room at the end on the left."

"Okay."

As I started down the hall, one of the doors on the right opened, and a man dressed in a polo shirt, khakis, and tennis shoes exited. He held a handful of pink towels. He looked at me and Drake and offered a smile. "Washer foul," he said. "Never put red socks in with white towels."

I didn't do laundry, so I had no idea what the etiquette was for putting clothes in the washer. Since I had household staff at my home, my dirty clothes disappeared from the hamper and appeared clean and pressed in my closet. As far as I was concerned it was magic. Well, more likely it was the steely-eyed glare and OCD machinations of Mr. Harold Keyter, who was the ruler of the staff and all things house-related. My grandfather had hired him twenty years ago, so Mr. Keyter had had the delightful experience of meeting me when I was fourteen. You know, right before I suffered my breakdown and went into psychiatric care. And I have been a delight to be around ever since. Mr. Keyter was respectful, but firm in his manner and tone. To this day, despite practically being family, he called me Dr. Jameson and I called him Mr. Keyter. Some things are just done a certain way, no matter what. And there is comfort in the unchanging, no matter how small. I knew too well how life could upend your expectations and screw with you.

"Hello," he said. The man looked odd. His skin was kinda gray, and he moved somewhat stiffly, like he had joint problems. "I'm Lenette's husband," he said.

"Nice to see you again," said Drake. "This is our archaeologist, Dr. Moira Jameson."

"You're here to address the pyramid issue," he said.

"Yes," I said. I was trying not to stare. I couldn't figure out what this guy was. Maybe he was a warlock since he was married to a witch? Or were males just called witches, too? Or was he something else?

"I'll let you get to bed," said the man. "Good night."

We wished him good night as well, and then he shuffled off. Drake led me to my room, unlocked the door with an old-fashioned brass key, and ushered me inside.

"Okay. What was he?" I asked.

"We don't quite know," said Drake. "Half zombie, maybe."

"How the hell can you be half of a zombie?"

"He was bitten by one, and he didn't die. Or turn into one. He's alive. Sorta." Drake shrugged. "Broken Heart has many different creatures from the parakind world."

"And nobody knows you guys are out here in . . . er, where are we again?"

"Oklahoma."

I blinked. I'd never had cause to go to this part of the

country. And if I had, going to Oklahoma wouldn't have been at the top of my list. I couldn't think of single thing I knew about this state. My brain files mostly had items about ancient cultures. Oh, wait! Oklahoma had the Heavener Runestone. Now that would be interesting to see. The theory that Vikings had traveled through our part of the American continent was an exciting idea.

"I would think a huge paranormal population in Oklahoma would be noticed," I said. I was intently aware that we were alone in a room with a four-poster with a mountain of pillows and a plush patchwork comforter. I couldn't wait to crawl in. If only Drake was crawling in with me. . . .

"We have taken precautions to protect the community. The Invisi-shield prevents people from knowing that the town is here." He looked at me, and reached out to brush his thumb over my jaw. "You are exhausted. Please. Go to bed."

It should've been a strange thing to have a man I'd known a couple of hours touch me so intimately. But it felt natural, as though he'd done so a thousand times before. And yet, an electric thrill pulsed in my belly . . . and in parts farther south. I'd never experienced the dichotomy of being both comfortable and excited in the same moment. A moment caused by one of the hottest men I'd ever met.

I suddenly felt sleepy . . . so sleepy, in fact, that my eyes drooped and my body didn't want to stay upright. "Whoa," I said, swaying.

Drake put his arms around my shoulders and led me to the bed. He unfurled the covers, and I crawled into the space. And by crawled, I mean I fell facefirst into the soft sheets and rolled onto my back. Drake moved aside the three thousand pillows piled against the headboard and tucked a big fluffy one under my head.

"So tired," I said. I could feel my brain shutting down. And my body felt like a bowl of fresh-cooked noodles.

"Ah. Well, we need you and Dove to rest deeply the entirety of the day," he said. He pulled the covers up to my chin. "Lenette added some ingredients to the food to ensure that you would sleep very well."

"Whaa . . ."

I slipped inside the dark warmth of sleep. But I could have sworn that Drake pressed a light kiss against my brow and whispered something sexy and German in my ear.

Or maybe I was only dreaming.

"Another human?" The gruff male voice practically barked. "Can our sons find no one among their kind?"

"What kind would that be?" asked a much more soothing female voice. Her tone held patient amusement. "Demigods aren't easy to find in these modern times. And Moira? You are dreaming."

Huh. This was new. I rarely remembered my dreams—"a blessing, child" my grandfather had once said to me, when I was older and complaining about my lack of imagination. Apparently I'd suffered terrible nightmares after my mother died. Well, duh. Death had taken her from me, and then left me with a grief so awful I couldn't breathe. I was five, for fuck's sake.

"It might help," said the man, "if you opened your eyes."

Oh. I opened my eyes, and found myself within a circle of trees so tall that their thick branches nearly blotted out the moon overhead. Something about this place seemed mystical and out of time. I felt the way I did right before I entered a new site, my fingers scraping rough stone, my lungs inhaling dusty air. Mostly, though, was the wholehearted feeling of hushed wonderment as I traversed the sacredness of the ancient past guarded by time and by ghosts.

I looked down. I wore the lavender dress I'd fallen asleep in, if it had been altered into the style of a Roman noblewoman's garment. My feet were bare, and I felt the soft tickle of grass beneath my toes.

Sooooo . . . I was definitely not awake. I'd been kidnapped by vampires, commandeered by werewolves, and zapped to some middle-of-nowhere town, but I couldn't fathom this scenario being at all real.

Then again . . . what was real anymore? Real had packed its bag, waved good-bye, and left the moment Karn demanded I dance with him. Or maybe it was when my formerly staid colleague Doriana had punched him in the face.

"Hello, Moira." Sitting on a throne carved from gleaming dark wood was a woman so beautiful I was reminded of the great known beauties of ancient times—Helen of Troy, Queen Nefertiti, Xi Shi. She had in real time (er . . . dream time?) those ethereal qualities that I could only imagine as I stared at effigies unearthed from the sands. She had long black hair coiled in tight ringlets that fell like silky ribbons to her waist. Her skin was perfect, as creamy and pale as cold milk. She wore a blue T-shirt that read, LYCAN THERAPY: ROCK BAND CHAMPIONS. And she wore a pair of faded jeans. Her feet were bare, too. She saw the direction of my gaze, and she wiggled her toes, which were painted neon pink.

"I am Aufanie and this is my mate, Tark. Drake is our son, as are Darrius and Damian."

My gaze was drawn to where the woman's hand rested on the jeans-clad thigh of a man who stood next to her throne. He was built like the Rock. He, too, wore a T-shirt proclaiming LYCAN THERAPY: ROCK BAND CHAMPIONS. He looked like Drake—not only that familiar green gaze and amazing waterfall of hair, but also the warrior vibe. Well, I should probably say that Drake had Tark's appearance and manner, since Tark was the father. The confusing part, of course, was that they looked like they were about the same age as Drake and Darrius.

Also . . . Drake had another brother?

"You may be wondering why we've entered your dreamscape," said Aufanie.

Actually, I hadn't wondered at all. A dream was a dream, right? Although since I wasn't used to remembering my dreams, much less actively participating in them, what did I know?

Aufanie shared a look with Tark, who leaned down and placed a comforting hand on her shoulder. "We feel we should convey certain information about the pyramid," he said in that gruff voice. "It is not particularly pleasant news."

"Wonderful," I muttered.

Aufanie nodded, and lifted her gaze to mine. "Tomorrow, you must be the first one to enter the pyramid."

"Whoa. You don't just go into a pyramid," I said. "You have to examine, plan, measure. Sometimes it takes weeks before we're ready to—"

"This is not the kind of pyramid you are used to excavating," interrupted Tark. "This one protects two Ancient vampires who went to ground more than three thousand years ago. These vampires are prophesied to return and rule the undead."

"Vampires," clarified Aufanie. "Not zombies."

"I believe zombies are dead-dead," mused Tark. "And do not fall under the purview of vampire rulership."

I didn't even know what to say. How on earth could I contribute to such a bizarre conversation? "I know that part . . . the part about the pyramid, not the zombies. "

"Yes," said Tark. "Karn wishes to kill the slumbering vampires, Amahté and Shamhat, and lead the vampires himself. Also, he wants to drink the ambrosia that was buried with them."

"And then he wants to reveal supernatural creatures to humans," I said. "I understand all of that."

"We once lived in harmony with humans, but they eventually turned against us," said Aufanie. "Even in these enlightened times, we would risk too much—if we reveal ourselves too soon. But with Amahté and his mate returned to the world, we gain ground toward the goal of revelation—and peaceful accord with humans."

"It's imperative to our world, and yours, that you ensure their safe return," said Tark.

I hadn't even seen the pyramid yet, and here I was being made responsible for its contents. Which were vampires. How did I get into this mess? I scrunched my toes in the grass and sighed.

"Drake will insist that he go in ahead of you," said Tark. "You must not let him. Your blood opened the first lock and made the pyramid appear. Drake cannot be the sacrifice."

I thought about Drake, about his eyes, and that body, and those plingy lust vibes . . . oh, wow. "Have you met your son? He doesn't seem the type to be bossed around." I blinked. "Wait. What do you mean, 'sacrifice'?"

I studied their concerned faces. Maybe Drake's parents were trying to protect him. Patsy had said the pyramid was booby-trapped. So, save him and sacrifice me? I was only a human, after all. Still, it seemed an odd thing to rescue me from Karn so they could use my archaeological expertise to trigger traps. Anyone could be thrown to the wolves . . . um, so to speak. "Why do you want me to prevent Drake from entering the pyramid?"

Aufanie offered me a gentle smile. "You must go in first, Moira . . . because it's imperative that you die."

Chapter 14

"Die?" I said.

"Oh, it won't be right away," said Aufanie. She took a look at my expression and added hastily, "Nor will it be forever."

"The blood of the person who opened the tomb is required to get through the traps. That would be you," said Tark. "If Drake enters first and tries to be the key, the pyramid will reject him and disappear again."

"And you know that how?" I asked. "Because I thought these vampires were lost, or something."

"We had a very enlightening conversation with the vampire who helped create the pyramid and its protections," said Tark.

"And whoever found the damned thing and unlocked it had the dubious honor of being a sacrifice?"

Tark and Aufanie exchanged a look. "Not necessarily."

"Well, that's not vague at all," I said, annoyed. "Can we have some further discussion on the sacrifice part of this business?"

"You will slowly be drained as you progress," said Tark. "It is your blood that will begin to awaken the Ancients. When you reach the end of your journey, you will be rewarded with the ambrosia."

"So it's really ambrosia? Food-of-the-gods ambrosia?" I asked. "Make-me-immortal ambrosia?"

"Yes." Tark looked at me as though he were questioning my sacrifice candidacy.

"Why would you come to me in a dream? And not tell Drake directly about not going in ahead me?"

"My son is stubborn," said Tark.

"All of our sons are stubborn," said Aufanie. She glanced at her husband and smiled. "I fear they come by it naturally." She patted her husband's hip.

"Drake will insist on coming with you."

"Our son is very fond of you."

"I've known him for two seconds," I said. "Granted, he's aces at the white-knight stuff—well, so far—but why would he care about some archaeologist he's never met before?"

"Oh. Well." Aufanie's smile crinkled, as though she was trying to prevent a secret from spilling out of her lips. "We know you have questions."

"Does she ever," muttered Tark.

"More will be revealed to you, I promise," said Aufanie. "But for now, we must have your answer, Moira. Will you enter the pyramid first, of your own free will, and traverse time and traps to bring forth the new hope of parakind?"

Her eloquence was moving, as was the sincere gaze she bestowed on me. Tark, for all his rough-tough exterior, seemed to be holding his breath as they awaited my answer. Well, what was I supposed to say? Good luck with Karn, and your pyramid, and your paranormal problems. Nice knowing you. Also, I apparently started this whole process . . . and I didn't remember any of it. And if I could believe them, my grandfather had been involved somehow in all this before he died. In any case, how the hell was I expected to go back to my life knowing what I knew now? How could I ever look at another pyramid, another sand dune, another campfire, and not think of this moment?

"Well, the blood-draining thing doesn't sound like an optimal experience," I said. "But . . . I'm in."

"Excellent," said Aufanie.

"You are brave," said Tark. He studied me. "I hope you are strong as well."

"Votes of confidence are always welcome," I said.

Tark cracked a smile.

Then the forest and the dark and the trees shattered . . . and so did I.

I woke up with a pounding headache and my mouth so dry it felt like I'd been eating sand. For a moment, I tried to remember how much tequila I'd slammed and why on earth I'd let Ax talk me into another stupid drinking contest.

I propped myself up on my elbows, and moaned. "Someone kill me. Please."

"Never, my treasure."

The voice startled me so much my eyes flew open and I yelped. Drake stood next to the bed holding a delicate china cup.

"What the hell are you doing hovering over me like some kind of . . . of . . . stalker?" I sounded as cranky as I felt.

One dark eyebrow winged upward. "Not a morning person?" He glanced at the darkened window. The shade had been raised and the curtains opened to reveal the last vestiges of dusk. "Or should I say not an evening person."

I dropped my head to the pillow and put the back of my hand on my forehead. "Ouch."

"Lenette said that you might suffer some aftereffects." He sat on the edge of the bed and offered the cup. "Drink this. You'll feel better."

"Says you." I sat up slowly, and took the cup, peering at the amber liquid. "You drug my food, and expect me to drink whatever you put in my hand?" I snorted.

"I understand," said Drake. "Would it help to know we are protecting you?"

"Not really, no." My head pounded. I sniffed at the

tea, or whatever it was. It had a cinnamon fragrance. "Well, what could happen?" I took a sip.

"You could grow a tail and horns," said Drake.

Anyone else—anywhere else—I would have accused of being sarcastic. Instead, I stared at him suspiciously.

"I'm kidding," he said, offering one of those patented wicked grins. "One sip won't do anything."

I waited for Mr. Werewolf to say something else. He remained silent, so I drank another sip of the delicious brew.

"I remember now. It's two sips."

"You're hilarious." I tried to hand him the cup. "Forget it."

He pushed it gently back toward me. "Please. I promise the tea will help." He removed two pill bottles that had been tucked into his pocket. "Dove mentioned you need these."

Embarrassment clogged my throat. I took the bottles and looked away from him. "I'm a little crazy," I said. "Rough childhood."

"Your mother's death."

"Yeah, that was part of it. But there was something else, inside me, that was dark and angry and just . . . Well, I lost myself for a while. Anyway. The pills keep me from picking up sharp objects and embedding them in people."

He was staring at me, but not in a judgmental way.

"I would like to hear your story," he said. "I want to know why you believe you are crazy."

"Well, having three psychiatrists tell me I was nutballs contributed to the idea," I said. "Although they used words like 'delusional' and 'psychotic breaks.'"

"My sister-in-law used to be a psychotherapist," said Drake. "She never uses the term 'nutballs.'"

"Because she's probably kind."

"She is. And as are you." The teasing gleam in his eyes had disappeared, replaced by sincerity. Whoa. Serious Drake was even more effective than Sexy Drake. "Take your pills, Moira, and please drink the tea."

I popped open the plastic bottles, plucked out my pills, and took them by drinking the tea.

By the time I'd finished the cup, my headache had disappeared.

"What now?" I asked.

"Shower. Clothes. Breakfast." He plucked the teacup from my grasp, then stood up and offered a half bow. He glanced at me, that damnable gleam back in his gaze. "And then, my lady, your pyramid awaits."

"Does it really?" I asked.

"Not yet. But it should appear at your South Sudan dig site soon."

The bedside clock informed me that it was just after eight p.m. That meant it was just after three a.m. in Egypt. "Shouldn't it have arrived already?"

"There is time yet."

"But you don't know if it will appear."

"We're good guessers." He stretched out his hand. "C'mon, Moira. It's a brand-new night."

Vampires awaited us in the kitchen of the Three Sisters Bed-and-Breakfast.

A pretty brunette and a younger version of an undead Pierce Brosnan sat in the kitchen, eating scones and drinking coffee.

Dove sat across from them, her own plate full of pastry. Apparently, she had no qualms about eating the food around here. Actually, I didn't either because despite the witch's propensity to drug food like she was entertaining Hansel and Gretel, she was a damned fine cook.

"If you're wondering," Dove said as she swallowed a mouthful of pastry, "a fairy wish allows all the undead people to eat anything they want within the borders of Broken Heart."

Obviously, I needed the CliffsNotes version of Theodora's books. I hadn't considered the idea that vampires usually only drank blood, but here they were, eating pastries and drinking coffee like normal people. Or so I assumed. I didn't have a good gauge for what passed as "normal."

"Also, Theodora Monroe is the mother of Libby, who is a dragon. And she's married to a vampire. Well, now he's a half dragon, and alive-ish. But still . . . Theodora Monroe's books are officially *not* bullshit." She sent me a triumphant look.

I narrowed my eyes. "How many of those scones have you eaten?"

"One," said Liar McLiarPants.

"I'm Eva," said the brunette, offering me a kind smile. "This is my husband, Lorcan."

Lorcan offered me a formal nod. "Good evening."

"We'll see," I said.

He grinned.

"I'm Moira. I see you've met Dove. And her appetite."

"Bad waker-uppers suffer breakfast penalties," said Dove, primly blotting her lips with a napkin.

"Let's get this party started, then," said Patsy as she toddled inside with her husband close behind. They sat down and started loading up their plates.

Not wanting to be left out of breakfast, and slightly worried that Dove would eat all the damned scones before I could have one, I sat down and filled my own plate.

Eva waited until I'd finished coffee and two scones before asking, "Are you ready to get your memories back?"

"I have no idea," I said.

She smiled. Then she rose and rounded the table. I turned my chair to face her. She put her fingertips to my temples and looked deeply into my gaze.

I saw her eyes go red, and then it was if a door had been opened. All the memories acquired in the desert tumbled into my consciousness.

I couldn't decide if I was amazed or pissed off at Eva's ability to lock my experiences away. Getting a download like that was somewhat disconcerting at first, but eventually the rush of images and attached emotions settled.

Eva turned to Dove and did the same un-glamour move.

I watched my friend's eyes widen, and when it was over, she heaved a shocked breath. Then Dove looked at me. "We had a busy night."

"No kidding."

"Well, I can check that off my to-do list," said Patsy.

I rubbed my temples. "Why on earth would Karn risk public exposure by confronting me at the college gala? The asshole nearly poked my eye out with a knife! He couldn't have known I'd been glamoured. What if I had screamed or punched him when he introduced himself?"

"He understands the protocols of the Consortium," said Patsy. "We don't keep our policies secret. Unfortunately, the man's not a dipshit. The odds were in his favor that your memories were wiped."

This was scone-worthy news. I picked up another one from the serving plate and slathered it with clotted cream and blueberry jam. Eating my frustrations away was no doubt something a therapist would add to my "Reasons Moira Is Fucked-Up" list, but whatever. It was better than babbling incoherently while stabbing people with my butter knife.

Drake pushed another scone onto my plate, and I turned, giving him a questioning glance.

"I like watching you eat," he said. He had that look in his eyes—the one that made me tingle and think naked thoughts.

I was unnerved and fascinated by the sexual tension that arced between us. I didn't have a lot of practice with flirting. I was more of a "let's just do this and move on with our respective lives" kind of girl. This approach made rejection less painful.

With my gaze on Drake's, I lifted the scone and took a bite. Drake's eyes darkened with what could only be called raw lust. He reached over and flicked a crumb away from the corner of my mouth. That small gesture sent electricity racing down into the tingly parts.

"Wow," said Dove. "And I here I used a napkin."

Everyone laughed.

Then a tiny werewolf howl echoed into the room and cut everyone's giggles short. We all turned to Drake, who offered a sheepish (that's right, I said it) grin as he removed his cell phone from his jeans pocket. "Darrius gave me a replacement for the one stolen from me," he said, "and he has a stupid sense of humor." He touched the screen and put the phone to his ear. *"Ja?"*

He listened for a moment, and then his eyes widened. "We're coming now." He clicked the phone off and turned to Patsy. "It seems we do not have to go to the pyramid after all."

"What?" she exclaimed. "Why?"

He glanced at me. "Because the pyramid has come to us."

"Holy shit."

The expletive pierced Dove's lips, and echoed my own shocked thoughts. We stood at the base of a pyramid. Not a crumbling pile of stone that showcased workmanship and culture of ages past, but an actual, beautiful, complete pyramid. White limestone covered it like thinly spread cream cheese frosting, and the tip was covered in gold. That night in the desert I hadn't had an opportunity to really study it, but here, in this field with the Oklahoma night sky stretched above it like a velvet blanket . . . it was beyond amazing.

"This is incredible," I said. "I've seen renderings of what they were supposed to look like, of course."

"Computer generated graphics are a poor substitute," said Dove.

Patsy and her husband stood next to each other, and then to my surprise, although with not as much OMG, a dude sparkled into existence on the other side of Patsy. He was a good-looking, casually dressed gentleman with silvery-gray eyes, longish black hair, and a drop-dead smile. He reached out a hand toward me. "I'm Ruadan," he said. "You're a real blessin', you are, Dr. Jameson."

I blinked. A hazy childhood memory formed, the one so recently unlocked. A man with eyes like shiny nickels, sitting on the bed, placing a hand on my fore-head, and whispering, *"Déan dearmad."*

"Do I know you?" I asked. "I do, don't I?"

"I was a friend of your grandfather's," he said. "He wanted to protect you."

"There's a lot of that going around these days," I said.

Something flashed in his eyes, almost like sorrow, and that made my heart turn over in my chest. "You look like Patrick and Lorcan," I said. "Older brother?"

"Father," he clarified. Then he said, "And who's this lovely girl?"

"Dove," she said, offering her hand. "Just Dove."

"A beautiful name for a beautiful woman," he said. He kissed the top of her hand.

Dove blushed.

I had never seen Dove blush. Not ever. Not . . . well, ever. I was so stunned by the redness tinting her cheeks, I couldn't think of a single sarcastic thing to say about it. Even so, she looked at me and said, "Shut up."

"You shut up," I said, because I am obviously mature and articulate.

We all turned toward the pyramid and gazed upward once more.

"So, we go in, survive the traps, and . . . what?" asked Dove.

"Wake up two Ancient vampires who haven't had human blood in three thousand years," I said.

"Oh, is that all?" asked Dove. She shared a look with

me, and I noted that she looked particularly young in just jeans, a T-shirt, and ballet flats, especially without the kohl eyes, red lipstick, and goth clothing that usually hid her fresh-faced looks. It was all camouflage armor, small ways she'd learned to protect herself from the world. She rejected the world first, so it wouldn't reject her. I wasn't so much into rejecting the world with my clothing choices. I mostly just flipped it off or, when needed, punched out anyone who annoyed me. I wore khakis, a T-shirt, and hiking boots—clothing provided by Drake. New clothes, in my size, that had been presented right before I took a shower. I also had a flashlight, a Swiss Army knife, and two bottles of water tucked into the various pockets. I didn't have my usual excavation tools because (1) I hadn't had the opportunity to bring them, and (2) I wasn't actually excavating anything.

"Well, then," said Patsy. "Let's get to it." She pointed at a small gold circle. The hieroglyph's basic interpretation was simple enough: "Enter here."

"You know what to do, Moira. You open it. We'll follow you inside."

Gabriel cleared his throat.

Patsy rolled her eyes. "Everyone else will go inside. I'm too busy being pregnant."

I studied her expression, and decided she didn't harbor the same knowledge that had been imparted to me via dreamland. I hadn't mentioned the dream, not to anyone, especially not to Dove. She would've tied me

to the bed and fended off anyone who tried to cart me
into the pyramid with only her bad attitude and that
blade she kept tucked in her boots. It was her bad attitude that was the more potent of the weapons.

In any case, I remembered the dream in detail, and
knew, somehow, that it was real. At least, real in the
sense of truth. And I'd made a promise. I remembered
what the voice in my head said when I stuck my hand
into the keyhole the first time. *Love will lead you. Be worthy.* I had no idea what that meant. Even so, I would
enter the pyramid and be the first meal of Amahté and
Shamhat. It wasn't like I had a choice. I had opened the
pyramid, and now I had to follow through with the
whole sacrifice thing.

Yay, me.

I could only hope that Aufanie and Tark hadn't lied
about the ambrosia, or today I would be entering my
last pyramid ever. "I will go first," said Drake. He
reached out his hand, but I stepped in front of him.

"The hell you will," I said, looking at him over my
shoulder. "You don't know what you're doing."

"Neither do you," he said tightly.

"Oh, stop," said Patsy, exasperated. "That's the way
it works, Drake. It's her blood that opens the damned
thing."

He looked supremely irritated, but gave a short,
quick nod.

I stuck my hand inside the hole. Something sharp
raked my wrist.

We heard a rumble, and then a doorway appeared. It pushed back, inward, and then slid to the side. A blend of female and male voices invited, "Enter, chosen."

"Step aside, Moira," said Drake.

"She's the one to go first," said Ruadan. "She's been chosen, Drake. You can't change that."

Ruadan looked at me. "Your destiny is what you make it, love. Remember that."

"Fate can be a real bitch," I said.

He laughed. "That is the truth, sure enough."

I had every intention of getting out of this pyramid alive. Well, alive-ish. After snacking on some ambrosia.

I stepped inside, and smelled the dust of the ages in the suffocating dark. Drake followed, so close I could feel the warmth of his body against my backside. I had to stay in front of him, make sure he didn't go around and set off the blood-drinking traps. I didn't know if he'd be ejected out of the pyramid, too . . . or just get plain ol' dead from trying. Sheesh. He really was as stubborn as Aufanie had said.

Behind me, I heard Dove gasp, and then her vivid cursing streak made my ears bleed . . . at least until the door shut behind us.

Drake and I turned around.

"That's not good," I said.

The door was completely gone.

"It only let two of us inside," he said. "Why?"

"Well, I'm the chosen," I said with mock haughtiness. "So you're probably screwed."

He snorted a laugh. "We'll see. Let's get through as quickly as possible, shall we?" Drake said, placing his hand on my shoulder. "Let me pass, o chosen one."

Ha. As if. I slipped out of his grasp and move onward. The passage was so narrow that he wouldn't be able to scoot around me unless turned and pressed my back against the wall. I heard his hiss of impatience, and then a string of German words that had the feel and tone of "fucking fuckety fuck."

Then I heard the *whoom* noise made when a lit match strikes gas-soaked wood. Torches on either side of the wall lit up, one by one, stretching several feet down the hallway until they illuminated an intricately carved stone door.

"Ach," said Drake. "Let me by, Moira. We don't know the dangers here. It is better if I go first."

"No, it's not," I argued. "I have more experience with pyramids."

"Not this pyramid," he said. "Move aside."

"No." I sprinted toward the door, hoping that the first trap wasn't some sort of spike-infested pit, or spears spinning out of the walls in *Indiana Jones* fashion.

Drake cursed some more in German, and followed. I reached the door seconds before he skidded behind me. I studied the hieroglyphs, and puzzled out the meanings. I don't know how much time passed, but as I crouched down to view the final set of glyphs, I heard Drake sigh.

"What does it say, *Liebling*?"

"Archaeology takes patience," I said. I straightened, and peered at the carved hole in the middle of the door-way. "Basically, it's a bunch of threats about being in this pyramid. Death-on-swift-wings kinds of stuff," I said.

Drake stared at me blankly.

"Not a fan of *The Mummy* movies?" I asked.

He cocked an eyebrow.

"Ancient Egyptians often wrote prayers and threats on their tombs to protect their resting places. This one is a little different." I pointed at the hole. "And then there's this." I encircled my finger around the images that surrounded the hole. "These are instructions. It says: 'To know the beginning is to know the answer.'"

Then I stuck my hand into the hole.

Chapter 15

Dove

"**Y**our knowledge of swear words is impressive," said Patsy. "Still, don't get your panties in a bunch. You didn't get to go on the field trip. Suck it up."

How could I explain to the queen of the vampires that Moira needed me?

Or that I felt completely weirded out being left in the company of vampires?

Or that Moira had abandoned me and it hurt. Even though she hadn't done it on purpose. Probably.

I inhaled deeply. Oh, yeah. I needed to suck it up. Quick.

"What's there to do around here?" I asked.

"Are you kidding me?" asked Patsy. "It's Oklahoma. You can tip cows, skinny-dip in the pond, or watch reality TV."

"Spectacular."

"How do you feel about babysitting?" she asked.

I stared at her for a full thirty seconds. "How do you feel about dead children?"

She blinked, and then she snorted a laugh. "Jesus, you're a pistol." She looped her arm through mine. "C'mon, buttercup. We have plans to make and bad guys to defeat."

I perked up. "Now, that sounds fun."

Chapter 16

"Moira!" Drake's shocked exclamation made me feel guilty. Well, I had to be sneaky, damn it. He was trying to protect me, but I was saving the world. His parents had told me so.

I stretched out my fingers, wiggling for . . . ah, there it was. I felt a sharp, swift prick as I pressed my palm down onto the point. Blood welled, dripped, and then . . .

I passed out.

I floated. Like a feather tossed by the wind, I danced and whirled in the night sky. Another dream? Below me was a silver trailer, and I swooped down, lower and lower, until I melted through the metal roof.

Now I was in a white room.

Below me, a woman with brunette hair lay between the legs of a spectacularly naked man.

I kept floating, floating . . . until I sank into her skin. Melded with her essence. Became her.

I was a woman named Jessica Matthews.

And she was just waking up . . .

I was latched on to the velvety inside of a muscular male thigh, my teeth embedded in the flesh near his groin, my mouth soaked with warm, very tasty liquid.

After another minute or two of sucking on the stranger's thigh, I felt firm, long fingers under my chin.

"That's enough, love," said an Irish-tinged voice. "You're healed now."

With great reluctance, I allowed the fingers cupping my jaw to disengage me from the yummy thigh. I sat up, licking my lips to get every dribble of blood smeared on my mouth.

So, I was Jessica. Only I was me.

And apparently, I liked blood.

Or was she the one who liked the blood?

Oh for—gah! Well, if I wasn't nutballs before, this kind of shit should do the trick.

"Ssshhh. Everything will be explained." He tilted his head, looking me over in a way that caused heat to skitter in my stomach. Or rather, Jessica's stomach.

"So . . . with all the, uh, bloodsucking, I'm guessing I'm a vampire now." These words were spoken by Jessica . . . and I was just inside her head, inside this dream, with her. It was *a weird sensation to be inside another person, even if it was a dream, or vision, or . . . me, finally sailing over the edge of sanity.*

"Yes. We Irish vampires call ourselves **deamhan fola.**" He grinned at me. "It means 'blood demon.'"

"Oh. Well, that's certainly . . . descriptive."

We were in some sort of small white room. It had a long, uncomfortable steel slab sticking out from the wall and we were on it. About six feet from the steel slab on the left side of the room was a door without any visible knob or handle. That was it. White room. Steel bed. Naked man. Jessica was in some sort of white hospital gown and smelled like antiseptic.

Jessica was a vampire.

The guy who'd been the lifesaving snack leaned against the wall, his knees drawn up slightly. Raven black hair feathered away from his face, the ends of it curling on his shoulders. He watched me, or rather her, with the strangest eyes I'd ever seen. Of course, I knew this was Patrick. And his brother Lorcan looked exactly the same. As did their father, Ruadan. Following the vampire bloodlines was probably going to require a chart. And someone who understood how to explain charts to people like me.

I heard a steel scrape, then clang, clang, clang. *Patrick had put his hands on his knees and revealed that he was chained to the wall. The chains, maybe as thick as those that secured bicycles, looked too delicate to hold him. Swirls and weird words emblazoned the silver cuffs.*

"You're a prisoner?" Jessica sounded aghast. "I thought vampires were super-duper strong."

He chuckled. "We are very strong. But these little beauties"—he shook his arms—"have special charms on them. I cannot break them."

"Special charms? As in . . ." Jessica wiggled her fingers in a bad sorceress impression.

He nodded. "I had to be bound, love. Because of that ring you're wearin'."

On the ring finger of my right hand—well, Jessica's right hand—was a beautiful silver ring. I looked at it, as if doing so would make it clear why the vampire needed chains to protect him from it. "My claddagh ring?"

"It's a fede," said the man. "It's made from the purest silver and it's very old."

I woke up with my face buried in werewolf thigh. I pushed up and sat back, staring at Drake in shock. My lips felt swollen. "What the hell?"

He seemed dazed. "You . . . were acting out something," he said weakly. "I'm afraid I had no choice but to . . . do as you wished." He grimaced as he adjusted himself, and my gaze was drawn to his crotch.

He had a hard-on. A really big, delicious hard-on.

"Wow," I said.

He looked down, then at me, and sighed. "You were nibbling," he said. Then his gaze tracked down my arm, to my stinging upraised palm that I rested on my thigh. Did I mention the stinging? He frowned. "You are bleeding."

My heart was pounding, either from the vision or

from lust or from excitement. Maybe all three. I looked at my palm and noted that the first blood sacrifice had been minimal. More like a scratch. But yeah, the wound was still bleeding. I looked at Drake and batted my eyelashes. "Are you going to rip off a piece of your shirt and wrap it around my hand?"

I think my voice held too much hope. Drake offered me a wicked grin and then leaned to the side and dug into his front pocket. "Patsy gave me a handful of Band-Aids," he said, pulling out said Band-Aids, along with a pack of peppermint gum. "She also wanted me to have fresh breath."

I laughed. I went to take one of the bandages, but he said, "*Nein.*"

He chose a Band-Aid, stuffed the rest and the gum back into his pocket, and undid the wrapping, which he tucked into the opposite pocket. Then he put the bandage over my minor wound. He looked at me with that smoky gaze that made my stomach squeeze, and then placed a kiss on top of the bandage. "It is my understanding that kisses help boo-boos heal faster," he said.

"I've heard that, too." I grinned.

"Any other boo-boos?" he asked in that smoky voice. My thighs shivered.

"I'll let you know."

He cocked his lips into a half smile, a reminder that his lips could be on my body anytime.

"So, what do we do now, Moira?"

Well, I had some ideas (see: trembling thighs), but they didn't involve pyramids, Ancients, or blood. Drake caught on to my line of thought rather quickly. Actually, he was probably already skating in the same direction, waiting for me to catch up.

Here I was, stuck in a pyramid, where my blood would be drained drop by drop, and all I could think about was getting horizontal with Drake. I hadn't forgotten that he was a werewolf, either. I couldn't imagine what the sex would be like. Oh, wait. Yes. Yes, I could.

Drake slipped his hand around my neck and leaned close. "For luck," he whispered. Then he kissed me.

Just one, sweet, soft meeting of lips. A promise, really.

My heart skipped a beat, and I felt lust take flight in my belly. I'd been in relationships. Or tried to be. Not many men in my social circle could understand my archaeological mind-set, much less allow themselves to be put aside so I could constantly go to Egypt. Some had been concerned for my safety, others were under the impression that I needed a reason to stay home (i.e., them), and yet others believed I just needed a man to guide me. And that, of course, was before they understood that I was highly medicated because I had the crazy in me.

So, I guess I mostly dated idiots.

I had a feeling that Drake wouldn't expect me to be anyone other than myself, and that was a nice thought . . . someone who accepted me for who I was without expectation that I would change to suit him. And he hadn't seemed to give a rat's ass about the pills I had to take, either. That was a refreshing change. But maybe parakind was more understanding of humans who were different.

"You were obviously having a vision earlier," said Drake. "Unless you were looking for an excuse to nibble on me." He brushed his thumb across my lower lip, and that light touch made my mouth tingle. "For the record, you can nibble me anytime."

"Noted," I said. We stared at each other, both of us breathing a little too heavily. It was probably because we were in a space with limited oxygen or because we wanted to fall on each other like rabid hyenas. Hmm. Would a reference to the werewolf and Red Riding Hood be more appropriate here?

Ahem.

I explained what had happened to me, and as the words tumbled out of my mouth, the frown that formed between his eyebrows deepened into a V.

"You experienced a memory, I think. Patrick and Jessica's first meeting is very well known. But what has that to do with our current circumstances?"

"To know the beginning is to know the answer," I said.

"The beginning of our presence in Broken Heart?" He shook his head. "Why would that matter so much?"

"There's a clue in what I experienced." I held up my non-bandaged hand and counted off my fingers. "I would say that the important elements that jump out at me are . . . magical cuffs . . . silver . . . and a ring." I wiggled my ring finger.

"The *fede* ring," he murmured. "Jessica's prized possession, held even above her swords, which she adores nearly as much as she does Patrick."

I remembered how good Jessica had been with those swords in the desert, and how she and Patrick, like most Broken Heart couples I'd met, seemed so in tune with each other. Two halves of a whole—I couldn't quite wrap my brain around the idea that true love was real. But if vampires and werewolves and banshees were real . . . then why not soul mate love? "Why wouldn't a pyramid made three thousand years ago have ancient clues? Why toss me into the memories of two vampires with a recent history?"

"Maybe it's using our location to create the clues— and if so, then the traps as well. Magic is powerful, especially spells cast so long ago, when magic was more present in the human world."

"Magic," I mused. "So, the pyramid draws from Broken Heart . . . and from me . . . to know the beginning . . . er, of what?"

"Broken Heart. And you."

"The beginning of me? That makes no sense."

"Perhaps it will as we get through the pyramid."

"Maybe." I sat back, studying the blank walls, my gaze scraping over Drake, who leaned against the wall, one leg bent and an arm casually draped over the knee.

Silence thickened as we tried to puzzle out meaning from the strange vision.

"I got nothing," I said.

"We have something," he replied, nodding toward the door. It was gone. An entrance beckoned us to the next phase of our pyramid adventure.

Drake stood, and then reached down a hand, which I took with my non-injured one. He pulled me to my feet, and we both turned to consider another narrow passageway lit with torches.

"Huh," I said. Then, in order to keep ahead of Mr. Stubborn, I marched on through the arched doorway. I grinned at him over my shoulder. "This is *eeeeeeeeee*—"

Chapter 17

I was falling.

Because I had thrown all my caution and archaeological experience out the window, I'd stepped right into the yawning blackness of a pit.

My descent stopped as suddenly as it had started, and I found myself dangling in the dark. I yanked my feet up because I didn't know what terrible things were below me . . . snakes, spikes, broken bones of other archaeologists. Then I realized that Drake's hand was clamped over my wrist.

I looked up and found him staring at me, his expression etched with shock and worry. "Are you all right?

"Not particularly."

He hoisted me up, easily, with just that one hand, and then set me on my feet next to the rectangular pit.

"Do not do that again," he admonished.

"No problem." I gently slipped my arm from his grip, and turned to consider how we were going to cross the pit. There was enough of an edge for us to turn sideways, press against the wall, and scoot.

"I will go first," he said. "I insist."

I figured if he stayed stubborn, I could get around him once we got to the other side, and then get to the next door/trap/blood sacrifice before he did. I might have to push him down and hop over his prone body, but that was okay. I was determined to see this thing through.

Also, there was no going back.

Drake slipped around me, pressed his back against the stone wall, and began shuffling across the narrow strip of stone. I did the same, and we spent an eon or so slowly, carefully inching our way along the ledge. When we reached the other side, I heaved a sigh of relief.

"Onward," I said. I caught his gaze, leaned toward him, saw his eyes go expectant . . . and then I wiggled past him and headed down the narrow hall. I know. Mean, right?

Drake grabbed my arm, spun me around, and said, "No, Moira." Then he pulled me back and moved toward the door, practically towing me behind him. When he reached the stone door, he hesitated.

"Did you miss your Hieroglyphs 101 class?" I asked sweetly.

"I was too busy taking advanced Kick Your Ass

courses," he replied. He spent useless seconds staring at the images he could not possibly interpret, and then sighed. He stepped aside and gestured eloquently. "My lady."

"Thanks." I moved past him and studied the hieroglyphs, which were the same as the others—prayers and threats. There wasn't a circular opening like the one in the other door, but there was a particular glyph in the middle. I stared at it. "Shit."

"What?" asked Drake. He looked over my shoulder. "What does it say?"

"Basically? It's a closed exit sign. This is a false door." I turned, and found myself practically nose to nose with him. He stayed put, his gaze on mine, hushed expectation falling between us, stretching into a moment so fine and thin it cut like a blade. And then he stepped back. The spell was broken, but my body hummed. *Him, him, him,* it seemed to chant. *Now, now, now.*

"We have to go into the pit," I said.

"It says that?"

"Not exactly. But it's our only option." I walked to the pit, and Drake followed. I pulled the small flashlight out of my pocket and aimed the beam into the darkness below.

As far as I could tell, there weren't any spikes or skulls or snakes. It was too far down for me to just leap, but when I glanced at Drake, I could see him contemplating the distance.

"I'll jump down there," he said in all seriousness.

"That's a terrible idea! What if you land on a sharpened stake?"

"It will hurt."

"Or kill you. Werewolves aren't immune to death, are they?"

"Most aren't," he conceded. "There is nothing down there." He tapped the side of his temple. "Werewolf vision. I'll jump and then you follow. I'll catch you."

"You'll catch me?" I asked. "Um . . . no."

"I cannot lower you down first," he said reasonably. "Even if I did so, the distance would still be too great for you to land safely." He put his hand on my shoulder. "Trust me."

I considered the pit, then him, then the pit. I didn't really have a choice. I'd entered the pyramid with sparse equipment, not that there was exactly a place to put in a pulley system. I was all about trying to control situations, and I was used to considering all the angles and making quick decisions. In archaeology, you didn't always have the luxury of time. So, my initial blood sacrifice got us inside the pyramid. After that, I had no idea what else awaited us, or how much blood I would be giving in the name of saving the Ancients. Getting through this mess as quickly as possible suited me just fine. I was hopeful, but not exactly confident, that I would leave this pyramid alive.

"Okay." I kept the beam aimed at the dirt floor below, and Drake stood, then jumped.

He landed on his feet.

In the narrow light, I saw him curve his arms. "C'mon," he said. "Jump."

"Yeah. Sure. No problem." I considered how long the drop was, the equivalent probably of jumping out a second-story window of a house, and felt my heart skip a beat. I wasn't usually afraid, but this was big leap . . . of faith. It wasn't like there was another option, though.

"Catch," I said, and threw the flashlight down.

He caught it one-handed and set it upright, so the beam shined upward.

"I will catch you, Moira."

I took a big breath, and then . . . jumped.

The three seconds of free fall made my stomach roil, my lungs heave, and my heart pound.

Then he caught me.

He didn't even "oof" or stumble backward. He just caught me like I was a pillow that had been lightly tossed at him. He cradled me to his chest, and then said, "What I catch, I keep."

"Interesting philosophy."

He chuckled and then swung me down. When my feet touched solid ground, he let me go. I picked up the flashlight and aimed it around the four walls. The nearest wall was the only one with any glyphs—a narrow series of brightly painted hieroglyphs. We stood and walked to it. I studied the glyphs.

"They're in a random order," I said. "If you try to

read them, it makes no sense, not even for ancient Egyptians." I paused. I thought about my vision of Patrick and Jessica, and the clues offered by that experience. Damn. None of the glyphs was the equivalent of "ring" or "chains." But there was one for "mate." Was that the clue I was supposed to get from the first vision? I studied the other glyphs. Different words, but none that made sense when put together . . . and I couldn't puzzle out a particular phrase or meaning. I kept returning to the word for "mate." Love will lead me, right?

I pressed the glyph.

The gold-rimmed circular hole appeared instantly, and I knew it was time for another round of blood sacrifice.

"Moira," warned Drake, "do not—"

I stuck my hand inside, and felt something sharp, like teeth, clamp onto my wrist. Pain flared, but I resisted the urge to cry out. This was no mere prick of a needle to release a drop or two of blood. Whatever had my hand was ensuring that I couldn't move while the blood flowed.

I don't remember passing out.

But I did recognize the floating.

What? Again?

This time, I hovered above a small brick building. From my vantage point, I could see a trailer in the back, tucked near a copse of trees.

Then I descended into the building, melting through the ceiling, and there I saw Patsy, puttering around a beauty shop.

I had no choice but to sink into her skin, and I became Patsy Donahue, the vampire she'd been before she became queen of the undead . . .

Someone pounded on the back door. She yelled, "Who is it?"

"Gabriel. Please, let me in!"

My fingers, her fingers, clenched the bolt, but didn't turn it.

"Do we have to talk through this blasted door? Please, Patsy. Trust me."

She unbolted the door and swung it open. Gabriel nearly fell into our arms, but managed to stagger inside on his own. He looked a mess. He wore only a pair of jeans. His chest had been clawed. Blood dripped onto the floor.

We slammed the door shut and locked it again.

Gabriel sank to his knees, swaying. His face was tight with pain.

Patsy knelt down, and I felt her confusion, her terror. Her hands hovered over his shoulders, but she was afraid to touch him. "What can I do?"

One corner of his mouth hitched. "Ask me that again later, okay?"

His gaze dipped to Patsy's breasts, leaving no doubt what he meant by the question. She shook her head, amused. "Get into the chair and I'll clean your wounds."

He stood up and Patsy, or me as Patsy, gently guided him to the nearest styling chair. His moon white hair needed a good brushing. Patsy got paper towels and soaked them with warm water. As I, or she (this was goddamn confusing), leaned over to wipe the blood off his ribs, Gabriel's hand snaked around her neck and pulled us close.

"I need blood."

"Lycans don't drink blood."

"I do." He opened his mouth and needle-point fangs descended. He licked his lips as he leaned forward, aiming those sharp babies right at my neck.

Panic erupted inside Patsy. We jerked out of his grip and lurched back. "What the hell are you?"

"Patricia."

Her full given name held a world of hurt. He reached one arm beseechingly toward us. "Why do you fear me? I am no different than Lorcan or Eva or any of the other vampires who share my abilities."

"Lorcan was cured, so he's not a beast anymore. And Eva isn't a werewolf."

"The cure for the Taint comes from the blood of royal lycanthropes," he said quietly. "But there is side effect. The vampires who survive the cure retain the ability to shapeshift."

Patsy believed he was full of . . . malarkey. But she couldn't help but think the werewolf side effect would explain why the Consortium hadn't released the cure to all vampires seeking it.

"Is that what happened to you?"

"No." He grimaced. "I was born with this . . . anomaly."

A lycanthrope born with vampire tendencies? How in the

*world had such a thing happened? Patsy was insanely at-
tracted to Gabriel, which upset her. Even though she was
scared of him, she wanted to touch him. Wanted to make him
feel better. His wounds had not closed. Blood flowed onto the
chair and pooled around its base.*

"Why haven't you healed?" I asked.

"Demon scratches are poisonous, even to mutants such as
I." *His words held bitterness. He sucked in a sharp breath
and squeezed his eyes shut.*

"Why did you risk coming here?"

His eyes flickered open. "To claim you."

"I'm not checked baggage." *Patsy put her hands on her
hips and looked him over. All Gabriel needed was a little
blood to help him heal. She wanted to get closer to him—and
that uncontrollable urge to be near him confused her. Terrified her. I recognized these feelings . . . because I felt the same
way about Drake.*

*Patsy approached Gabriel. He watched her, his expression
solemn. She gripped the armrests of the barber chair, leaned
down, and offered her neck. His lips brushed her skin. She,
and of course I, felt electrified by that single, soft touch. Then
his fangs sank into her neck and he drank.*

When I came to, I was wrapped around Drake like a
stripper hugging the brass pole. My lips were pressed
against the hollow of his throat. He smelled so good,
like man and cologne and . . . something else. Something dark and sexy and . . . oh, I was tingling.

"Moira."

His voice was hoarse, and given the vision I had just had, I could only imagine what sorts of things I'd done to him in the throes of another couple's passion. Also, it was damned weird to be forced into the body of someone else so I could relive certain memories. To what end? I had no clue how to piece it all together. And what would be the next one? Would there even be another one?

Poor Drake.

I unwound myself from him, feeling shaky and strange. He seemed reluctant to let me go, and I wasn't exactly in a hurry to leave his embrace, either. He found the wherewithal first to release me, and I stepped back. I offered him a trembling smile. "Sorry. I have no control over this shit."

"I know." He sucked in a breath. Then his gaze met mine, and I saw the raw lust sparkling in his gaze. My knees nearly buckled.

"I want you," he said.

Chapter 18

"You know I want you," he echoed.

"Yes," I said softly. "I want you, too." I waved my hand around. "Granted, these are not ideal conditions for exploration of our attraction."

"No," he agreed, regret heavy in his voice. His gaze fell to my breasts, and then I saw him look farther down. At my vagina? Really? Way to be subtle, werewolf.

"You're bleeding again."

"Oh." He'd been gazing at my bloody arm. Oops. Now that I was in my right mind again, I could feel the pulsing pain in the wrist that had been pierced. I lifted my arm and stared at the wound. "Yeah, that hurts."

"I think it's time to rip my shirt," he said. He untucked his black T-shirt and ripped a section from the bottom. He wrapped the piece of T-shirt around my wrist. He tied a bow at the top.

"I don't suppose you have any Advil in one of those pockets?"

He shook his head. "Sorry. Human medication doesn't work on werewolves, and most paranormal creatures have no need for pain relievers."

"Especially when you have the goddess of healing on call," I said.

"True." He looked over my shoulder. "There is another passage."

I turned to see. Just as the other one had, the wall here had disappeared. Once again, magical torchlight flickered off stone walls, beckoning us on to the next part of the journey.

"Shall we?" I asked. I felt tired, no doubt from the blood loss. I really needed to, pardon the vampire humor, suck it up. I had a feeling the vampires weren't on the other side of the door. We were on a journey here, and if I was going to die from blood loss, it might take a few tries.

Awesome.

Drake grasped my non-injured hand, and stalled my progress. I was hyper-aware of him, not only because he was gorgeous, but also because I knew I had to keep ahead of him so I could conquer this pyramid with this whole blood sacrifice thing.

I only hoped the ambrosia was real. I would be really pissed off if I died.

He pulled me back, swung me around right into his embrace.

"One kiss," he murmured.

I could not deny him—or me—that one simple request. He cupped my face, staring deeply into my eyes. Electric thrills raced up my spine and spun like an out-of-control Ferris wheel in my belly. He pulled out the band holding my hair in its requisite ponytail and spread his fingers through the silky layers. (Okay, look, I know describing my own hair as having silky layers is somewhat arrogant, but it's also the truth. I have an awesome stylist.)

"Beautiful," he said.

He angled his head and brushed his lips over mine. My entire body went still, except for the tingles. Oh, holy hell, these were some bad-ass tingles, too. His lips cavorted over mine, teasing me. He captured—again and again—but did not conquer.

By the time his tongue pierced the seam of my mouth, I was clinging to him, if only because my legs were so shaky I didn't think I could stand on my own.

His tongue drew mine into a mating dance. My heart pounded erratically, and I felt so electrified, so hot for him. The passion of our kiss intensified, and I started to think that we had too many clothes on. And there were others part of me that needed kissing. And other parts of him that I wanted to kiss.

Then he drew away, panting, his eyes dilated, his lips swollen and wet. He leaned forward and licked my bottom lip. "Later," he promised in a growling voice. "I will take you, Moira."

"That's the best news I've heard all day." I looked up at him and brushed my fingers over his cheek. His kiss, his passion, had quite the rejuvenation effect. My exhaustion faded, and I felt ready for the next task. I looked at him and smiled. "I'll hold you to that, Drake."

He gifted me with that wicked, wicked grin, and suddenly I had a whole new reason to get out of the pyramid and, you know, not die.

Not dying would be good.

At least, not dying *forever*.

I moved through the door, and down the hall. I could see stairs through the next archway, and as we made our way up the stone steps, I explained my second vision to Drake.

"You experienced the first time Gabriel took blood from Patsy?" he asked.

"Seems like," I said. "But there wasn't any talk of objects. I mean, unless we take into consideration the beauty shop aspect . . . combs . . . scissors . . . hair."

"I do not think what you are supposed to learn has much to do with objects," mused Drake.

"Then what?"

We reached the top of the staircase, and found yet another narrow hallway lit with torches. "Well, here we go again," I said.

For whatever reason, Drake felt compelled to take

my hand, and as I stepped into the hall, cold air blasted us from the other end.

An otherworldly voice rang out: *Know the beginning . . .*

I blinked against the fierce wind, and when it stopped, we were no longer in the pyramid. Or so it seemed. We were walking in a faded landscape. It was not like the previous visions I'd experienced, the main difference being that Drake walked beside me, still clasping my hand. It was like we had been tossed into the ghost of the land that had once been ancient Egypt.

I was enthralled.

Ahead of us walked a tall man with a shaved head wearing some sort of white dress that looped over one shoulder. I knew from the wall reliefs and the architecture that we were in a temple, one devoted to the god Anubis.

"It seems we are visiting a memory," said Drake. He nodded toward the man. "That's Amahté."

"How do you know?"

"Who else would it be? Amahté was the high priest of Anubis. Khenti, his son, once told us that the god gave him the ability to speak to the dead and he also gave him the ability to raise the dead."

"His son was a vampire, too?"

"All Ancients turned at least one of their biological children."

"Well, that's weird." I pondered that idea for a moment. "Ruadan is an Ancient, isn't he?"

"Yes. He was the first to make his own children into vampires. His twin sons, Patrick and Lorcan, were both Turned."

Patsy had mentioned Lorcan in her conversation with Gabriel. Something about suffering from the Taint, and vampires who could turn into werewolves. Shape-shifting didn't seem to be a common element of being a vampire.

"What exactly are Patsy and Gabriel?"

"Werewolves who must drink blood to survive. It is a very small pack. Only Gabriel, Ren, and Anise existed, until Patsy was Turned and had children with her mate."

"I'm starting to feel like I need a flowchart," I said.

He nodded to the ghostly image of the priest. "Every vampire family has certain abilities. Amahté's Family gift is the ability to see ghosts and communicate with them."

I remembered the strange moment during our rescue/re-kidnapping when Patsy had gone off to a corner to have a conversation with the air. Gabriel had said then that she could speak to spirits. "So, Patsy was a vampire before Gabriel . . . er, made her into a vampire-werewolf?"

"Yes. She was part of the Amahté Family. But now she is also *loup de sang*. And as queen of the vampires and, for a time, the werewolves, she absorbed seven powers of the Ancients."

I stared at him. "You know that I have no idea what's going on, right?"

"I'm not a flowchart kind of guy. I'll tell Lorcan to

make you one when we return to Broken Heart. He keeps track of all the vampire history."

We reached the end of the temple's hall. The man ahead of us had barely cleared the doorway, which led outside, when we heard noises of a scuffle.

We stepped out of the temple and saw three men, all of whom were naked, struggling with Amahté. He was putting up an impressive fight, and for a moment I thought he might actually win.

Then the attacker behind him took out a dagger. He drew it across Amahté's neck. The blade slit his skin easily.

Blood spurted everywhere.

The man dropped his victim, then fled with his companions.

Amahté lay on his back, his hands pressed against his gurgling throat.

"You see why they wore no clothes," said Drake. "They can go to the Nile and wash off the blood. Then get dressed, and no one would know they committed murder."

"Bastards," I muttered. "Why would they kill him?"

"Jealousy about being a favorite of both a god and the ruling pharaoh," said Drake. "At least that's what Khenti had told us."

Amahté was a handsome man, mid- to late forties, with doe-like brown eyes and muscles that denoted hard work. Not what I would call a priest's body, which I figured should be soft and pudgy.

No one was around the temple. The path was lined with trees and bushes, and down the road I could see flickering lights. I realized the lights were torches left on the outside of buildings. That was a village down there. In the far distance, the pyramids glowed big and white against the night sky.

We heard the sound of running feet and then a stream of words I didn't understand, but the musical flow of them was familiar.

Ruadan appeared.

"Wow. What's he doing here?"

"He's not only an Ancient, Moira, he's also the first vampire ever to walk the earth," he said. "He made all of the Ancients."

"Holy crap! I met the first vampire *ever* and I didn't even know it?"

"Ruadan likes to keep a low profile."

Ruadan looked horrified as he knelt down and spoke to Amahté, this time in a different language. And yet we understood the words.

"My friend! It is me, Ruadan. We have talked much these last few nights, remember?"

Amahté's eyes clearly showed that he did.

"I can save you. But my gift has a price. You will not be able to see the sun again, but you will live forever. You will be among those I have chosen to rule our kind. Do you accept my offer?"

Amahté took an inordinate amount of time to decide. Blood seeped from between his fingers and pooled blackly on the ground. Finally, he managed a weak nod.

Ruadan removed Amahté's hands from the wound. The blood poured out. My stomach jumped. I could barely stand to keep my eyes on the action. Ruadan didn't move, merely watched the life drain from his supposed friend.

"I thought he was supposed to drink the blood."

Drake shook his head. "What would be the point of drinking from a dying human? Ruadan's dark blood is what Amahté needs to become a vampire."

Ruadan watched calmly, waiting patiently as Amahté bled to death right in front of him.

"If vampires get different powers from the various Ancients . . . ," I whispered. Silly, but I just couldn't raise my voice with all that was going on with the vampires. ". . . then why isn't everyone just from Ruadan's line?"

"His grandmother is Morrigu, and it was she who made him into a vampire—after he was killed in battle."

"I know that story." I liked ancient myths and legends, though I tended to save most of my brain files for ancient Egyptian facts. Still, I thought about what I knew of the fae battle for Ireland. I blinked. "If Morrigu is Ruadan's grandmother, then Brigid is his mother."

"Yes. Ruadan asked Morrigu for the secret for making others of his kind. She gave him the spells and the instructions, but said he could choose only seven others to Turn. And only they would be his equals with their own powers. I'm sure she hoped it would cause strife and grief." He glanced at me. "She really takes the queen of chaos thing seriously."

The crow queen was real, too? How many more gods and goddesses from the mythologies of various cultures were actual beings?

Now, Amahté lay still, his caramel skin graying, his eyes wide and unstaring. Ruadan muttered over Amahté, pressing his palms against the man's chest. I couldn't understand these words and I looked at Drake, frowning.

"I've seen a few Turnings," said Drake. "Once the human's blood is drained, you must keep the soul within the body. Ruadan is uttering a spell designed to do that. If any part of the process goes wrong you can kill the person you are trying to Turn."

"What about those who try it without knowing what to do?"

"The person merely dies, which is the better option."

After Ruadan had secured Amahté's soul, he removed a small gold knife from his wide belt. He punctured his forefinger and rubbed it on Amahté's neck wound.

The skin started to mend.

Then Ruadan began to carve symbols into Amahté's flesh: one on each wrist, one on the top of each foot, one on the forehead, one on the chest, and two on the belly.

He pierced his finger again, and with his blood, he

retraced all the symbols he'd cut into Amahté. As he did so, they all glowed gold.

"Only the Family's symbol must be cut into the flesh of the one being Turned," said Drake. "Each Family was assigned one of the sacred symbols given to Ruadan by Morrigu. That's why all eight are used to make Ruadan's equal."

"Eight?" I murmured. I seemed to recall that Monroe's book had mentioned seven vampire lines.

"Everyone believed that the eighth vampire line was destroyed when Shamhat died. It was centuries before Ruadan let a few know that Shamhat lived . . . but barely."

I heard what Drake said, but I was fascinated by Ruadan's actions. Now Ruadan slit his wrist and pressed it against the lips of the man he hoped to save.

For a moment the blood merely seeped into Amahté's open mouth. Then, somehow, he revived and began to drink.

Minutes passed, but it felt like years before Ruadan finally pulled his wrist away.

When Amahté's body started to convulse, I yelped and jumped back. What happened to him was a terrible thing to watch. His eyes rolled back in his head and his arms and legs went wild. The symbols went bright white and Amahté screamed.

He went still. The symbols burned into his skin. The blackened marks faded slowly, until they couldn't be seen anymore.

"Some vampires can lose their souls," said Drake quietly. "They become *droch fola*. They are vicious. They have no conscience, and do not conform to the rules created by the Ancients."

"Like the one you killed in the Sudan. And Karn is a *droch fola*."

"Yes. And so are most of his minions. They tire of staying in the shadows, of keeping parakind hidden."

"Not to mention that they think they're the top of the food chain."

Drake nodded. "Exactly."

We returned our attention to Ruadan. He had finished his gruesome work. Blood splattered the man on the ground, staining his white clothes. Ruadan had fared no better—his own clothing was soiled with his victim's blood.

Ruadan picked up the priest and carried him away.

The scene faded, just like a movie getting ready to switch scenes, and we found ourselves at the end of the hallway, facing another stone door with its familiar circular hole.

"I won't let you do that again," said Drake. He moved in front of me, his expression stubborn. "Step away, Moira."

His tone rankled me. I got that he was a he-man type, or he-werewolf type, but I was strong, capable, and already bleeding for our cause. I stepped into his space, jutted my chin out defiantly, and said, "Or what, wolf boy?"

"That's wolf *man*," he corrected. "And I will put you over my shoulder and carry you the rest of the way. With your mouth bandaged shut." He patted the pocket with its stash of Band-Aids. "I can better survive being the blood key."

"Blood key" was a good way to describe my current role in this situation. "You can't," I said. "It requires my blood."

"I know," he said, his gaze narrowed, "but I don't have to like it."

"Just for the record, I don't like it, either. I have to do it, Drake. So just let me stick my poor, abused hand into the creepy hole, and move on to the next phase of Rescue the Ancient Vampires, okay?"

His lips thinned, and he crossed his arms. For a moment I thought he wouldn't move, and we'd be stuck staring daggers at each other—at least until one of us thought of some way to outwit the other. But then Drake begrudgingly moved aside. I have to admit, I was surprised he'd given in so easily. I hadn't expected him to be reasonable.

No need to have two injured hands, right? So I took off the T-shirt bandage, handed the bloodied cloth to Drake, inhaled deeply, and stuck my hand into yet another hole.

Something cold and metallic slithered over my entire hand. For the first time, fear chilled me. The sacrifices required were getting more profound. I wonder how many more doorways were left, and how much more blood I would have to give to the Ancients, and their pyramid, before I breathed my last.

My entire hand started to burn, and the pain sizzled up my arm. I couldn't stop my scream, or my instinct to pull my hand out. But it was too late.

I was floating again, this time in a room that felt . . . strange. It was a living room, but felt almost like I was on a movie set rather than in an actual space where people lived. And maybe that was the real issue . . . I don't think these were people.

Unlike the previous visions, in this one I wasn't slipping into someone else's skin. Instead I was like a ghost, floating among the people in the room.

A woman stood in the doorway.

She was otherworldly: pale-skinned, with bow-shaped lips as red as candy and green eyes as soft as moss. She wore a ribbed green T-shirt, tight black pants, thick-soled black boots, and on her waist was a weapons belt. On one side was a Glock and three cartridges, and on the other a series of small silver daggers. Her raven hair hung in ringlets down her back, like those of a medieval princess. "Beautiful" wasn't a decent enough word to describe her. The only visible flaw I could see was the jagged pearlescent scar that wrapped around her throat like an ugly necklace.

Information floated into my head . . . her name was Larsa, and she was a vampire . . . and she was the daughter of Shamhat.

"The demon Lilith killed my mother," Larsa explained to the room of people. Obviously I had arrived in the middle of

a conversation. "The Ancients learned a harsh lesson the day Shamhat died. All of her line died when she did. Because of the bonding magic, all of their mates died, too."

"Shamhat was the eighth vampire line. Vampires with earth magic," said Larsa. "They're very sensual creatures, in tune with creation. With life. Ironic, in a way, since we're undead. But you know how it was. Ruadan sought out others who had supernatural abilities. It's no coincidence that all the Ancients have specific gifts."

"Why?" The question came from a lithe brunette. Her name floated into my mind: Phoebe.

"Eight vampire Families had existed once," said Larsa. "And Lilith had effectively wiped out one-eighth of the vampire population by killing its founder.

"Ruadan always had the goal of bettering the world. Even then, belief in magic was dying out, giving way to science and cynics. He wanted to preserve as much as possible, to pass it along to the world when it was needed."

"Patsy saved the vampire lines because she was the queen of all," mused Phoebe. She sent a questioning glance to Larsa. "If Patsy dies . . . we all die?"

"Probably," said Larsa. "Unless there comes a time when that burden is lifted from her."

"I missed the connection with Amahté," Phoebe said. "And the sorta-dead thing for Shamhat."

"Amahté was powerful," said Larsa. "Even before he was Turned. He could leave his body and travel into the Underworld. That ability, and being an Ancient, gave him the power to retrieve Shamhat's soul. But her body needed some serious *healage*. So everyone believed she'd died. And he went to ground with her. To protect her."

"Isn't three thousand years long enough to heal grievous injuries?" asked Phoebe.

"Yep," said Larsa.

I found myself being pulled toward Phoebe. Into her thoughts. She was thinking about the Consortium . . . about when the vampires came to Broken Heart. There had been talk about an archaeological dig in the Sudan. At the time, we'd been told the Consortium was looking for the source of the Taint. The disease had flared up now and then throughout undead history, but the modern-day version had taken them by surprise.

"They were looking for Amahté," she said. "In the Sudan."

"Nobody knows where they are. And the Consortium aren't the only ones looking."

"I'm from the Family Shamhat," said Larsa. "I was the last. Lilith hacked off my mother's head and nearly severed mine." She fingered the scar on her neck, one that had never completely healed because she shouldn't have survived it. "When Amahté pulled back her soul and returned her life, however feeble, it revived me. But none of the others. At least, none that I've ever been able to find." She shrugged. "It took a long time to heal. By the time I was recovered enough to dig out from my grave, more than a hundred years had passed. Everyone believed me dead, and I let them think so. Until my mother is found and awakened, I am the last of my Family line."

I guess that was the extent of the information that needed to be conveyed, because I found myself being yanked out of the vision and tossed into the darkness.

When I awoke, I was sagging against the wall, being held up by Drake, whose arms were wrapped around my waist. My hand was still clamped in the hole, and my blood still draining. I felt dizzy, and a little nauseated. I didn't know if I should feel relieved or disappointed that I hadn't been wrapped around Drake again.

I was leaning toward disappointed.

And feeling like crap.

Then my hand was released, and I dragged my arm out of the hole.

"Ow," I muttered.

Drake lowered me to the ground and cursed softly as he removed his entire shirt and wrapped it around my mangled hand.

"These locks are demanding too much blood from you," he said.

"We have no choice but to move forward."

"*Ja*," he said. It was a short, angry burst of a word. He finished securing the shirt and leaned back to study my face. "You are pale."

"I feel light-headed." I used my uninjured arm to grab water from one of the side pockets of my pants. Drake gently took it from me and twisted off the cap. When he gave me the bottle, I drained half of it. He put the lid back on and then tucked it back into the pocket for me.

"What did you see this time?" he asked.

"Nothing sexual. Disappointed?"

His lips split into a quicksilver grin. "Immensely."

I managed a laugh and then I told him about the strange room, the people, and the information I'd learned about Larsa, Shamhat, and Amahté.

He nodded. "Yes. It was revealed not so long ago that the eighth family line still existed. And Larsa was alive. But how does that vision fit in with the others?"

"To know the beginning," I said. "So, Jessica and Patrick were the beginning of what became Broken Heart. Patsy and Gabriel were the beginning of a new kind of leadership. And knowing what happened to Shamhat and Amahté is the beginning of . . . well, this. Why we're here right now."

"What are we supposed to do with the information?"

I liked that he'd used a pronoun: "we." I think I liked being part of a "we." It was nice. I looked over my shoulder at the doorway that had been revealed. That last round of blood sacrifice had been intense. "Hey, it's not a hallway. Do you think we've reached our destination?"

Fat chance, I knew, since my apparent death was part of this gig. Still . . . who was to know anything for sure?

"Let us find out." Drake popped up and reached down a hand, which I grasped.

I wobbled to my feet, took a breath, and turned. We stared at the room beyond, and then looked at each other.

Torches rimmed the small room. The only object in it was . . . well, a bed. Right in the middle. The smooth, flat stone was covered in a pile of silky furs—which shouldn't look comfortable or like they'd just been fluffed by servants of the palace. And yet it looked as though it had just been made up, and was waiting for us to . . . what? Take a nap?

We walked to the bed and studied it. On each corner was a small statue of Bastet, who was part cat, part woman. In her clasped paws were sticks of incense. Their fragrance wafted into the air.

"We should look for glyphs," I said. But I had a feeling already of what would be expected of me. Well, of us. "Do you think they sent us here on purpose? I mean, male and female? Would anyone know . . . um, to do that?"

Drake sent me a strange look. "What do you mean?"

"That's a bed," I said, pointing to the item, "and those effigies are of Bastet. The goddess of sensuality, sexuality, and fertility."

Drake moved over to study one of the statues. "I see."

I walked to the nearest wall, then took a circuit of the room. Hmm. Nothing but smooth stone and the magical blue-flamed torches. No hieroglyphs. No paintings. No clues.

"Moira."

Drake had crouched down to view something on the edge of the bed. I joined him, and looked at the series of glyphs inscribed there. And it confirmed my suspicion about what was supposed to happen next.

"'To know the beginning, is to become the beginning,'" I said. I studied the other images, and hesitated.

"That is all it says?"

"No." I glanced at him. "This next part isn't a blood sacrifice. If we want to progress, we have to invoke the magic of Bastet."

Realization dawned in Drake's gaze. "You mean we must unlock the next doorway . . . by having sex."

"Yes," I confirmed.

We both stood up, then because I was still feeling unsteady, I sat on the edge of the bed. The furs felt unexpectedly nice. I couldn't help but wonder now if the reason the pyramid closed behind Drake was because of this part. Or was it the magic? Had this all been created because of the whole emphasis on love and mates? And wouldn't that make sense given what we now knew about Shamhat and Amahté? Because, hell, anyone could've accessed this chamber. Two girls. Two guys. Two goats. Okay. Maybe not goats. But still.

"Shamhat and Amahté have never known modern times," said Drake. "Whoever created this"—he waved his hand to indicate the pyramid—"did so during a time when the world was different."

"I've studied the lives, the religious practices, the

deities of ancient Egypt," I said. "Believe me, I know quite a bit about the sexual mores of Ancient Egypt. It makes sense that they might have something like a sex rite to unlock the power of the god. Or to wake up two very tired bloodsuckers."

Drake gave a short laugh, and then he joined me on the bed. He pushed a lock of hair away from my face, and then grasped my chin, his thumb resting on my upper lip. Butterflies fluttered in my belly.

"Ah, my beauty," he said in that smoky voice. "Shall we?"

Chapter 19

"Now?" I squeaked, even though I knew it was imperative that we keep moving forward. I mean, time was literally ticking. Drake was appreciating the idea of having sex a little too much. Not that my libido was complaining. Besides, if we didn't . . . um, do the deed, get the next doorway to unlock . . . then both of us were worm food.

"We cannot go back," he said, glancing over his shoulder.

I followed his gaze to the doorway and saw that it no longer existed. Whoever created this pyramid wanted to make damn sure the sacrifices kept moving forward. Drake's slight touch was setting off lust alarms all over my body. I wondered if anyone had attempted to wake Shamhat and Amahté before.

Somehow I doubted it.

"You've been looking for a while in the Sudan. Looking for them. Why?"

"To honor a promise made by Ruadan."

"Maybe he's the one who created all of this."

"It's possible," said Drake in a distracted voice. His gaze was on mine, and he was getting . . . whew, *intense*. "He does have a flair for the dramatic. But still . . . I don't believe he hid Shamhat and Amahté. They never meant to be gone for so long. But the vampires lost them. Or so we thought."

Drake didn't seem particularly interested in his words. His eyes were dilating, and I could have sworn they seemed to change entirely, becoming more animal-like.

I swallowed the knot in my throat.

"Moira."

"Yes?"

Drake's voice had a sensual quality that made my nerves prickle. The intent gleam in his jade green eyes warned me, but before I could protest, he lowered his head and pressed warm, soft lips against my mouth.

Oh, he'd kissed me before.

But this was more than just a hello kiss. This was an introduction-to-ravishment kiss. My whole body responded to the sensual invitation he offered.

Drake pulled me closer and deepened the kiss. He tasted like mints, and I wondered vaguely if he'd been chewing that gum Patsy had given him.

Damn, it had been a long time since I'd been kissed. And I don't think I'd ever been kissed like this. His tongue flicked the corner of my mouth and a jolt of electricity zapped my very core.

Then he invaded, his tongue sweeping inside, drawing mine into a sensual mating dance.

Heat coiled in my belly. Arousal liquefied my protests and fogged my mind. Whatever doubts I had about this situation, about what was being asked of us by two vampires we'd never met and yet somehow owed, dissolved under Drake's sensual onslaught.

On some level I knew that what I'd been searching for in the sands all these years, following in the footsteps of my grandfather, trying to honor his work and his legacy . . . that maybe I'd been looking for the wrong things in the wrong places. I was searching through time and civilizations for this feeling, for this . . . Oh, whoa. *This* man. I wanted this experience, these feelings.

I wanted Drake.

He stopped kissing me, his breathing erratic as he pulled back and offered me a lazy grin. Oh, if we only had all the time in the world. How tangled the sheets would be, how sweaty our bodies as we . . . He grinned.

I guess my thoughts showed on my face.

I was clinging to Drake's shoulders, feeling unnerved. My mouth throbbed.

His face was all sharp angles, softened only by the fullness of his mouth. I considered the leather band that held back his wonderful hair. He guessed at my thoughts, I supposed, because he reached back and loosed his hair.

I drew my fingers through the fine raven waves. They were gorgeous and felt like silk.

"Wow," I murmured.

He clasped the wrist not wrapped in his T-shirt and tugged me forward. "I want to kiss you again," he said.

"If you insist."

Desire flared in his eyes, and then he pushed lightly on my shoulders. I took the hint and moved fully onto the furs, lying down.

Drake did not lie down beside me. Instead, he got between my legs and tugged on the button and then the zipper of my khakis.

"What are you doing?"

"I'm going to kiss you."

"My lips are up here."

"There are some down here as well." He stroked me through the pants, and I gasped.

"Wait a minute. You don't have to go to all this trouble." I stared at him. I felt my skin prickle and my heart turn over in my chest. It wasn't like I was afraid of sex. Or of Drake. Two people engaged in copulation was an act as old as time, and didn't necessarily bear the hallmarks of love. I couldn't remember a time when I thought I was in love. Oh, there were the typical high school crushes, but in my adult life . . . nothing. I wanted men. I liked men. But I was easily bored.

I didn't think Drake would ever bore me.

And that was the part—that he was different, that he could make my heart pound and my blood thicken, that an inexplicable tenderness wound through the heat and dark of my lust—well, *that* was the scary part. I suddenly wanted to get the whole sex thing over with. I was afraid this moment might mean more if we actually took the time to enjoy each other. And really, did we have the time? "We could just . . . you know, do it."

He met my gaze. "No."

He took precious minutes to unlace my boots and take them and my socks off. Then he returned and grasped the top of my pants. Before I realized what my body was agreeing to do, I'd lifted my hips and allowed him to shimmy my pants and underwear off.

Talk about feeling vulnerable! There I was with my lower half exposed to the hungry gaze of a werewolf. And he was fully clothed, which somehow made my capitulation more submissive—and erotic.

But he wasn't finished.

Through my thin shirt, he cupped my breasts, stroking and molding. My nipples puckered, aching to be touched, to be kissed. But Drake tormented me for hours, days, eons, before pushing my shirt up, then reaching around to unsnap the bra. I realized he wasn't going to take off my shirt or bra, if only because it might bump against the makeshift bandage on my hand.

His gaze feasted on my flesh. He just . . . looked. And my body responded with a terrible ache, a need so great that I trembled. He made that happen without even touching me. Then, *oh, then*, he circled one finger around my aureola, teasing my nipple with a flutter of a single fingertip. He moved to my other breast and tormented it just the same.

For the longest of moments, he did only those feather-light touches. And the only sounds echoing in the chamber were my harsh intakes of breath.

My stomach quivered.

I ached for more of his touch, but I didn't ask. I wanted to beg, really, but I stayed silent. He placed his hands on either side of me, and leaned down, his gaze intent. He captured my gaze, kept it hostage, and continued a slow downward arc to my breasts.

His lips closed over one hardened peak.

I made a noise I don't think I've ever made before—a cry of need and a sigh of longing tangled together.

Then he sucked my nipple into his mouth, his tongue swirling against the sensitive flesh.

A low moan rose from my throat. He cupped my other breast and lightly pinched that nipple while using his tongue to torment the other.

I clenched the furs with shaking fingers, and I moaned again.

He released my breasts, his fingers dragging down the sides of my rib cage as his lips kissed inch after inch of my flesh. He took his time, as if we had all the time in the world, and I swear I nearly melted.

I'd heard women refer to feeling like they were

"afire" during lovemaking. I knew what it took to reach orgasm. I mean, pleasure was pleasure, right? And I'd always believed that the term "making love" was for people intent on romanticizing a normal biological function.

But I'd never felt this way.

I'd never had a lover who wanted to devour me. Given that he was a werewolf, that phrase had a whole new meaning.

I was awash in sensations that ebbed and flowed like ocean waves hitting the beach. Wow. I was so overwhelmed with how Drake made me feel, I couldn't even come up with an original metaphor.

Drake's hands coasted to my hips; his mouth pressed on the skin above my pubic bone. He paused there, long enough to drag his fingers over my thighs, and then he pushed my legs up and settled into a prime position. My feet now rested on his back.

He layered kisses on the inner edges of my thighs. I was already slick, and my very core trembled as he stroked the flesh with lips and tongue. Just the edges, too. Never the center, where the ache bloomed and need pulsed.

Bastard.

I released the furs, my fingers digging into his beautiful hair. He murmured something in German, and the words vibrated against my agitated flesh.

"Oh, God!"

He lifted his head, that wicked gleam made brighter

with his own desire. Then he said, "You can just call me Drake."

I bopped the top of his head. "I'll call you dead if you don't—"

He slipped his tongue inside my swollen flesh, and rendered me speechless. He tasted me fully, and his tongue flicked over my entrance, then back up . . . and down again.

My erratic breathing hitched even more, and my body, already *afire*, damn it, seemed to burn even hotter.

His hot breath ghosted over my clit.

Then he sucked the sensitive nub into his mouth and flicked it with his tongue.

I think I blacked out for a second.

I couldn't remember sex being like this before. Either Drake was really, really good, or I'd picked some really bad lovers.

Pleasure spiderwebbed through me, gossamer strings that pulled taut, that felt electric. I could barely stand being in my own skin.

His tongue started stroking my clit in a rhythm that drove me wild.

I could feel the rise of an orgasm, that first sweet swell of pleasure, and then Drake . . . stopped. He just fucking stopped.

"Argh!"

"Patience, my beauty," he said in a hoarse voice.

I was reminded then that he'd received nothing

from me, no stroking or touching, unless you counted frantic hair pulling. I had eagerly accepted the gift of his unselfish pursuit of my pleasure.

"Patience," I agreed. And I would so pay him back for his torment. We'd see who had patience then. *Mwuhahahaha*—"*Oh,*" I said as his tongue slid over my clit, offering me both relief and agitation.

He slowly stroked me with that talented wolf-man tongue, building the fires again, and then I felt two of his fingers penetrate me. Whoa. He began to pump his fingers in the same rhythm as his tongue.

I sucked in deep breaths, but I couldn't get enough air. The sensations incurred by such devoted skill forced my thoughts into a foggy daze. I couldn't think beyond *Ohmyfreakingawdmoremoremore.*

Because Drake apparently knew exactly what he was doing, because he was single-minded in his purpose, and because he could make me almost die from the pure, raw wanting . . . he curled his fingers upward and found a knot of flesh just inside my entrance.

He relentlessly licked my clit.

And that spot he'd found was a very sensitive bundle of nerves, which he stroked in a rough, wonderful way, matching the rhythm of his tongue once more.

I felt the swift rise of my pleasure, the orgasm that ballooned into heat and sound and light . . . and then burst like the crashing crescendo of every great song. My thighs clenched around Drake's head, but he didn't seem to mind. He slipped his fingers out of me, and slowed his tongue's movements to soothing strokes.

I wanted him to experience the same as I had. I wanted him to feel as shaken as I did.

And I wanted him inside me.

I tugged on his shoulders until he took the hint and slid up to lie beside me. I turned into his embrace and saw the animal eyes. I was reminded that Drake was, quite literally, an animal. A werewolf.

"Are you afraid?" he asked.

"No," I lied. But it wasn't him that I was afraid of. It was this unfolding moment, this feeling that I had been changed by Drake's lovemaking.

And it wasn't over.

I kissed him.

I tasted my own essence on his lips, and merged my tongue with his. We melted into each other's arms, deepened our contact. We both smelled like sex, and like need.

Desire and need streaked through me, pooling wet and hot between my still trembling thighs. Reaching between us, I stroked Drake's cock through his jeans. Good Lord, he was huge.

He growled.

And I felt powerful.

I was provoking a werewolf.

I pulled away from his lips and kissed his jaw, dragging my mouth down his neck, then back up again. My fingers curled under the edge of his T-shirt, which I pulled up to expose the muscled planes of his body.

Drake was built. The man had nice abs. Hell, he had nice everything. Brown hair lightly furred his pecs and stomach. Feast! I worked my way over his pectorals, taking a detour to one coin-sized aureola and its tiny, hard peak. I tugged it between my teeth, flicking the tip rapidly. He groaned, his hands threading into my hair as I attacked his other nipple and gave it the same treatment.

"*Liebling,*" he said. "Moira."

I moved farther down his chest, exploring the muscled ridges of his stomach with my hands, my mouth, my tongue.

I slipped between his legs and tugged open the button to his jeans. I couldn't get the goddamned zipper over his penis, so he choked out a laugh and helped me.

I removed his boots, then pulled off his jeans and silk boxers.

Then it was like Christmas morning and I had a new toy to play with. I grasped his cock, loving the silky hard feel of it against my palm.

Cupping his balls, I squeezed them lightly as I licked the tip of his cock, and then, because I didn't have his patience, I leaned down and sucked him into my mouth. I swirled my tongue around the rim of his head.

His breathing went ragged and his thighs tensed.

He was breathing harshly, his hands cupping my head as I took him as far down as I could. I really liked the feel of his cock invading my mouth, and though I couldn't admit to porn-star skill, I certainly had enthusiasm.

"Moira." My name was both plea and demand.

I released his cock, gave the tip one last flick of my tongue, and then straddled his hips. I gripped his shaft and guided it inside me. For a moment I sat there, impaled, and enjoyed the feel of his penetration as he stretched, as he filled me.

He cupped my breasts, brushing the hard peaks with his thumbs. I leaned down, and he drew a nipple into his mouth and flicked his tongue rapidly across the peak. He switched to the other breast and gave it the same treatment.

Pleasure sparked, spreading heat through me . . . the fire again. The only sexual fire I'd ever experienced—like this act, and this moment—would burn me up until I didn't exist.

Drake gripped my hips, his gaze on mine as he thrust upward.

I gasped.

We stared at each other, and I knew my eyes probably held the same glazed passion as his. I certainly *felt* dazed. My knees dug into the furs as I rode him.

Then, next thing I knew, Drake grasped my waist and lifted me off. He lightly tossed me to the side. I landed on my stomach. He was breathing hard, and now I heard him growl.

Excitement raced through me. And maybe a little fear, too.

He got behind me, lifting my hips, and slid his cock between my thighs, penetrating me.

I leaned forward on my elbows and let him take me.

For the longest time, our harsh breathing echoed in the chamber. Sweat beaded my spine and dripped off my temples, and still he pumped into me, and he was hitting the sweet spot just right.

I felt the rise of another intense orgasm.

"Drake!"

I fell over again, into the sparkling bliss, and as my orgasm pulsed around his cock, he gave a strangled cry, penetrated me deeply, and came.

I almost expected him to howl.

But he didn't.

I don't know how long it was before he slipped out of me and we both collapsed onto the furs. He lay beside me, rolling to his side, and leaned up on his elbow. He brushed a lock of hair away from my face.

"How are you?"

"Really, really well," I said.

He grinned.

Then we heard a noise.

Blue and green sparkles rose from the four corners of the bed and wound into one long ribbon that flowed toward the wall. As soon as the magic made contact, we heard a pop, and a sliding noise—stone grating against stone.

We both sat up. The wall facing us had opened, revealing total darkness. No torches magically lit up.

Since the opening was quite large, I couldn't imagine it was another hallway, so it was probably another room.

A hissing noise erupted from the endless dark.

"What the hell is that?" I asked.

We both scrambled up, grabbing at our clothes. Drake got completely dressed before I'd even shimmied my pants on. Talk about supernatural speed. Sheesh.

I got my pants buttoned and zipped and my bra snapped. I couldn't find my socks, so I decided *Screw it* and shoved a bare foot into my hiking boot.

The hissing noise got louder and louder.

And then . . . the creature emerged.

Chapter 20

Dove

Patsy and I had returned to the bed-and-breakfast and now sat at the table in the kitchen of perpetual food. Lenette had made mini quiches and finger sandwiches, along with tea, coffee, and some kind of magical lemonade I was fairly sure I wanted to marry. Then Lenette had disappeared, muttering something about husbands and Laundry 101.

I poured my second glass of lemonade. "So what's the deal with Karn? Why is he so grumpy?"

"Karn is damaged," said Patsy.

Sitting at the table to the left of me, she reached out and chose a peanut butter cookie. I liked Patsy for a number of reasons, one of which was that she wasn't a nibbler. She took real bites and enjoyed her food like a regular human being. Well, like a vampire-werewolf, I supposed.

"The vampire who made him didn't do the job right," continued Patsy. "He was an inquisitor . . . you know, those Italian priests who tortured people accused of heresy."

"I know what an inquisitor is," I said.

"Well, that makes one of us," muttered Patsy. "He shouldn't have survived, but he did. The thing is . . . Karn doesn't have the full skill set. He can't glamour at all. Anyway, he caused a huge problem for vampires and humans alike . . . apparently he was really good at his job of torturing poor folks. The vampires got tired of his shit and hunted him down. He was busy burning a village at the time, so they shoved him into the nearest fire. Everyone thought he was ash." She sighed. "But he survived and just went to ground. He popped up a couple months ago. Just as crazy and mean as before, and two hundred times more pissed off."

Yeah, yeah, fascinating stuff. If Karn wasn't such a dickhead, I would probably be interested in his take on the Inquisition. All of these vampires who'd been walking around for thousands of years had seen history unfold. No guesswork needed. But getting the historical 4-1-1 wasn't my priority. I eyed the quiches.

"What do you think's going on in the pyramid with Moira and Drake?" I asked.

"I have no idea," said Patsy. "I've given up trying to figure out the why and the how of the world. I just try to keep my head above water and try not to kill anyone."

Coming from anyone else, that last declaration would be an exaggeration. But from a supernatural being, it was probably truth. "You . . . uh, feel murderous impulses a lot?"

"Yeah," she said. "But then I remember I love my kids, and I go have vodka instead."

I laughed.

Then a huge spray of red sparkles exploded next to me.

I dropped my quiche and stared up at a really pissed-off Karn. Fear shot through me like a cold, sharp spike.

"What the fuck?" Patsy exclaimed.

Neither of us had time to do anything else.

Karn put a hand on each of our shoulders, and in the next instant the world tilted and went black.

"Hey, kid. You okay?"

I woke slowly to the soft voice of Patsy calling to me. Metallic clanging rattled into the headache crawling around my skull. I tried to raise my arms to rub my temples, but I couldn't move them.

My eyes fluttered open.

"Dove. You alive?"

I groaned as I moved my head, trying to find the source of her voice. She was about three feet or so away from me, chained to the wall.

Then I realized that I was pinned to the floor with the same kind of chains.

"What the hell?" I murmured. I had very little range

to move, and when I did, the chains scraped the concrete floor. I shuddered. It was like someone was scraping the inside of my skull with a dull blade.

"They're magicked," said Patsy. "I can't use any of my vampire powers."

I was able to bend my head a little more to look at her better. "Are you okay?" I asked.

"Believe it or not, I've been in worse circumstances," said Patsy. She glanced down at her belly. "But not with a passenger on board."

Despite Patsy's bravado, I could see that she was pale—paler than usual. Worry wormed through me.

"Do you have any idea where we are?" I asked.

"The old Thrifty Sip," said Patsy. "He really knows how to treat a girl . . . sticking us in the basement of a burned-out convenience store."

"How did Karn get through the maxi-pad thing?"

"I don't know," said Patsy. "Obviously he figured out a way."

I didn't want to think about what Karn was planning. He hoped to use me to ensure Moira's cooperation. Patsy was queen of the vampires, probably the most valuable kidnap victim on the planet.

"Okay, you can't use your powers, but can you still leave your body?"

Patsy arched a blond eyebrow. "Can I do what now?"

"I read Theodora's book. She said the vampires of Amahté's line could do soul travel like he did."

Patsy shook her head. "I have no idea. I've never tried it." She stilled. "Someone's coming down the stairs."

Seconds later, Karn arrived, looking as smarmy as usual. He came alone, no minions needed, apparently, and stopped next to me. He crouched down and tapped my neck with his forefinger. "Your friend has something I want," he said. He gave me a cold smile. "And so do you."

Chapter 21

Moira

I stared at the monster scorpion that crawled out of the dark and paused in front of us, its pincers clacking and its feet skittering on the stone floor as it danced, trying to decide which of us to eat first.

"A scorpion? Really?" I asked, lacing up my boot as fast as possible. My heart raced, and adrenaline roared through me. "Dove would just die."

Drake, standing a few feet from me, glanced over his shoulder, shooting me a look of profound disbelief. "*Dove* would die?"

"She loves those goddamned *Mummy* movies, including the *Scorpion King* one. She'd be in heaven right now." I was chattering idiotically, I knew, but I was having a hard time getting my other boot laced because my hands were shaking so badly. "Do you have a sword?"

"Yeah, but I left it in my other jeans," said Drake. His voice was so heavy with sarcasm, it nearly crushed me.

"Why the hell didn't we bring any guns?"

"Ruadan recommended against it."

"Well, he's stupid."

"Agreed," said Drake. "Any other ideas?"

"Stay away from its ass—that's where the poison is."

As if to punctuate my warning, the scorpion propelled itself forward—*skitter, skitter, skitter*—and waved its deadly tail around.

I screamed, left off tying my boot, and leapt off the bed on which I'd been sitting.

The sharpened tip of the tail slammed into the stone.

The bed exploded, and the destruction echoed harshly in the chamber—like a thousand gunshots.

Stone and furs flew everywhere.

A statue of Bastet, mostly intact, rolled toward me, and I picked it up and wielded it like a baseball bat.

Drake's response to facing a monstrous poisonous creature was to take off his ragged shirt.

"What the hell are you doing?" I yelled.

"These are my only clothes," he said. "If I shift while wearing them, they'll be destroyed. And I'll have to walk around naked."

"I don't see the downside."

He barked a laugh as he yanked off his boots.

The scorpion apparently didn't like the idea of a werewolf striptease and scurried toward us, wielding that stinger like a cat-o'-nine-tails. It was going for

Drake, so I ran forward and slammed one of its pincers with my Bastet statue. The beast made a horrible, trains-braking-on-metal-track noise and reared back.

I ran toward the other side of the room, and it followed, still screeching and skittering, and now aiming those claws at me.

"Are you insane?" yelled Drake.

"Clearly," I yelled back. "Hurry up, wolf boy!" I whirled around, which the scorpion didn't expect, and bashed the other pincer.

It screamed in that same horrible metallic way, moving back just a little, and then its stinger sailed toward me. I scurried backward as fast as I could, but I tripped on one of the broken stones and went down hard on my backside. My lungs felt like they'd collapsed and pain shot up my spine. My gaze was riveted on the stinger, on the sharp, ugly death headed straight for me.

A fierce, aggressive howl cut through the room, and the ferocity of the sound impressed even the scorpion, especially since a huge black werewolf landed on its back and began tearing at its head. I knew a few awful facts about scorpions because I'd had to deal with them on dig sites. Several pairs of eyes were located on the head, and that was the only spot on its armored body vulnerable to real damage.

Even though my body ached from its violent fall, I managed to scramble to my feet. I picked up my handy-dandy statue and backed up, trying to figure out how I could help Drake.

The scorpion was thrashing back and forth, trying to use the violent movements to knock Drake off its back. It was also coming at him with its pincers, but not quite reaching him.

Drake was definitely going for the eyes, and being rather successful. I had an iron stomach—archaeology wasn't for sissies—yet witnessing a werewolf viciously take out a scorpion's eyeballs was . . . well, gross . . . times one thousand. *Blech!*

Blinding the damned thing didn't seem to be slowing it down, though. It got more pissed off, and more desperate, and more erratic.

I didn't know what to do. I felt helpless as hell.

The scorpion's belly was plated, just like the rest of it. But as it moved, I could see the ribbons of scales reveal soft pierceable flesh. If I could get under there, time it right, and use every ounce of strength I had, I could potentially puncture something vital and kill this thing before it killed us.

Drake yelped as one of the pincers made contact, forcing him away from the head. He slid down the back, growling and barking.

The scorpion was listing like a drunken sailor, but still had a lot of killing energy. I was sure the blindness and the blood loss was making it less than effective in its efforts, but certainly not less dangerous.

Drake returned to his position and continued the gruesome work of blinding the scorpion. The pincer made another swipe at Drake, and barely missed.

I couldn't wait a second longer.

I ran between the legs, under the massive, swaying body.

It didn't notice.

Sweat poured off me, and fear rolled around in my stomach like icy marbles. I swiped away the hair clinging to my forehead and watched the undulation of the scorpion's belly scales. There was no rhyme or reason to the monster's movements, so it was difficult to gauge the right moment.

Then I heard Drake's yipping cry of pain.

I jumped, lifting the statue up like it was the pointiest sword in the world, and—hit a fucking scale. The impact shot down my arms, agony lancing me.

Argh!

My hands were slick, but I held on to the statue.

I heard a terrible cry, a cry that pierced my heart, and watched as Drake plummeted off the scorpion's back. I watched his magnificent wolf body land with a terrible thud.

He didn't move.

Shit. The idea that Drake was hurt . . . or something so much worse . . . sharpened my focus. The scorpion was adjusting its position, and to my mind, trying to find Drake to finish him off. Or maybe it had remembered it had a second adversary and wanted to get me next.

"The hell," I muttered. I waited for the scales to retract, and when I saw those strips of black armor push apart, I jumped with everything I had left and pushed the statue up as hard as I could.

This time it pierced the flesh, so much so that the three-fourths of the obsidian Bastet was lodged inside the scorpion.

I was shaking, sweating, cursing.

Above me, the scorpion screamed and tottered. For an awful moment, I thought that the monster would fall on Drake and that even though I was skidding toward him, reaching out, I wouldn't get there in time.

But the scorpion danced away, its pincers clacking, its screeches echoing with pain and fury. It hit the wall, hard, and collapsed. Its pincers gave one final wave—a good-bye to the world—and then it stilled completely.

And then . . . because this day hadn't been creepy-strange enough, it burst like a smashed piñata . . . into a very big pile of sand.

Huh.

"Drake!"

I ran to the werewolf, and good God, he was huge. I think I could've saddled and ridden him like a pony. (Only, I guess I'd done that already, right?) I knelt next to him. He was lying on his side, covered in sand. I assumed that whatever blood or gore had gotten onto him had also turned into sand when the scorpion was dispatched.

I wasn't sure how to check for a pulse on a wolf. I put my ear up to his snout, hoping I could hear him breathe.

Something wet and flat smeared my cheek.

"Ugh!" I reared back and looked down.

Drake's eyes were open, and it seemed to me that they were shadowed with pain. Well, who wouldn't be hurt after falling several stories off a monster scorpion?

"Are you all right?"

He heaved himself onto his belly and looked at me, cocking his head. His big red tongue lolled out of his mouth.

"I don't speak werewolf. Or German. How's your French?"

He offered a weak *woof*, then laid his head on his paws and closed his eyes.

"Oh, honey," I murmured. I stroked his silky fur, and I thought about Drake the man. And here was Drake the wolf. It was a crazy concept to believe. But no crazier than anything else I'd seen today.

"Drake? You . . . er, feel like moving? Or changing back into a human?"

He didn't respond. He was breathing, though, steady and strong. What should I do? If I stayed here and tended to him, I risked us both. If I went on without him, and he woke up . . . well, he'd be pissed off. But it would be easy to follow my trail . . . at least until some magical door closed up behind me like all the rest had. Yikes.

"Sorry," I murmured. I patted his head. "A girl's gotta do what a girl's gotta do."

I gathered his clothes and left them next to his resting wolf form. I also stopped to finish tying my boot.

Then I crossed the room and paused before the yawning darkness of the room beyond.

"Hey."

The female voice made me stumble forward and yelp. Heart pounding, I whirled around.

Patsy floated a few feet away, staring at me with arms crossed.

Okay, it wasn't quite Patsy. She was faded, like an old photograph. She was sorta bluish, too, and her bottom half looked like smoke. She was either a ghost or a djinn.

"Oh, my God," I said. "Are you dead?"

"Well, I've been dead. And undead. And alive again. But this is weirder." She stretched out her arms and examined her own ghostly pallor. "I didn't even know I could do this." She wiggled her fingers at me. "Out-of-body experience."

I blinked at her. "So, you're just visiting?"

"Yeah," she said. "I decided, hey, why not pop out of my seven-month-pregnant body and risk my baby, freak myself out, and float on in to a deadly pyramid so I could see you." She huffed in impatience. "Where's Drake?"

I glanced over her shoulder at the unconscious werewolf, and Patsy followed my gaze.

"What happened to him?"

We had the most awesome sex on the planet, and then a giant scorpion tried to eat us. "It's a long story, but it ends with him needing a really big nap."

She returned her gaze to me. "Men."

"Yeah. What can you do?" My stomach was starting to squeeze a little. Patsy showing up, well, her . . . er, soul anyway, probably didn't indicate anything good. She didn't strike me as the cheerleader type. And what mother would intentionally leave her pregnant body behind so she could go spirit-visit a crazy archaeologist and a werewolf?

"You have bad news, don't you?"

Patsy sighed. "I'm sorry. We tried to protect her."

"Protect her? Who . . . *Dove*?" My stomach dropped out and I pressed my palm flat against my belly. "What happened? Is she okay?"

Patsy's expression did not offer hope. For a second I couldn't breathe. I never should have left her in the company of vampires. I should've found a way to protect her myself, to drag her into the pyramid, which for all its trials seemed to be a safer place than a town supposedly protected by an invisible shield and supernatural creatures.

"Karn found a way into Broken Heart. Him, and half a dozen other assholes. They snatched me and Dove and then holed up at the Thrifty Sip. It's an abandoned burned-out convenience store on the edge of town."

I wanted to scream. Fury roared through me, but I sucked in a deep breath because I knew being reactionary wouldn't help the situation. My hands fisted at my sides, and I swallowed my anger. It pulsed like a second heartbeat inside me, but I quelled it. For now.

"Is she alive?"

"She's breathing," she said. "But she doesn't have a lot of time. Karn's bleeding her out."

My vision blurred, and I sucked in a grief-stricken breath. "He's going to kill her."

"Worse," said Patsy. "He's going to Turn her."

It took me a minute to process the information. "Turn her? Into a vampire?"

"No, into a pumpkin. Look, the process isn't always successful," she said. "We estimate only one in ten humans make the transition."

Well, that was just more good news. *Karn couldn't have Dove.* Although I was fairly sure Dove wouldn't mind being undead, she sure as hell wouldn't want Karn to do the Turning. Oh, my God. What was I thinking? Dove would die. She was tough, street tough, but a bad attitude wouldn't help her now. I thought about watching the Turning of Amahté, and I could see why humans might not make it. It was certainly difficult to be made the undead, and damn, it shouldn't be easy. In fact, the kinder option seemed to be death.

But not for Dove.

"How do you know Dove is still breathing? You're not taking his word for it, are you?"

"I know because I'm sitting in the fucking basement with her. Karn got me, too. And I'm trussed up like a Thanksgiving turkey, and the manacles are magicked, so my powers are muted. Otherwise I'd kick his ass, or call up a zombie army to do it for me." She held out her arms and looked at herself. "I guess the magical cuffs can't prevent me from soul traveling."

I was still wrapping my brain around the idea that Patsy could call up a zombie army. I imagined all the mummies in Egypt shuddering to life and marching on Cairo.

"I'm sorry," I said. "But I'm glad you're there. For her." Honestly, Patsy being there was saving Dove's life. Not from Karn's perspective, certainly. But having the queen trapped meant the other vampires would be very, very careful about how they approached Karn. Otherwise, they might've gone in full bore, not particularly concerned about saving one small human's life.

So, Patsy was their priority . . . and Dove was mine.

"There's not a lot I can do," she said. "Watching that bastard tor—" She stopped, and shook her head. "I didn't know I could pop out of my body. Dove was the one who told me to try. She knows all about us . . . Theodora's books, you know. She said Amahté could do it, so I probably could, too."

"She's smart," I said. My voice quaked.

"He wants the ambrosia," Patsy said softly. "It'll fix his vampire problems and make him unkillable."

Shit. "Is that all?" I asked.

"He wants you to murder Shamhat and Amahté. Obviously, we don't want you to take out the Ancients," said Patsy. "My understanding is that waking from a three-thousand-year nap takes a while. But once you get them free, we can help you."

"We who?" I asked.

"Everyone who is not Karn's prisoner," she snapped.

"How long do I have?" I asked. Now, there was a ticking clock that was counting down even as I had this conversation with Patsy. Karn's little nightmare clock where he was killing my best friend.

What a fucking jackass.

"Not long. She's such a little thing."

"Could the ambrosia save her?"

"Yes," said Patsy. "Brigid told us that ambrosia is extremely rare. It's a cure-all, though. And there is that whole immortality thing that goes with it."

"If you can't save Dove, then promise me you'll give the ambrosia to her."

It didn't appear that Patsy knew I was supposed to receive the ambrosia as a thank-you gift for handing over my blood-filled body to the Ancients. And that was fine. If the last earthly thing I managed to do was save that kid, then that was worthwhile.

"I'll be goddamned if Karn gets it," said Patsy. "You're doing us a huge solid, Moira. Once you awaken the Ancients and get the ambrosia to us, I promise you I'll use it to save her."

I believed her. I didn't have a choice, really, because if I was dead, I couldn't make sure she fulfilled the bargain. But all the same, I did think she would try to save Dove.

Patsy looked around the room, her gaze once again falling on Drake. "Are you almost to their chamber?"

"I have no idea."

"Well, that su—" Patsy's eyes went wide, and then her form started wavering erratically. She sent me a look of regret, and said, "Aw, shit."

Then she was gone.

For a few seconds I stared at the empty space.

I guess Patsy had no real control over the whole soul journey aspect of her powers. However, I was relieved that the queen was back with Dove. I couldn't imagine what she was going through, and I was making a promise to myself right now that Karn would pay for hurting her.

I took a breath, tried to gather my thoughts into some kind of workable plan. Okay, all I had to do was find Shamhat and Amahté, steal the ambrosia, kill them, and try to get to Dove before I died from all the blood loss.

Yeah, right. I gnawed my lower lip. That scenario wasn't under serious consideration. Doing what Karn wanted only meant everyone would die faster. He was too smart to think he could do anything other than kill us all. We were obstacles standing in the way of his goal. And if he let us live, we'd figure out a way to stop him. I mean, the people of Broken Heart could certainly take the phrase "Never say die" really, really far.

I heard a noise, and looked over my shoulder.

Drake the man had returned. My gaze feasted on his naked form. He was still prone, groaning as he rolled over and put a hand against his forehead.

"Are you okay?" I called out.

He sat up slowly and offered me a tired smile. "I will live, *Liebling*."

"Glad to hear it." I moved toward him, relieved that he was conscious, selfishly happy that I would be able to spend a few moments more with him. Granted, we'd consistently been in peril, but it had been a helluva first date.

"Chosen, present thyself to thy fate."

The booming voice echoed through the chamber, rolling out from the darkened place behind me.

I heard Drake's strangled cry, but I couldn't turn to see what had placed that look of shock on his handsome face. I was surrounded by a paralyzing Arctic chill, like a giant icy hand had closed around me. And it was pulling me inside.

"Moira!"

I saw Drake leap to his feet and run toward me.

But it was too late.

I was dragged into the darkness.

Chapter 22

Even preternaturally fast Drake couldn't get to me quickly enough. I saw raw frustration and worry bleed into his expression, right before the doorway disappeared.

My heart pounded so hard I could hear the beat of it inside my eardrums. My breathing had gone shallow, and fear added to the intense chill caused by my invisible captor.

Being enveloped by darkness so quiet and thick was like I imagined it would feel being tucked into a sarcophagus. I wasn't claustrophobic, but the feeling of having nothing around me was disconcerting.

Know your beginning . . .

The voice echoed in my head. I knew the feeling by now, the floating sensation that happened right before a vision. This time I found myself suddenly hovering at ceiling level in a room I recognized right away.

The classroom was typical. A big, solid desk sat in front of a white board and a chalkboard. A series of desks for the students took up the rest of the room, except in the back, where big black supply cabinets stood like sentinels.

Oh, God. I didn't want to be here.

But wishing wouldn't make me disappear.

So I had to watch . . .

The little girl wore a blue checkered dress and white shoes. Her red hair was pulled into two ponytails. The little fasteners had white daisies on them. She sat in the first desk in the first row, concentrating on the coloring book page. The unicorn was pink, all except for its horn. That was currently being made into a rainbow. Because unicorns had rainbow horns. Everyone knew that.

The mother sat at the big desk marking her way through a stack of papers. "Almost done, honey," she said. "You okay?"

"Yes, Mommy. I'm okay dokay!"

Regina smiled.

My heart clenched. I hadn't remembered her smile. Just the feeling of her love. My grandparents had loved me tremendously, had given me everything. But they couldn't give me that. A mother's love was unique, precious.

"Want to see my picture, Mommy?"

"Yes, darling."

I took the page and skipped to the desk, crawling onto my mother's lap. I put the drawing on the desk.

"That's beautiful, Moira!" She gave me a smacking kiss on my cheek, and I giggled.

"Do me a favor, babe? I need a new red pen to grade my papers. You remember where they are?"

"In the back room, first cabinet on the left. Third shelf." I preened, obviously proud that I'd gotten my mother a red pen before.

"Perfect." She twirled the chair around and lifted me off her lap. "Scoot now. As soon as I get these papers graded, we can go home."

"And have ice cream?" I asked.

She smiled. "After dinner . . . absolutely."

"Yay!"

I skipped to the back room and went to the cabinet. The boxes holding red pens were lined up neatly, and I was careful about picking one off the shelf. Opening the top took a little longer, but finally I was able to extract one red pen.

I replaced the box. Then I walked the short distance to the door that led to the main classroom. It was halfway open, and I went to slip through it, but then I heard a deep male voice.

I hesitated. My heart hitched in my chest, and I gripped the red pen as I poked my head through the door.

"Your mother is dead. And with her, all that lovely magical protection you've enjoyed."

My mother rose from the desk and faced the man standing in the doorway. "I didn't know who I was," she said. "They didn't tell me. But you did, Bran. You knew."

"Of course I knew. You were the pot of gold at the end of

the rainbow, Regina. The proof I needed. And our little tryst . . . well, I had hoped for better results."

"You're a bastard."

"And you're a lying bitch. I've seen the girl. I bet you wish I'd stayed buried under that pile of rocks." He laughed, but it was not a joyous sound. "That little tumble down the mountain didn't kill me. By the time I recovered, your mother had enacted the spells. I couldn't get near you. Or her. My daughter."

"She's not yours."

"Oh, yes, she is."

Something about the man seemed strange. His eyes were too bright, and there was a sweaty sheen to his skin. He was tall, but on the lean side. He had short blond hair and was dressed in an oxford-cloth shirt, black pants, and black shoes. He looked feverish and pale.

My mother kept her voice calm and edged away from the desk. I got the feeling she was trying very hard not to look in my direction. She didn't want the man to notice me. I shrank back, but kept an eye on what was going on. I had a very bad feeling in my tummy.

"I want what's mine." He stepped into the room. "So long as I have her, I don't need you." The man raised the knife. The blade was made of a white stone. The hilt was made of beaten copper. I recognized it instantly. My grandfather claimed to have excavated it from an Indus Valley site. He'd displayed the knife in a locked glass case in his study. To this day, it was in the same location. After he died, I hadn't touched my grandfather's study, leaving it intact because I so enjoyed the

memories invoked when I tucked myself into his big leather chair and stared at his books and archaeological treasures. Now, I was astounded that he'd openly displayed his own daughter's murder weapon.

I knew how this would end, I knew and I didn't want to see. I wasn't only a victim of tragedy, but also a witness to it. I had spent the entire rest of my life trying to forget, to not deal with it, to . . . oh, God. My father. My father took everything from me.

"No." Her voice broke. "Please."

Sorrow pressed in on me. I was formless, merely a soul visiting my so-called beginning. I was so fearful, so immersed in that awful feeling of helplessness and fury and grief that I couldn't bear it.

With a swift grace, the man crossed the distance between them and stabbed my mother.

"Nooooo!" I yelled, and then I bounded out of the doorway. My mother held on to her side.

"Run, babe," she cried. "Run!"

The man turned his feverish gaze on me. "Don't worry. Ssshh. I'm your daddy. You're mine. My little unicorn."

"You are not my daddy!" I screamed.

He moved toward me, the knife quivering. My mother, wounded and bleeding, somehow found the strength to throw herself on her attacker. They wrestled for the knife. A father's insanity could not trump a mother's fierce love. She managed to wrest the knife from him, and with a furious cry, she dragged the blade across his throat.

He grabbed at the wound and sank to his knees, falling

onto his side as he gurgled, his life ebbing away as his blood spilled across the floor.

My mother stumbled toward me. "Go, Moira. To your grandfather. Remember where his office is?"

I nodded. But I didn't want to leave her.

She whispered, "I love you." She swayed, the knife tumbling out of her hand as she fell to her knees. "Love is worth sacrifice," she said. "Remember that, Moira. Remember. And be worthy, my darling."

She slid to the floor, lying down as though she was merely trying to take a nap.

I watched, both apart and within, as the little girl stood for a moment, tears falling as she saw her mother die.

I came to in my body, swaying, trembling, blinded. It took me a moment to realize that I had solid ground under my feet and for my eyesight to adjust. I couldn't quite get my breath back, either. I was being suffocated by grief on so many levels. I felt betrayed. They'd kept the truth from me. The memory I had about Ruadan and my grandfather's conversation made more sense. My grandmother passed away just a couple of months before my mother had been killed. I didn't remember much about my grandmother. My mother had been my world—a world shattered because some goddamned man claiming to be my father shoved a knife into her. Why would Grandfather keep that blade?

I heard the *whoosh* mere seconds before the blue-flamed torches lighted. The chamber was much smaller

than the previous room. I stood between two beauti-
fully decorated sarcophagi. It was as though this king
and queen had been put to rest just a minute ago, so
spectacular was the craftsmanship and painted imagery.

Even though I was no doubt moments away from
being the first meal of two Ancient vampires, I couldn't
help but marvel at the burial chamber. The torches reflected obsidian walls that held no decorations. Shamhat and Amahté had not included their death journeys
because, technically, they didn't go on any.

I was stunned by the idea that I would soon witness
an actual ancient Egyptian arise from his coffin. I almost wished Dove was here. She was the only one who
could enjoy this situation in the same way I did. Well,
except she'd probably hyperventilate before she experienced any giddiness because she really did hate en-
closed spaces.

Blue and green magic appeared over the sarcophagi,
looping over the lids in sparkling ribbons. The lids
trembled and slowly, creepily, slid forward until the
heavy painted stones thudded to the stone floor. The
magic dove inside, and I heard rustling noises.

I couldn't move. Whatever had dragged me into this
place hadn't exactly let go. It was as if I'd been ce-
mented to the floor. All I could do was watch . . . and
wait.

Most sarcophagi had interior coffins, making the discovery of royal mummies like opening up a morgue

version of nesting dolls. But these didn't seem to have that feature. I knew that because two wizened forms sat up, and both turned to look at me at the same time.

I screamed.

The vampires didn't seem to mind.

It wasn't like the *Mummy* movies at all. They weren't decrepit, eyeless, dirty-bandage-wrapped corpses. They looked human-ish, just really starved and horribly gaunt. Both had caramel skin, and both of their gazes were pinpoints of red. They were dressed in fine linens that looked as though they had just donned them. Amahté's hair was shorn, but Shamhat's was brown and gold and fell in waves to her waist.

If I hadn't been glued in place, I might have collapsed. Instead, my legs trembled violently. Oh, I wanted to run. It was a natural compunction because the undead were currently creeping out of their coffins.

They didn't say anything, but their gazes were riveted on me. The only noises were my heavy breathing, and the whispering sounds of the corpses climbing out of the sarcophagi. I wasn't exactly sure what to do . . . or what to expect.

Shamhat got to me first. Her bony fingers gripped my shoulder, her fetid breath rolling across my face. Fear tumbled through me. I couldn't move. Couldn't run. Screaming wasn't doing much for me, so I stopped wasting my breath. My breathing was so shallow that I was barely getting air into my lungs. And I was fairly sure my heart would explode any second. Sweat rolled down my spine, my neck, my temples.

I had chosen this moment.

Destiny.

Fate.

Choice.

All intertwined . . . and it was okay, I realized. It was . . . what I wanted. What I needed to do.

And I couldn't exactly change my mind now.

Shamhat waited for him, for her husband.

Even though fear fogged my mind, clouded my lungs, liquefied my knees, a small part of my brain wondered about a love for all time. Shamhat and Amahté were truly a love for the ages. He had gone to the Underworld to save her soul. And chosen to lie with her, buried and undiscovered for three millennia, because his life was not worthwhile without her in it.

And I wanted to believe that kind of love was real.

What was I thinking? Two vampires were getting ready to reconstitute their forms by feasting on mine. I was promised ambrosia, but I realized now that it was a pipe dream.

My death had arrived.

The truth was . . . in this moment . . . this moment when Amahté grasped my waist . . . and showed his fangs . . . this moment when two mates rejoined . . . this awful, beautiful moment when my flesh was pierced . . . my blood eagerly imbibed . . . I wished for so much more. Drake filled my thoughts. We'd had little time to know each other. But I suspected he would've been the one for me.

Love.

Sacrifice.

Always.

Chapter 23

"Are those stories of Dean and Sam Winchester truly a historical account of humans who track and kill paranormal creatures? Is that the purpose of the television? To show what other people are doing?" The fluid female voice held fascination and concern. "I do not blame them for killing the wendigo, but I do not agree with killing werewolves. I've always liked werewolves."

Me, too. My mind felt mushy, like someone had put my brain in a blender and hit PUREE. I heard the word, tried to process the question, and somewhere there was an answer. My response, however, came out as "Ooooooouch!"

"I do not think that is an appropriate response. Do you suppose I am speaking this new language incorrectly?"

"No, dear. I think the poor girl is trying to wake up."
I felt a poke on my shoulder. "Are you alive?"

My eyes fluttered open, and I stared up at two really gorgeous people. They looked rather worried.

"We learned your language through imprinting with your memories," said the beautiful woman. "And we learned about the world as it exists now. I would like a car. I think it would be far more fun than a chariot."

"You drove chariots very well."

"Thank you." She leaned over me, her curtain of silky hair falling across my face, and kissed the man.

Shamhat. Amahté.

Holy shit. I was alive.

"Did I drink the ambrosia?" I asked. Panic consumed me. Dove needed it. And I was alive, and I really shouldn't be.

"Why on earth would you need ambrosia?" asked Shamhat. "You're a . . ." She frowned, looked at Amahté, offered a word I didn't recognize.

He looked at me, smiling. "Unicorn."

I laughed. It came out more like a rusted croak, but I couldn't stop. "Unicorns aren't real." But they were, weren't they? What a silly statement to make. I sat up, and I honestly didn't feel too bad. "Where's Drake?"

"What's a Drake?" asked Shamhat. "Is it a car?"

"No, he's a werewolf. He was in the other room."

"Oh," said Amahté. "That explains all the howling and banging." He lifted a hand, and the wall disappeared.

A very pissed-off Drake, who apparently had forgotten to get dressed, marched into the space looking as though he might kill something with his bare hands. "Moira!"

"You're naked," I pointed out.

"See? That's why I like werewolves so much." Shamhat sent a sly glance to Amahté, but he only gave her an affectionate look and then tweaked her nose. She giggled.

I hadn't expected an Ancient vampire to giggle.

"I think her mate would like to see her," said Amahté. They moved aside, and Drake, still very much naked, dropped to his knees and scooped me into his arms.

"Are you all right?" he growled. (No, really. He did.)

"I'm alive." I know I was echoing this sentiment a lot, but . . . hey, *alive*, all right?

He crushed me into his embrace and kissed the everliving hell out of me. Oh, my God. Being alive was so, so awesome.

"Never sacrifice yourself again," he demanded. "Do you understand me?"

Then he kissed me again.

"I didn't know werewolves could mate with unicorns," said Shamhat. "The world truly is a different place."

Drake turned an incredulous gaze to the woman, who offered him a radiant smile, and then he frowned down at me. "Unicorns are extinct."

"Extinct? As in, they really lived?" I asked. But I knew, didn't I? It was why my mother had died. To protect me. And protecting me was protecting our secret, too. My heritage.

"Only a unicorn could open the pyramid and survive it," said Shamhat. "So, no, unicorns are not extinct."

Drake stared at me.

"Why are unicorns extinct-ish?" I asked.

"Unicorn blood and horns were coveted by humans and paranormals alike. The horns were used to make weapons and other objects because of their mystical properties. And a unicorn's blood can heal anyone of anything." A gruesome kind of worry entered his gaze. Uh-oh. That wasn't good.

"And unicorn horn can kill anything," said Shamhat. "Even an immortal. And that's also the only way to kill a unicorn."

My mind flashed to the memory that was embedded in my soul like a poisoned thorn. The white blade with the beaten copper hilt. Unicorn horn. The only way to kill my mother . . . and the only way to kill me?

"Moira?"

"Still alive," I said. "And not crazy. Well, not crazier. I think." I glanced down and got a gander at his penis. "I really think you should get dressed." Shamhat was ogling his backside, and while Amahté thought that was all cute and shit, I did not.

"Yes," he agreed. "We should get back to Broken Heart."

I realized then that he hadn't been around for Pat-sy's visitation. I explained the situation as quickly as I could, and Drake was up and out of the chamber even before the last word echoed off the walls. He returned less than a minute later fully dressed. Well, he hadn't donned the shirt. Wow, that man had some abs. He eyed the Ancients. "How do we get out of here?"

"Wait," I said. "Where's the ambrosia?"

Shamhat and Amahté looked at each other. After a moment, Amahté nodded. "It is in another location," he offered. "We'll tell you how to get it. It will be your reward, Moira."

I stared at them. "Wait a sec. No ambrosia?"

The vampiric couple actually looked abashed.

"Ruadan and I created this place from magic—with the help of one of your unicorn ancestors," said Amahté. He took his wife's hand and drew her into his embrace. "We had not intended to stay asleep for so long."

"You've been lost to us," said Drake. "The vampires have been searching for you for a while."

Amahté nodded. "The only way to awaken us was through the blood of one such as Moira. It was neces-sary to create those protections with that magic so that no one else could enter."

"So only unicorn blood would've worked," I said. "That's why my grandfather was hunting for your temple. Because he was the one who was supposed to open it."

"Unicorns are female," said Shamhat. "Your blood must be from your grandmother's side."

I wasn't buying that I was a unicorn. Come on! I'd accepted so much about this world already, but I couldn't wrap my brain around the idea that I was like that innocent, tragic figure from *The Last Unicorn*. No, I wasn't that girl who tried to find her destiny, only to find love . . . and to know eternal regret.

"So what was the deal with the sex magic, then?" I asked.

"That's why only two could enter the pyramid," said Amahté. "Sex magic is very, very strong. And it was that essence, along with your blood, that we needed to revive."

"And what was the deal with the scorpion?" I asked.

"The scorpion was meant to protect us if something went wrong in the final chamber." Amahté offered an apologetic smile. "Oops."

"Oops?" I said. "Really?"

"We need to go," said Drake. "We do not know if Broken Heart has fallen to Karn."

"What's a Karn?" asked Shamhat.

"He's an asshole," I said. "A big one."

"Sounds unpleasant," she said, wrinkling her pert nose.

That was the understatement of the century. Drake helped me to my feet, and we looked at the Ancients.

"Do we walk?" asked Drake.

"Let us use alternative transportation," said Amahté.

He swept me into his arms, and Shamhat did the same to Drake.

"I'd rather walk," I said. "No. Really. Don't—"

Once again I found myself imploding—like a window shattered by a brick.

Fucking vampires.

We arrived outside the pyramid, and I was so dizzy I had to hold on to Amahté for a full minute until the world stopped spinning.

"I hate that," I said as I stumbled out of Amahté's arms. "Thanks."

"You are welcome. I think."

"Traveling that way is wonderful fun," enthused Shamhat. "You can go anywhere in the blink of an eye!"

Drake studied me, frowning. "Are you all right? You look a little green."

"Well, I'm still breathing, so I can't complain."

He nodded. He was all business, his expression serious and his body tense. Warrior vibes rolled off him.

Behind him, the pyramid gleamed white against the night sky. And then it slowly faded, like a memory, like a dream. It was as if it had never existed, and part of me regretted its disappearance.

"Can we get Dove now?" I asked.

"Drake!"

Across the field, several people hurried toward us. Gabriel and Ren I recognized right away, and then I realized I recognized some of others as well. There were Jessica and Patrick from my desert memories. There was also a blond man who carried himself like military. And then there was Larsa. She looked exactly the same as she had in my vision.

"Mother!" Larsa broke free of the group.

"Larsa!" Shamhat enveloped her daughter in her embrace, and they shared a sweet moment of reconnection.

"It's so nice to see you," said Larsa, pulling away, seemingly caught between embarrassment about this show of affection and happiness that she was no longer orphaned. I had a moment of envy. What would it be like if my mother suddenly showed up after so long? Regret was a terrible ache in my chest.

"It is good that you lived," said Shamhat. Then she pulled her daughter in for another hug and made a sobbing sound, even though no tears fell. One of Theodora Monroe's factoids came to mind—vampires couldn't cry.

Drake had joined the others, and they were having an animated discussion. While Shamhat and Larsa continued their reunion, Amahté and I walked to the group.

Everyone quieted all at once, and their gazes slid away from me.

"What?" I asked. My heart started to pound, and foreboding dropped like a cold, wet stone into my stomach.

"We managed to rout them," said Gabriel. "We killed all but three."

"Karn got away again, didn't he?" I asked.

"Him and two others," confirmed the blond man. He offered me a grim smile. "I'm Braddock Hayes. I head up security for Broken Heart."

I nodded toward him, and waited for the bomb to drop.

"They have my wife," said Gabriel. "And Dove."

"Did Patsy visit you, too?" I asked.

"Yes," said Gabriel. "I'm sorry. Your friend is . . ." The look of empathy on his face made my stomach roil.

"She's really bad off," offered Jessica. "But still breathing." She sent Gabriel a testy look. "Don't be a Negative Nelly, Gabe."

"Don't call me Gabe," he muttered.

"What's the negotiating point?" I asked.

"The ambrosia," said Gabriel. "Do you have it?"

I had a feeling that if I had the ambrosia in my possession, he would've taken it and popped off to wherever to get his wife. I understood his anxiety. His pregnant mate was chained up and at the mercy of a vampire who had no soul and no conscience. But Patsy was a paranormal being. She was strong. She would survive.

Dove would not.

"The ambrosia is elsewhere," said Amahté. "We have released our claim on it and gifted it to Moira. Now she's the only one who can retrieve it."

"Your claim?" I asked.

"Ambrosia can only be gifted by the gods—but the

people who receive the precious substance can also give it another," said Amahté. He looked apologetic. "The ambrosia was a backup for our revival. In case the unicorn blood was not enough."

Well, apparently the unicorn blood was plenty. I waved my hand, dismissing all guilt associated with the current situation. "So . . . retrieve?" I asked. I was terrified for Dove. She was dying. And these people . . . these non-people didn't care . . . And now I had to go on another scavenger hunt for the ambrosia? Hadn't I earned it already? "Can't you just use your almighty vampire powers to get it?"

"No," said Amahté. "You must be the one to get it, Moira. Claiming it yourself is the only way for you to use its powers."

"Where is it?" I asked. Anger coiled around me like pythons, squeezing the patience right out of me.

Drake reached over and clapped my shoulder. I don't know if he meant to calm or to comfort, but I wasn't in the mood to be coddled, damn it. I shrugged off his hand. "Amahté?"

"Are you sure you want to know?" he asked softly. "Your hatred of Karn may well impede your journey. You must be stronger than your anger and your fear, or you will fail."

"Stop bullshitting," I snapped. "Where. Is. It?"

"Ambrosia can only be found in one place." Amahté searched my face, and then he sighed. "The Underworld."

Chapter 24

"You mean hell?" I asked. I'd been to a lot of dangerous places, which is why I wasn't scared to fight or to use a gun. I'd excavated sites where I'd had to pay drug lords for protection and make deals with rebels to dig in their part of the jungle. It was part and parcel of what I loved to do, and I'd gotten used to it. But the Underworld? How was I supposed to prepare for that?

"Not hell," offered Amahté. "That's a lower realm. Planes of existence are in layers. The Underworld is . . . er, on top of hell, if you wanted to think of it like that. It's more a gateway location to the other realms."

"It's not the World-Between-Worlds, is it?" asked Jessica.

Amahté shook his head. "That is a place that cannot

be accessed easily. It exists everywhere . . . and no-
where."

"Yeah. Okay." Jessica shrugged, and then offered me
a tight smile. "The Underworld is probably the same as
going to Florida. It'll be hot and muggy and filled with
old people."

I had to crack a smile at that. You know, I think me
and Jessica could be friends. If I survived the Underworld, procured the food of the gods, and managed to
save Dove.

"Where am I supposed to go in the Underworld?" I
asked. "How long will it take? And what do I have to
do to get the ambrosia?"

"When I open the gateway, you'll find the path,
which will lead you to the ambrosia." He pressed a
thumb against my forehead, and I felt a surge of tingling heat. "This gives you a pass, if you will, into the
Underworld. Don't leave the path! It's your safety.
Once you claim the ambrosia, follow the path back to
the entrance. I will know when you've returned, and
I'll open the doorway again."

"That sounds too easy," I said. "Will I run into Anubis?" I asked. The idea was both thrilling and terrify-
ing.

"Pray you do not," said Amahté. "He will not be
pleased that a living human has entered his domain."
He frowned. "Perhaps he has forgiven me for stealing
back Shamhat's soul."

"You think Anubis might be holding a three-thousand-year-old grudge against you?" I asked. "That's just super."

"I will go with you," said Drake. His tone brooked no argument, which was unnecessary. I wasn't going to argue. I may have been stubborn, but I wasn't a fool. I had a feeling I would need all the help I could get on this little adventure.

"And I as well," said Larsa. She and Shamhat had joined us, and Larsa sent me a grateful look. "You risked all for my mother and her mate. I can do no less for you."

My anger receded. I had to believe that Drake wouldn't take the ambrosia from me, and Larsa had the same kind of surliness I'd found in people with strong moral character. Or maybe she was just a righteous bitch. Either way, she was the lesser risk as backup, considering that everyone else's motives were related to saving the queen.

Not that I begrudged Patsy her safety, but Dove wasn't a vampire. She had one fragile life that was bleeding away while we kibitzed about ambrosia. God-damn it, if I didn't save that irritating little brat, I would never forgive myself.

"Fine," I said. "Just the two of you." I eyed the group of supernaturals, and no one complained about not being included. I was quite sure they weren't afraid of me or my ire. More like no one else wanted to travel into the Underworld. And I didn't blame them. Then again, if paranormal creatures were reluctant to venture there, I was probably screwed. "I need Ax, too."

"You will not need an ax to get into the Underworld," offered Amahté. "I told you, I can open the door for you."

"Trust me," I said. "This Ax will come in damn handy." And I knew I could trust Ax. He always had my back. All I had to do was explain that monsters were real, the Underworld was an actual place, and we needed ambrosia to save Dove.

"All right," I said. "Can we do the instant transpo? I hate it, but time's wasting."

"If you will think about the location of this Ax," said Larsa. "I can take you to him."

"I'll go as well," said Shamhat. "That way we can bring them both back at the same time."

"Okay," said Larsa. She looked at Drake. "Get ready. We'll return soon."

He nodded at her, and slanted a gaze at me that I didn't understand, but I sensed that I had somehow wounded him. I was feeling agitated and worried, and I couldn't be concerned about his feelings. I mean so far all I had with him was a one-night stand with a werewolf. It wasn't like we were married, right?

"I'll be ready." Drake turned, and walked away. No good-byes or good lucks, and I had to admit that stung. But really, what were we to each other? Still, my heart ached because I knew, soul-deep, that Drake meant something to me. I didn't know what, not yet, but I'd always gone my own way. And being that stubborn was its own kind of hell.

Speaking of hell . . . I eyed Larsa. "Let's get this over with."

Shamhat kissed Amahté, and I saw the worry shadowing his gaze. But he said nothing, and I realized he trusted in the strength and abilities of his wife. It showed me, yet again, the value of having a partner who believed me to be his equal, who had faith that I was smart enough and strong enough to handle anything.

To my surprise, Larsa and Shamhat put their arms around me, and I realized they both needed Ax's location, which was in my brain.

"Wait," I said. "Er . . . what day is it?"

"After midnight on a Saturday," said Larsa. "We are risking much—it's only a few hours until dawn."

"Okay," I said. I thought about Ax, and where he'd be on a Saturday night. That was easy enough to figure out. I squeezed my eyes shut, and felt that awful tingling sensation that occurred right before my atoms got scrambled.

Shit. I really hated this part.

"At least I don't want to throw up this time," I said, swaying in the parking lot of Velvet and Lace: A Gentlemen's Club. Larsa and Shamhat had let go of me and were currently staring up at the neon-framed sign of gorgeous women with huge, barely covered breasts blowing out kisses to the people zooming down the nearby freeway.

"There is an important ax here?" asked Shamhat suspiciously. "What is this place?"

"It's called a strip club," said Larsa. "It's where women dance around naked and men give them money."

"These women are like Godswives . . . and the men offer worship and tributes?"

"Close enough," I said. "Let's go."

Velvet and Lace was an extremely popular club. On the weekends the lines were crazy long, and tonight, even after midnight, a bevy of horny men snaked around the building. As we made our way toward the front, I heard the grumbling from the line monkeys, and rolled my eyes.

"Hey, Moira," said Neal. He was sitting on a barstool, studying the crowd, looking for trouble to nip in the bud. He was a bruiser, as big and solid as an oak tree, with the kind of flat, scarred face that held reminders of more violent days. He opened the velvet rope and motioned to the three of us to come through. We sailed past the college boys who were at the front.

"What the fuck, man?" groused one of them. "We've been waiting two hours to see premium pussy."

I could tell he was drunk, and so were his companions. I stared at him, and he sneered. "You better be the talent, honey."

"Leave." Neal stood, rising to his full six-foot, seven-inch height. "Now."

The idiot looked up at Neal and gave him the finger. Neal reared back and cold-cocked him. The little shit slithered to the ground like a limp noodle, and his friends stared down at him openmouthed.

"I don't repeat myself," said Neal.

The dudes gathered up their unconscious friend and left as fast as their Nikes could carry them.

"You could've broken his jaw," said Larsa, sounding impressed. "But you tapped him just right. Nice."

"Thank you." Neal assessed her for a moment, obviously liked what he saw, and offered a quicksilver smile. He turned his gaze to me and quirked an eyebrow. "Anyone who breaks the rules doesn't get inside. One of the rules is that no one insults you. Ever."

I grinned. "Thanks, Neal. Ax at the bar?"

"Where else?"

The booming beat of the music greeted us even before we opened the door. Like most strip clubs, it was dark. Squiggles of neon on the wall offered some light, as did the muted stage lighting on the three girls performing on three different catwalks. Unlike most strip clubs, it didn't smell like desperation and cigarettes, and there wasn't an unidentifiable haze hanging in the air. Ax owned the club, and he ran a clean establishment. The girls had health insurance as well as paid vacation, a 401(k) plan, and child care. The girls had to be free of drugs, could not prostitute themselves, and did not have to put up with one ounce of asshole-ish-ness from the clientele. They also had to have an actual life plan that did not include working at Velvet and Lace past five years. I had yet to meet to a girl that made it to the five-year mark. Nearly all of them used the opportunities provided by Ax to create better lives.

The place was jam-packed. The booming beat of the music was like an excited heartbeat. We weaved through men-laden tables and scantily clad strippers selling fantasies and high-priced drinks until we reached the bar. It was elbow to elbow. I went to the end, flipped up the hinged countertop, and rounded the corner. Ax was one of three bartenders mixing up drinks and handing out cold beers. He looked up, studied me, then the two women behind me, and gestured for me to follow him.

We left the bar area and went to the back, through the kitchen area, where cooks were making up the batches of food preferred by the inebriated—everything fried. Finally we reached another door, and I knew this one led to his office. He opened the door, smiling, and made a sweeping gesture for us to go ahead of him.

We entered, and Ax followed, shutting the door behind him. The space was small, crammed with a desk, bookshelves, and file cabinets, so it took a few seconds to find an area to turn around in and face Ax.

By the time the three of us managed to turn around, Ax was in front of the door, the pump-action shotgun in his hands aimed at us. His expression was pleasant, but his gaze was as hard and cold as polished obsidian.

I nearly wet myself. I'd seen Ax in action, but had never been on the receiving end. He was a scary son of a bitch.

"You're sure keeping strange company these days, Moira," he said. He racked the shotgun. "You wanna explain what you're doing with a couple of vamps?"

Chapter 25

"Put down your weapon," ordered Shamhat. She let her fangs show, and her eyes went red. "Or I will rend your flesh from your bones."

"Mother," said Larsa, sounding pained.

"What? Rending flesh from bones was a very effective threat three-thousand years ago." She frowned. "Although really not that easy to do." Her eyes went back to their original color and her fangs receded. She crossed her arms and glared at Ax. "Hmph. He doesn't scare me."

I could tell that Larsa stopped short of rolling her eyes.

My gaze met Ax's. "You know about vampires?"

"I know all about parakind." The shotgun never wavered. "I used to hunt them."

"Do you know Sam and Dean Winchester?" asked Shamhat. "They are hunters, too."

Incredulity slid across Ax's expression. "Is she serious?"

"She's been asleep for a while, and has missed a lot," I said. "She hasn't quite grasped the concept of television shows."

"Do you still hunt us?" asked Larsa.

"Not since I escaped ETAC," he said.

"What's an ETAC?" asked Shamhat. "Is it a car?"

"It's a black ops government-funded organization that went off the rails," said Ax.

Larsa flashed a grim smile. "You are one of their experiments."

"Yeah," he said, "so don't think you can fuck with me."

"Experiments?" I asked.

"ETAC liked to mess around with paranormal and human DNA. Sometimes they were successful . . . and most times they weren't."

"You are still just a human," said Larsa. "Easily killed."

"Not as easy as you think, sister."

Okay, so Larsa and Ax were getting into a pissing contest, and I didn't have time to mess around with who had the bigger set of balls. However, for the record, I suspected Larsa had the winning clangers. (Sorry, Ax.)

"Dove's dying."

"*What?*" He gaze swung toward me, and the gun

trembled ever so slightly. His mouth pulled into a tight line. "One of these vamps hurt her?"

"No. Another one named Karn. He kidnapped me and Dove, and then we were rescued—" I eyed the shotgun. "It's a long story. I'll give you the short version, Ax, but I gotta ask you to trust me here."

He studied our faces one more time, and then nodded. He lowered the shotgun, but didn't put it down. "Tell me."

We arrived in the same field we'd left from because that was the only other space Shamhat knew. How she and Amahté had managed to get us outside the pyramid without being able to visualize the location boggled my mind. We could've easily ended up inside a tree or, hell, on another planet.

Drake, Gabriel, and Braddock waited for us. Drake was dressed in black combat fatigues and loaded up with weapons. He tossed some gear at Larsa, who caught it and put on the weapons belt, then sheathed daggers into slots on the side of her boots.

"Braddock," said Ax. He shook his former ETAC's hand. "You put the word out about Broken Heart as a haven for former ETACers."

"Yeah. Didn't think you'd ever come through the doors, though," said Braddock.

"I'd do anything for Moira and Dove. They're kin."

Braddock nodded, and the two moved away for a private convo. I was stunned by Ax's assertion that

Dove and I were his family. Now that I thought about it, we had been a family—an odd one, to be sure, but in this crowd, who'd notice?

"Moira." Drake handed me a black duffel bag. "Clothing and weapons." He pointed over my shoulder to a copse of trees. "More privacy there, if you need it."

Honestly, I had no issues getting naked and dressed right here. I'd done it a million times on job sites. Like I said, archaeology wasn't for sissies, or for prudes. All the same, though, I felt unaccountably vulnerable around Drake. I was trying really hard not to think about him, about these feelings that kept popping up when I thought about him. He was different. I mean, yeah, there was the whole werewolf thing, but different as a man, too. Huh. Maybe that was the werewolf thing in play.

And see, here's the part where my brain got all mushy, and my heart welled with this . . . emotion, and I wondered . . . no, I wanted. I wanted him in the same way I wanted to see my mother one more time. It was that ache . . . that yearning you felt when you wanted, so badly, the things you could never really have. I would never see my mother again.

Drake would never be mine.

How could he?

It was scary and confusing and fucking weird.

"Thanks." I took the bag and headed into the trees. It wasn't my modesty I was protecting, but my pride.

The trees offered plenty of protection from prying eyes. I opened up the duffel and removed the same kind of black combat clothes Drake wore. I yanked off my shirt and went to unzip my pants when I heard the snap of a twig.

I whirled around, taking a fighting stance, and saw Ruadan leaning against one of the trees. He grinned at me. "Sorry, darlin'. Didn't mean to scare you."

"Waiting for the pants to come off before you announced your presence," I accused.

"I do miss the days of the frolicking nymphs. And you do so remind me of them, Moira."

"Did they kick you in the balls, too?"

He laughed. "A time or two, love. Nymphs are fickle creatures."

"I hope there's another reason you popped in," I said. I shimmied out of my khakis and put on the black pants. "I have to get to the Underworld in a few."

"We vampires owe you a debt for rescuing Shamhat and Amahté."

"Yeah. I was just the meal, Ruadan. I should be glaring down at you from the Fields of Offerings right now."

"I would've never sent you in if I hadn't thought you'd survive."

"I remember that night you glamoured me, so I wouldn't remember how my mother died. Or what I was. You always knew that one day I would be here, releasing your ancient vampires." I put on the black T-shirt. "You knew the ambrosia wasn't there, didn't you?"

"We couldn't put the very last portion of the food of the gods in the same place as our Ancients. Seemed a dangerous thing to do."

"You're avoiding. You blocked the memories of my mother's death. My grandfather knew you. He was on a lot of digs in the Sudan looking for your Ancients. And you knew about that whole unicorn thing."

He watched me shuck off the hiking boots and sit down to pull the black combat boots on. "We had to protect you, Moira. Your secret needed to stay a secret. You truly are the last of your kind."

I tied the boot strings into tight loops. "So my mother died because she was a unicorn? And my father was a raving lunatic, apparently."

"Unicorns were shape-shifters, Moira. They were unique even among the unique. Beautiful creatures."

"I heard they were hunted to extinction because their blood and their horns were so awesome."

"That's true as well. People and paranormals can be real bastards." He watched as I tightened the loops on the other boot. "Your mother was the last unicorn, Moira. And before her, your grandmother, Camille."

"And my father?" I couldn't keep the bitterness out of my tone.

"Your mother didn't know her heritage, either. She loved unicorn mythology, though. When she was a little girl, she saw your grandmother in her unicorn form, and that sparked something inside her."

"Why wouldn't my grandparents just tell her?"

"They wanted to protect her. Only pure-bloods can shift, and your grandfather was a human. Regina had the blood, yes, but not the abilities. And neither do you. But you were asking about your father. Regina went to China to join a famous professor, Dr. Cecil Brannigan. He was the foremost authority about the Ki-lin. Chinese unicorns—long extinct. But he knew about your mother . . . about her unicorn blood."

"How? If it was such a big secret, how did he know that?"

"That answer I do not have. After he seduced your mother, he managed to keep up the ruse of love for a while. Then she discovered the truth about his intentions. They fought, and she left. He fell off a cliff, and she thought him dead." He smiled at me. "My mother and I helped deliver you into the world. You could say I'm your godfather."

"You delivered me?"

"Regina insisted. She knew about the paranormal world, but not her own heritage . . . until her grandparents revealed it. After she came back from China pregnant and scared. Your grandmother used her magic to place a powerful protection spell around you two. In case . . . well, she thought Dr. Brannigan was dead. And after your grandmother passed away, her magic did, too."

Ruadan, the Father of all vampires, considered himself my godfather. He'd delivered me into the world, and five years later, he'd wiped my memory of my mother's murder. And nearly thirty years after that, he made sure, somehow, that I would find and unlock the pyramid. "I'm a unicorn."

"Yes." Ruadan smiled at me. "You're not crazy. When you hit puberty, your body was trying to shift. Trying to become unicorn. Your mind couldn't grasp what your body was trying to do. It appears that neither you nor Regina has the shape-shifting ability."

"My grandmother could, though."

"Yes."

I was silent, and Ruadan stood there watching and waiting, while I absorbed all this information about my family, about my so-called destiny, about my sanity.

I was in a rage. The world had gone dark inside my mind, and I was . . . I tore up my room. I destroyed it all, and my grandparents were there. They couldn't reach me. Not even her, the one like me. Ax was there, too. He lived with us while he was attending college, and I liked him. He was big and strong and he let me cuss in front of him. And he gave me a beer once. I thought he was so cool.

"I tried to kill myself," I said softly. "I slashed my wrists, and I ran toward the window. I was bleeding and wailing and I had every intention of throwing myself out of my bedroom window. I was on the third story. Ax stopped me. He grabbed me and held on. He just . . . held on."

"I'm sorry, love," said Ruadan. "You've had a terrible time of it, I know. At least you don't have to worry about someone cutting off your horn. But your blood . . . well, that's plenty magical."

"You knew that," I said. "And you used Drake's parents to send me a message. You knew I wouldn't die."

"Not everything can be done straight on," he said. "No one can know you're a unicorn."

"And why did you send Drake in with me? Did you know about the . . . um, last part, too?"

"I may have," he said.

Incorrigible bastard. "Well, Shamhat and Amahté know. And Drake knows, too."

"Ah. Well, don't worry about that now," said Ruadan. "Just don't confide in anyone else. It's the only way to protect you."

"I'm not going to take out an announcement in the *Post* or anything." I thought about Doriana, who'd seen that I was in trouble and intervened. And I thought about my grandfather knowing about parakind. "So, there are all kinds of people, or whatever, watching over me . . . but they don't know I'm a fabled creature?"

"They're honoring the debt of service owed to your grandparents. They have no idea they're keeping an eye on the world's very last unicorn."

"How will I ever go back to that life?" I asked him. "I'll never stop looking over my shoulder. Not ever."

"You never know where you'll find your destiny." He gathered me into his arms and gave me a hug. I hadn't expected this move at all. It was so fatherly of him. It made me miss my grandfather, and because of that, I hugged him back. Even though I kinda wanted to punch him, too. "Go, Moira. Get the ambrosia. Save your darlin' Dove. Everything else will work out." He winked at me, but the friendly gesture wasn't enough to wipe the sadness from his gaze. "Did you ever look over your shoulder before?"

"No, not really. There's something to be said for blissful ignorance."

"Well, then. Maybe if you had, you would've seen a certain werewolf watching out for your lovely ass."

"You really do like talking in circles, don't you?"

"I'm Irish," he said. "Getting to the point isn't our style."

"Try this time."

"Drake," he said. "He's been watching out for you since the Sudan."

"Did you forget the part where I was kidnapped by Karn?"

"Drake had been tossed into a sewer and left for dead. He's been pissed at himself ever since for letting you down."

I thought back to the night of the gala, which seemed like eight thousand years ago, when I'd been so disturbed by something in the parking lot. One of Karn's goons had been tracking me, and Drake had gotten hurt trying to protect me. He seemed to do that a lot.

"Drake was yours even then, Moira. Love always find its way. Be worthy."

Exactly the words I'd heard when I opened the pyramid. My jaw dropped. "Was that you?"

He laughed, and then he disappeared, gold sparkles trailing in his wake. Ruadan was wily. I had no doubt he was harboring information, secrets, and God knew what else. Keeping it all from me. From everyone.

"Moira?"

Drake's voice filtered through the trees.

I stuffed my clothes into the duffel bag, and zipped it up. "Yeah?" I called back.

He stepped between two trees, his gaze traversing the area. "Are you ready?"

"Yes," I said.

His gaze swept over me. Then he suddenly grabbed my arm, yanked me into his embrace, and kissed me. It was ravenous, this kiss. He plundered my hair with his hands as his tongue stroked mine.

He pulled away just as suddenly, his eyes dilated, his lips swollen from mating with mine.

"We are not over," he said.

"No," I said just as fiercely, "we are not."

He gave me one of his wicked grins. "Glad that's settled, *Liebling*." He gave me a quick kiss. "Let's go to the Underworld."

Chapter 26

We stood in the field, and Amahté placed his
thumb on our foreheads: mine, Drake's, Ax's,
and Larsa's. As soon as we all had the all-important
pass to the Underworld, Amahté strode a few feet
away, lifted his arms in a wide arc, and shouted some
words in his ancient language.

A slit of darkness formed, the wink of a god's eye,
and then it slowly opened into an oval. We joined
Amahté, and I looked into the portal and sighed. Nothing but darkness. No discernible shapes, no hint of
sound, and certainly no yellow brick road. Going into
the black of supposedly nothingness was turning into
the theme of my life.

Ax saluted us, gave us a give-'em-hell grin, and
stepped inside. Larsa gave her mom and Amahté a

quick hug, and then she stepped into the portal without hesitation. Drake kissed me, winked, and said in that luscious German-tinted voice, "After you, my beauty."

I grinned at him. Then, I, too, stepped into the breach of the beyond.

As soon as I had entered, the Underworld formed around me.

It was a dance club.

I shit you not.

The Underworld, or at least this part of it, was a get-your-groove-on, booming-beat, neon-splattered, crammed-bodies-undulating par-*tay*.

Wow. Anyone who'd ever written about the Underworld had gotten it way, way wrong.

Larsa and Ax stood less than a foot away, pushing at the jostling dancers, trying to maintain a perimeter. I felt Drake's arm snake around my waist, and pull me close.

"Where do we go?" I shouted.

"Anywhere you want, sweet cheeks."

The chocolate-smooth male voice did not belong to Drake. Eep! I pushed out of the embrace and whirled around. The . . . um, demon, I supposed, shot me a sex-me-up smile. His skin looked like it was made from red leather, and his eyes were completely, totally black. His head was free of hair, which really made me focus on the two black horns curving out of his forehead. He was dressed in shiny, tight black pants, black cowboy boots, and a bone white shirt open to the belly button. He left the shirt open to show off a multitude of gold chains.

He grabbed his horns and stroked them. "You like what you see, babe?"

"Sorry," I said, caught somewhere between a laugh and a scream, "I'm with someone."

"Who?"

"Him," I said, pointing behind his shoulder.

He turned to look, just in time to get a fist full of werewolf fury. The demon, or whatever, went down like a pile of whipped cream, which kinda surprised me. I'd thought demons were more bad-ass. But no, red guy slid to the floor and lay there like a sad Mob reject. Drake stepped over him and said, "You are mine."

"So long as I'm not his," I said, ignoring the thrill caused by Drake's words. I know, I know. The feminist in me should probably protest the male-ownership angle, *blah, blah, blah*. But instead, I decided to like it. Because you know what? Drake was mine, too.

"If you're done flirting, Moira," said Ax from behind us, "we should probably go."

Ax took the lead. Larsa followed him, and I followed her. Drake stayed behind me. Ax was an expert at making a path through the gyrating crowd of supernatural beings. He had no problem shoving the creatures aside, and they didn't seem to take offense.

I wasn't sure if Ax knew where he was going or if he

was just trying to get to a place where we could have conversation to decide the next course of action.

The place seemed endless. The farther we went, the more frenzied the dancers, the louder the music, and the more dizzying the multicolored strobe lights.

"There!" shouted Ax. He pointed to a large metal door. Above it was an EXIT sign.

Amahté told us to stay on the path, that it would be revealed to us when we entered the Underworld, and we would be safe so long as we didn't veer off it. Well, safe-ish. So was the club somehow the path? Or would going through the EXIT door take us to the path? And where was the ambrosia?

Ax pushed the long metal bar, and the door opened outward.

"Fuck!" Ax jumped back, and the door slammed shut. He looked at us over his shoulder. "Everything's on fire out there," he said. "That's definitely not the way."

We all gathered into a tight little circle.

"We should look for another exit," said Ax. "There are probably several. My guess is that only one of them leads to the ambrosia." He grimaced. "Splitting up isn't an option. Even if one of us found the right door, there'd be no way to tell the others."

"This is going to take forever," said Larsa. "It's good that time is not the same here as it is on the earthly plane."

"What are we talking about, gang?" Red leather

arms slinked around mine and Larsa's necks. The demon with the horns and the terrible taste in clothing poked his head into our huddle. "You didn't try going out that door, did you? Because you don't have on enough sunscreen." He snort-laughed, and then gave me a come-hither look. "Stick with me, kitten. I'll show you what you want."

Larsa and I shoved him off at the same time, and he stumbled backward, smacking into the backside of a huge green-skinned dude wearing a fur kilt and red boots. It was at least eight feet tall. The creature turned around, grabbed the demon by the throat, and tossed him. The demon sailed over the dancers, and plopped like a big red rock into their midst.

The creature looked at us, and snarled.

"We don't even know that guy," said Ax. "We're leaving, all right?"

Once again Ax led the way, and Larsa followed. Drake snagged my hand, and this time he followed Larsa, keeping a tight grip on me as we once again wound through the crowd. We got bumped on all sides, but managed to stay together.

Ax led us to another door. This one was a plain wooden door. A sign above it said, RESTROOMS.

Ax was slightly more circumspect when opening this door. He took one quick look and backed away, gagging. "No. Fuck, no."

I didn't even want to know what he'd seen, and neither did anyone else. Frustration burned through me. Damn it.

It wasn't like I'd had any idea what the Underworld would be like, not really, but trying to navigate through a paranormal rave hadn't even been on the list of expectations.

Ax wheeled around and started another push through the boogying Boogey Men. We reached another wall, another door—this one had peeling paint and what looked like bullet holes in it. Above it was the sign OFFICE.

"Oh, I wouldn't go in there," said a familiar voice. Red arms slipped around my waist and pulled me close. "The manager doesn't like unexpected visitors." I looked up into the face of the really persistent and idiotic demon. "Hi, there," he said, wiggling his eyebrows.

The growl made us look at Drake. He curved his lips in a feral smile. "Take your hands off her, or I will remove your arms. Permanently."

The demon let me go, stepped back and lifted his hands up in a gesture of surrender. Drake grasped my hand and pulled me behind him.

"You need a Xanax, my friend." The demon reached into his trouser pocket and pulled out a prescription bottle. "You want?" He looked Drake over. "Oh, right. Medicine doesn't work on werewolves." His gaze moved over Larsa. "And the undead are stress-free enough." He grinned at me. "How about you, kitten? You look like you could use a chill pill."

"Will you go away?" I was supremely irritated with

this asshole. What was his deal? Everyone else in the place was ignoring us.

The demon actually looked hurt. "Amahté didn't mention you were all such party poopers." He sighed. "Look, I know I owe him for that whole Thira thing. Now, those Minoans, they know how to party." He looked at us and tsked. "Unlike you."

"Wait," I said, fascinated despite everything. "You're responsible for the volcanic explosion on Santorini?"

His expression turned sheepish. "My little shindig got a weensy bit out of hand . . . and well, we blew up the island. It happens, you know."

We all stared at him, and he stared back.

"What?" he asked. "Do I have brimstone on my face?"

"Who the fuck are you?" asked Drake, sounding exasperated and pissed off.

"Oh! I'm sorry. I should've introduced myself." He offered his hand. "My name is Path."

Chapter 27

"Amahté could've mentioned that we should be looking for some*one* instead of some*thing*," said Ax.

"Oh, don't blame him. He never knows what form I'm going to take," said Path. Since no one had taken him up on the handshake offer, he withdrew his hand. "So, gang! Let's go get us some ambrosia!" He rubbed his hands together. "Ready?"

I said, "For wh—"

Blink. Blink. Boom!

"—at?" I finished.

We stood on a hillside. All around us were verdant, rolling hills. Above us was a light purple sky dotted with fluffy silver clouds. And on top of the hill in front of us was a single golden tree, its branches curving up to the sky like a dozen prayerful hands. It had no leaves at all. On a single limb about midway up was a single golden fruit about the same size and shape as a plum.

The ground around the tree's base was blackened, as though it had been scorched, though the tree itself looked untouched.

Path saw the direction of my gaze and nodded. "You would not believe how many have tried to get that last piece of ambrosia." He rolled his eyes. "Such a kerfuffle!"

"And why can't they get it?" asked Larsa.

"Oh, the tree won't allow it. You see, Anubis gifted one of the fruits to Amahté for his service—right before that whole thing with Shamhat. But once a god has gifted ambrosia, it's an unbreakable promise. He couldn't take it back. Of course, the tree had more fruit on it three millennia ago. Anyhoodles! When Amahté gave it to you, his claim on the ambrosia ended." He glanced up at the tree. "You're the only who can touch it now."

"And by touch it," I said, "you mean I have to climb up there and pluck it."

"That's what *she* said." Path snort-laughed. He slapped his thigh. "Oh, I kill myself."

"If only you would," muttered Larsa.

I studied the trunk, noting that it was completely smooth. Trying to climb it would be like trying to shimmy up glass. Damn.

We all walked up the hill. When we came within two

feet of the tree, I kept going, but everyone else acted like they had walked facefirst into a wall. A round of cursing and rubbing of noses occurred.

"Keep going, kitten," encouraged Path. He'd known to stop about two steps before the others. Perverse son of a bitch.

"I really have to climb this thing?" I walked around the base of the tree, and studied it some more. No footholds, no knots that I could grab onto.

"I think it would be very entertaining if you tried," said Path. "But you could just ask the tree for it."

"Ask . . . the tree." I looked at Path, and he nodded.

What the hell, right? I stood under the branch, my gaze on that fruit. It was Dove's life hanging up there. "Hi," I said. "I'm Moira. May I please have my ambrosia?"

For a moment, nothing happened, and I began to wonder if Path had been fucking with me just to see if I would ask a magic tree for its magic fruit.

Then the limb with the ambrosia on it slowly lowered until the branch was at my eye level. "Thank you," I said. And I grabbed the fruit and pulled it off the tree.

"Okay, kids, let's skedaddle." Path looked at me, offering me another skeezy smile, and before I could tell him to knock it off—

Blink. Blink. Boom!

We stood at the location where we'd entered the Underworld. The party continued, and I wondered if it ever stopped. Probably not.

"I wish I could say it had been fun, kids," said Path. "But I really can't. Good luck with . . . well, whatever." Path wiggled his fingers at us, and then turned, slipping into the crowd.

"Moira."

I turned at the sound of Drake's voice, and saw that the portal had opened. Drake went first, then me, Larsa, and Ax.

On the other side, in the same field that we had left, Amahté and Shamhat waited for us, along with Gabriel, Braddock, and Darrius.

"You have the ambrosia?" asked Gabriel. He sounded anxious.

"Yes, and before you get any ideas, I'm the only one who can touch or use it." I showed him the fruit. "And I'm using it to save Dove."

Gabriel lifted a moon white eyebrow. "You mistake my intentions. Patsy made a promise. And her promise is mine as well."

"Good," I said. "Shall we go kick some vampire ass?"

"What a bastard. Holing up in my house!"

We were crouched in the back garden. Ten feet away were the French doors that led to an informal entertaining area.

"You call this a house?" asked Larsa. "This place has its own zip code."

Team One of the Save Dove and Patsy effort consisted of me, Drake, Larsa, and Gabriel. Other teams lead by Braddock, Patrick, and Darrius were surrounding the house at various locations. I knew only what our goal was: Get to Dove and Patsy. I believed the goal of everyone else was to kill as many bad guys as possible before dawn.

"Do you know if my staff is okay?" I asked.

"I'm sorry," said Gabriel. "We have to assume there have been human casualties."

Meaning, the vampires had probably snacked on the people who'd been in my employ for years. Guilt scraped me like rusty razors. I had never thought to protect them. It had never occurred to me that Karn would make an assault on my house! Damn, damn, damn.

We waited.

Then we saw the first flash bomb.

We all had guns, and they were loaded with special bullets designed to maim vampires. We stood up from our hiding place, crouched low, and ran down the concrete path to the doors. One swift, brutal kick from Drake busted them wide open.

And the three bullets from his gun took down the vampire coming for us. Larsa decapitated him with her sword.

We moved on.

The consensus was that Karn had holed up in the basement with his prisoners simply because it was the safest place to be, and because he knew he held the trump card so long as he had Dove and Patsy (mostly Patsy from the paranormal perspective).

While the Broken Heart teams fought with Karn's minions, we made our way to the kitchen—to the door that led to my basement.

The door was open, and the invitation—or rather the demand—was clear.

Karn expected us. And he no doubt thought he had his bases covered. I really wanted to punch him in the throat.

What? We've established my unicorn anger issues.

"Shit," said Larsa. She gestured for us to split up and take either side of the doorway. Drake and I took one side. Larsa and Gabriel took the other. Then Drake and Larsa craned their necks to peer down the lighted stairwell.

"Oh, do come down," called Karn. "We have so much to talk about."

"I really hate him," I said.

"I heard that, Moira," he singsonged. "It's not a good way to begin negotiations for your darling Dove's life."

Drake swung around and started down the stairs.

Karn yelled, "Drop your weapons down the stairs first. All of them."

Drake stopped, and shared a look of frustration with me. Everyone grimaced, but we began the toss-down of guns, swords, daggers, and every other piece of dangerous equipment that we had attached to our persons.

Eventually the rain of weaponry ended, and we heard the sounds of everything being gathered.

"Impressive," said Karn. "Come down now."

Drake moved down the staircase; then I, Larsa, and Gabriel followed. We had no idea what we were in for, but what else could we do? Dove was depending on me. I'd be damned if Karn won.

The basement was well lit. This part was walled off, a storage area used for party supplies. Other parts of the basement had other uses, but I wasn't sure about the setup. Mr. Keyter handled that. Honestly, I didn't think I'd ever really had cause to be in the basement. I made a mental note to have Mr. Keyter vampire-proof everything once we'd dealt with Karn. If the house was still standing and all—and if Mr. Keyter was still alive.

Rescue now, guilt later, I told myself.

Patsy was manacled to the wall, her mouth duct-taped. Her entire body vibrated with fury, and when she saw Gabriel, the look in her eyes was a blend of relief and fear.

Dove lay on a table, looking too pale and shatteringly vulnerable.

A knot clogged my throat.

"She's alive," said Karn. "Mostly."

He sat on a folding chair. Two other vampires were in the room, too. One near Patsy and one near Dove. I couldn't believe that Karn wouldn't stack the undead favor in his odds, so I was sure other vampires lurked down here as well, hidden in the shadows and crevices.

My suspicions were correct. As we gathered in a semi-circle near Karn, several vampires appeared behind us.

Fear slicked my spine and made my stomach spin.

"You are such a clever one, Moira. I knew you were the key to getting to the ambrosia. Ah, but you didn't kill the Ancients, did you?" He wagged his finger at me. "Somehow I knew you wouldn't. You're stubborn. But that is, of course, part of the nature of your kind." He slipped a hand into his jacket and brought out the white blade that had ended the lives of my parents. "I've never seen one before. No one has . . . not in several lifetimes." He held up the blade by the beaten copper handle. "Unicorn horn." He shook his head. "Amazing."

"I have no idea what you're talking about," I said. "Unicorns aren't real."

Karn laughed. "Just like vampires and werewolves aren't real?" He offered me a smarmy grin. "Mr. Keyter knew your secret. I had to steal the memories from his mind because he was, unfortunately, terribly uncooperative. A tragedy, since good help is so hard to find."

"Bastard." The word caught in my throat, snagged on the edges of my grief. I might as well have killed Mr. Keyter. He'd been my great and wonderful friend.

"Unicorn tears are so shimmery. Like little diamonds. But not, I bet, as potent as your blood." He tucked the blade back into his jacket.

"Give me Dove."

"I'm afraid that's as close to her as you'll get." He

glanced at Gabriel. "We all know the real prize is your wife. She's precious to us all, isn't she? If she dies, we all do." He turned his gaze to me. "The ambrosia, Dr. Jameson."

"Sure." I took the golden fruit from the pocket of my cargo pants and tossed it at him.

He caught it . . . for a second. Then it disappeared.

It reappeared in my hand. I looked down at the ambrosia. "Sorry. I guess it doesn't like you."

"I am not stupid, Moira. I know you must gift it to me." He stood up, and seemed to disappear himself. But he'd actually used his preternatural speed to get to Dove. He flashed his fangs at us, then leaned down and pierced her throat.

"No!" I moved toward him, but the vampire behind me grabbed my arm and yanked me backward. "Stop, goddamn you!"

Karn reared up, giving us a bloody smile. "She tastes so sweet."

"Give her to me," I said. "And I'll gift you the ambrosia."

"No," hissed Larsa. "The ambrosia will make Karn invincible! It is better to sacrifice one human so that the world does not burn."

"Fuck that," I said.

Karn laughed. "Delightful." He took a handkerchief from his pants pocket and wiped his mouth. "Fine. Come get her."

I didn't hesitate. I rushed to the table and gathered

Dove into my arms. She was so small, so slight. I picked her up and took her to Larsa. She looked surprised as I handed over my friend, but I mouthed, "Go."

She understood instantly. And disappeared in a shower of sparkles.

"You think anyone else matters now?" asked Karn. "I'm getting bored. The ambrosia, Moira."

He couldn't take it from me, but he could hurt my loved ones until I relinquished it. He knew it, and I knew it. What he didn't know what that I'd had a private conversation with Gabriel. And I knew, thanks to Theodora's books, that vampire mates had telepathy. Karn had to know the same thing, but despite his brilliant psychopathic nature, he was too fucking arrogant to believe he wouldn't win the day. The problem with people who knew they were smart is that they constantly underestimated everyone else.

I plucked the ambrosia from my pocket and held it up on my palm. Karn's greedy gaze took on a razor-sharp focus.

"I gift the ambrosia to . . . Gabriel Marchand."

"What! No!" Karn's cry of outrage echoed in the basement. Karn disappeared in a shower of red sparkles. Coward.

The fruit disappeared from my hand and reappeared in Gabriel's. He took a huge bite, half the fruit, and swallowed it. Gold light encompassed him, so suddenly and so brightly, I had to look away. The vampires behind us screamed, and exploded into dust.

When the light dissipated, Gabriel had already moved to Patsy and ripped off her manacles. She removed the tape from her mouth. Drake and I hurried forward, going into a protection stance in front of the couple.

"I gift the ambrosia to Patsy Marchand."

The half-eaten fruit appeared in her hand, and she ate the rest in two bites.

The golden light surrounded her, too, blinding us all for a few seconds.

I had just made two werewolf-vampires unkillable immortals.

And I hoped I hadn't traded Dove's life to do it.

When the bright light dissipated again, Karn flickered into being before me. His eyes were crazed with rage. The thin veneer of civilization had been stripped away. "You take from me, you bitch, and I'll take from you."

I shoved Drake out of the way, and he was so startled by my sudden move, he actually stumbled out of the path of the blade.

Karn embedded the dagger to the hilt into my side.

Shock waves of pain ricocheted through me, and I fell to my knees, gasping. I felt the blood rise in my throat, and I choked on it.

"Noooo!" Drake's cry of outrage vibrated within me, filled with pain and grief.

Oh, shit. I was dying.

Karn whirled to meet the werewolf's attack, but he

couldn't defeat Drake in full fury. Drake knocked the bastard to the ground and wrenched off his head with his bare hands.

Karn turned to dust.

Honestly? Slightly anticlimactic. Except for me getting stabbed. That was an unexpected twist to the story.

"Moira." Drake dropped to his knees, tears in his eyes.

"I . . . th-think . . ." Pushing the words out of my mouth was such a trial. I felt so cold now, and my mouth felt stiff. My vision was graying, but the pain was receding. I lifted a trembling hand to his cheek. "Love. You."

Then I died.

Chapter 28

"Mr. Keyter is a vampire," said the woman. "I am not . . . in case you were wondering. Brigid saved me, and she tried to save you, but . . . well, you're being stubborn."

The voice was familiar . . . and yet not. That voice seemed to be missing something.

Sarcasm.

I searched my memory banks for something to attach to that voice. *Dove.*

She was alive.

Relief flowed through me.

"Anyway. For some reason, Mr. Keyter had sent the staff out for the evening. Isn't that odd? No one else got hurt, Moira, so you can stop worrying. I thought you would like to know that the household staff is fine—

because you're you, and you feel insanely responsible for anyone who gets inside your orbit.

"Oh, yes. You should know two things about Mr. Keyter. One, he is an excellent vampire. Two, he was a closet nudist. He fits in extremely well at the vampire senior citizens community. He visits you, too. I just hope he hasn't regaled you with that story about him and Mrs. Stoffenblatz in the hot tub. It was so TMI." The voice paused. "P.S., I have not forgiven you for being brave and saving the werewolf you love. It was entirely selfish. You really need to work on those little personality flaws of yours." I felt fingertips on my shoulder and the brush of lips over my forehead. Then that voice whispered in my ear, "Those witches make excellent cheesecake. And if you don't wake up, Moira, I will eat all of it. Every crumb."

When I opened my eyes, I was sitting at a school desk. I recognized the room well enough. My mother's classroom in Building A. But I had no fear, no panic.

I knew my truth now, my heritage, and the reason my mother died.

For me.

For our family secret.

"You're tryin' much too hard to be dead," said a pleasant Irish male voice. Ruadan sparkled into being, and looked super-casual in jeans, T-shirt, and black Converses, for an ethereal visit. He leaned against the big square desk. "When my mother can't fully heal you, there's a problem. And it's you. If you're wondering, Karn didn't get you with the unicorn blade. I switched out the real blade for a fake one ages ago. The real one is protected and where no being can get at it. I promise."

"Good. I don't ever want to see it again." I sighed and looked around the room. No ghosts here. "I would prefer to not be dead."

"Are you sure?" He glanced around the room. "You picked an odd spot to hide your soul in."

"I'm hiding?"

"'Twould seem to be the case." He eyed me. "Maybe you're lookin' for closure." He gazed toward the classroom's doorway.

My mother entered. She wore a blue summer dress and strappy sandals. And her red hair was pulled into a ponytail. She looked young, younger than I was now, and she was beautiful. Just as I remembered. Somewhere in my very adult mind was the excited wonderment of my five-year-old self. *Mommy was alive!* I was out of and around my desk in a flash, flinging myself into her open arms.

"I'm sorry, so sorry, for all that you've been through." She pulled back and placed her hand against my cheek. "I wanted to be with you, to raise you, and to introduce you to our heritage. I wanted things to be different for you. My parents meant well . . . but they let fear drive their choices. I don't know if learning about being a unicorn would've changed things, sweetheart. I don't think so." She smiled. "Don't be afraid anymore, Moira."

"It's really you?" I asked. "I'm not just . . . hallucinating?"

"You are not crazy," she said fiercely. "Stop thinking like that. And throw those pills away. You don't need them. Besides, you have him, don't you?"

My heart skipped a beat. "Drake."

"Oh, yes. Love is so wondrous. So worthwhile." She let go of me and stepped back. "He's waiting for you."

"Mom—"

"I love you, Moira. But you have a life to live. Now, go. Be happy, babe." She smiled at me, a smile full of love and promises and hope and the world. Then she turned and walked through the doorway. As she passed through it, the dark weight of my fear, my life-long companion, the awful thing I carried around and treated like a monstrous friend . . . lifted from me . . . and shattered . . . and then it was all cosmic dust.

I was free.

Ruadan put his hand on my shoulder. "Go home, Moira. 'Tis time."

My eyes opened to a semi-lighted room. I was tucked into a comfortable single bed, the sheets and thin comforter pulled tight against me. I heard a rhythmic *beep beep beep* sound that was both alarming and comforting.

It took a few seconds for me to adjust to the fact I was awake and I was in a hospital room. Also something heavy was pinned against my thigh. I looked down and found Drake sitting in a chair as close to my bed as possible, his head and shoulders resting on me.

I lifted my hand, noted the IV attached there, and placed my hand on his head.

He woke.

"Moira." He sat up, looking exhausted and like he hadn't shaved in a while. He stared at me, drinking in my features, and his lips lifted into a ghost of a wicked grin. "You said you loved me."

"I do," I said.

"I love you, too."

"Glad that's settled."

"Me, too." He gingerly crawled onto the bed, on the other side, where my arm wasn't impeded by an IV drip, and gathered me into his arms. "I thought you were lost to me. And without you, I could see no future."

"Does it matter that I'm a unicorn and you're a werewolf?"

"No," he said. "But we will have to talk about winters in New York."

I laughed.

He tucked my head under his chin, and I pressed against his solid, warm chest, listening to the beat of his heart.

Sacrifice.

Love.

Always.

Epilogue

I stood in the doorway of my own campus office and watched my new personal assistant and chief ass kicker at work.

"Stop bullshitting me," said Dove into her headset. She plopped her booted feet onto my mahogany desk. "Get me the paperwork by tomorrow or you can kiss funding for your program good-bye." She cocked her head and listened to what was surely a stream of blustery disapproval. "Oh, yeah? Well, just try that and see what it gets you. And dead is not an excuse. Trust me." She pushed a button on the headpiece attached to her ear and eyed me from her position behind my desk. "What are you doing here?"

"Glowing with pride," I said, pretending to wipe a

tear from my eye. "I bet whoever you just pounded into the ground is still bleeding."

"I learned from the best." Dove's gaze went over my shoulder and I turned to see Doriana standing behind me, her spindly arms on her hips.

"Sea urchins," she said. "We must have the research funding. It's imperative—"

"Whatever you want," I said. I looked at Dove. "Right, Dove?"

"Anyone who has punched Karn in the face has my approval," she said. She shooed me away. "Don't you have a mysterious and lengthy trip to take?" She waved Doriana inside. "I have a blank check, sister, and I'm not afraid to use it."

Doriana flashed me a quicksilver smile. "Excuse me." She paused. "There's a werewolf lurking down the hall. They can be quite brutish, dear. Be careful."

"Oh, I will." I waved at Dove, and then I turned and hurried toward my brute of a werewolf. "Everything's fine. She's kicking administration ass like a pro."

"We should get going."

Our trip would begin in Germany, at the castle home of Drake's brother and his family. Then we were headed to a dig site in Belize, and after that . . . well, who knew? Dove would be my eyes and ears at the college until I returned. Staying off the radar was not just about the honeymoon, but about protection. We weren't sure who knew about my unicorn blood, and who might want it. There were, unfortunately, a lot more Karns out there.

So, we'd stay off the grid and with each other. And that was fine by me.

Drake brought me in close for a soft, sweet kiss. Then he moved back and offered his arm. "Ready, my beauty?"

I took his arm. "Yes," I said. "I'm ready."

And I was.

THE BROKEN HEART TURN-BLOODS

*Jessica Matthews: Widow (first husband, Richard). Mother to Bryan and Jenny, and to adopted son, Rich Jr. Stay-at-home mom. Vampire of Family Ruadan. Mated to Patrick O'Halloran.

Charlene Mason: *Deceased.* Mistress of Richard Matthews. Mother to Rich Jr. Receptionist for insurance company. Vampire of Family Ruadan.

Linda Beauchamp: Divorced (first husband, Earl). Mother to MaryBeth. Nail technician. Vampire of Family Koschei. Mated to Dr. Stan Michaels.

MaryBeth Beauchamp: Nanny to Marchand triplets. Vampire of Family Ruadan. Mated to Rand.

*Evangeline LeRoy: Mother to Tamara. Teacher at night school and colibrarian of Broken Heart and Consortium archives. Vampire of Family Koschei. Mated to Lorcan O'Halloran.

Patricia "Patsy" Donovan: Divorced (first husband, Sean). Mother to Wilson, and to *loup de sang* triplets. Former beautician. Queen of vampires and *loup de sang*. Vampire of Family Amahté. Mated to Gabriel Marchand.

Ralph Genessa: Widowed (first wife, Teresa). Father to twins Michael and Stephen, and to daughter Cassandra. Dragon handler. Vampire of Family Hua Mu Lan. Mated to half dragon Libby Monroe.

Simone Sweet: Widowed (first husband, Jacob). Mother to Glory. Mechanic. Vampire of Family Velthur. Mated to Braddock Hayes.

*Phoebe Allen: Divorced (first husband, Jackson Tate). Mother to Daniel. Comanages The Knight's Inn in Tulsa. Vampire of Family Durga. Mated to Connor Ballard.

Darlene Clark: *Deceased.* Divorced (first husband, Jason Clark*). Mother to Marissa. Operated Internet scrapbooking business. Vampire of Family Durga.

*Elizabeth Bretton née Silverstone: Widowed (first husband, Henry). Stepmother to Venice. Socialite and jewelry maker. Vampire of Family Zela. Mated to werejaguar Tez Jones.

---

*Direct descendents of the five families who founded Broken Heart: the McCrees, the LeRoys, the Silverstones, the Allens, and the Clarks.

GLOSSARY 1

a stóirín: My little darling

a thaisce: My dear/darling/treasure

aiteacht: Inexplicable sense of thing or place that is not right

bard: Poet-druid (see: *Filí*). Storyteller and singer of Celtic tribes

céardsearc: First love/beloved one

damnú air: Damn it

deamhan fola: Blood devil

draíocht: Magic

droch fola: Bad or evil blood

druid: The philosopher, teacher, and judge of Celtic tribes

Filí: (Old Irish) Poet-druid (see: *Bard*)

Go dtachta an diabhal thú: May the devil choke you (Irish curse)

Is minic a bhris béal duine a shrón: Many a time a man's mouth broke his nose

Leamhán sléibhe: A Wych Elm (the only species of Elm native to Ireland)

mo chroi: My heart

Ná glac pioc comhairle gan comhairle ban: Never take advice without a woman's guidance

Níl neart air: (lit. There is no power in it) There is no helping it

Ovate: Healer-druid; healer and seer of Celtic tribes

Solas: Light

Sonuachar: Soul mate

Súmaire Fola: Bloodsucker

Tír na Marbh: Land of the Dead

Titim gan éirí ort: May you fall without rising (Irish curse)

OTHER WORDS/TERMS

Centurion/Centurio: Professional officer in the Roman army in charge of a century, or *centuria*, of men

Century/Centuria: Group of 60 to 160 men in the Roman infantry led by a centurion

Durriken: Romany boy's name that means "he who forecasts"

Fac fortia et patere: Latin for "Do brave deeds and endure"

Gadjikane: Romany for "non-Gypsy"

Muló: Romany for "living dead"

Roma: Member of nomadic people originating in Northern India; gypsies considered as a group (Also the term used for cousins of full-blood lycanthropes who can only shift during a full moon and who hunt rogue vampires)

Romany/Romani: The language of the Roma

Strigoi mort: Term for Romanian vampire

GLOSSARY 2

Ancient: Refers to one of the original eight vampires. The very first vampire was Ruadan, who is the biological father of Patrick and Lorcan. Several centuries ago, Ruadan and his sons took on the last name of O'Halloran, which means "stranger from overseas."

banning: (see: *World Between Worlds*) Any one can be sent into limbo, but the spell must be cast by an Ancient or a being with powerful magic. No one can be released from banning until they feel true remorse for their evil acts. This happens rarely, which means banning is not done lightly.

binding: When vampires have consummation sex (with any person or creature), they're bound together for a hundred years. This was the Ancients' solution to keep vamps from sexual intercourse while blood-taking. There are only two known instances of breaking a binding.

Consortium: More than five hundred years ago, Patrick and Lorcan O'Halloran created the Consortium to figure out ways that parakind could make the world a better place for all beings. Many sudden leaps in human medicine and technology are because of the Consortium's work.

Convocation: Five neutral, immortal beings given the responsibility of keeping the balance between Light and Dark.

donors: Mortals who serve as sustenance for vampires. The Consortium screens and hires humans to be food sources. Donors are paid well and given living quarters. Not all vampires follow the guidelines created by the Consortium for feeding. A mortal may have been a donor without ever realizing it.

Drone: Mortals who do the bidding of their vampire Masters. The most famous was Renfield—drone to Dracula. The Consortium's code of ethics forbids the use of drones, but plenty of vampires still use them.

ETAC: The Ethics and Technology Assessment Commission is the public face of this covert government agency. In its program, soldier volunteers have undergone surgical procedures to implant nanobyte technology, which enhances strength, intelligence, sensory perception, and healing. Volunteers are trained in use of technological weapons and defense mechanisms so advanced, it's rumored they come from a certain section of Area 51. Their mission is to remove, by any means necessary, paranormal targets named as domestic threats.

Family: Every vampire can be traced to the one of the eight Ancients. The Ancients are divided into the Eight Sacred Sects, also known as the Families. The Families are: Ruadan, Koschei (aka Romanov), Hua Mu Lan, Durga, Zela, Amahté, Shamhat, and Velthur. Please note: At this time only one known vampire of the Family Shamhat exists.

gone to ground: When vampires secure places where they can lie undisturbed for centuries, they "go to ground." Usually they let someone know where they are located, but the resting locations of many vampires are unknown. Both the Ancients Amahté and Shamhat have gone to ground for more than three thousand years. Their locations have yet to be discovered.

Invisi-shield: Using technology stolen from ETAC and ancient magic, the Consortium created a shield that not only makes the town invisible to outsiders, but also creates a force field. No one can get into the town's borders unless their DNA signature is recognized by both the technology and magical elements.

loup de sang: Translated as "blood wolf." The first of these vampire-werewolves were triplets born after their lycanthrope mother was drained and killed by a vampire. For nearly two centuries, Gabriel Marchand was the only known *loup de sang* and also known as "the outcast." (See: *Vedere Prophecy*) Now the *loup de sang* include his brother, Ren, his sister, Anise, his wife, Patsy, and his children.

lycanthropes: Also called lycans and/or werewolves. Full-bloods can shift from human into wolf at will. Lycans have been around a long time and originate in Germany. Their numbers are small because they don't have many females, and most children born have a fifty percent chance of living to the age of one.

Master: Most Master vampires are hundreds of years old and have had many successful Turnings. Masters show Turn-bloods how to survive as a vampire. A Turn-blood has the protection of the Family (see: *Family* or *Sacred Sects*) to which their Master belongs.

PRIS: Paranormal Research and Investigation Services. Cofounded by Theodora and her husband, Elmore Monroe. Its primary mission is to document supernatural phenomena and conduct cryptozoological studies.

Roma: The Roma are cousins to full-blooded lycanthropes. They can change only on the night of a full moon. Just as full-blooded lycanthropes are raised to protect vampires, the Roma are raised to hunt vampires.

soul shifter: A supernatural being with the ability to absorb the souls of any mortal or immortal. The shifter has the ability to assume any of the forms she's absorbed. Only one is known to exist, the woman known as Ash, who works as a "balance keeper" for the Convocation.

Taint: The Black Plague for vampires, which makes vampires insane as their body deteriorates. The origins of the Taint were traced to demon poison. After many attempts to find a cure, which included transfusions of royal lycanthrope blood, a permanent cure has been found.

Turn-blood: A human who's been recently Turned into a vampire. If you're less than a century old, you're a Turn-blood.

Turning: Vampires perpetuate the species by Turning humans. Unfortunately, only one in about ten humans actually makes the transition.

Vedere prophecy: Astria Vedere predicted that in the twenty-first century a vampire queen would rule both vampires and lycans, and would also end the ruling power of the Ancients. This prophecy was circumvented by a newer proclamation that the lycan crown prince would take a mate and rebuild his pack. Please note: Patsy was granted only seven powers out of the eight. No one is sure why.

World Between Worlds: The place between this plane and the next, where there is a void. Some beings can slip back and forth between this "veil."

Wraiths: Rogue vampires who banded together to dominate both vampires and humans. Since the defeat of the Ancients Koschei and Durga, they are believed to be defunct.

Read on for a peek at the very first book
in Michele Bardsley's
Broken Heart series,

I'M THE VAMPIRE, THAT'S WHY

Now available in eBook!

The night I died, I was wrestling a garbage can to the
curb.

I had a perfectly healthy fourteen-year-old son, who
should have taken out the garbage after dinner, but he,
and let me quote him directly here, "forgot."

Every Sunday and Wednesday night we had the
same conversation, usually five minutes after he crawled
into bed. Here's the script:

Enter the Mother into the Pit of Despair. I refuse to
walk more than a foot into the Pit because I'm afraid a
radiated tentacle might emerge from a gooey pile of papers and clothes and drag me, screaming and clutching
at the faded carpet, into the smells-like-lima-beans clut-

ter. I open the door, try not to inhale any noxious boy-room fumes, and delicately scoot one Keds-protected foot inside. *Cue dialogue.*

"G'night, honey. And, Bry? Did you take out the garbage?"

"Oops."

"It's twice a week. It's your only chore. I pay you ten bucks every Friday morning to do it."

"It's a heinous chore."

"I know. That's why I pay *you* to do it."

"Sorry, Mom. I forgot."

At this point in the twice-weekly argument, variations occurred. Sometimes, Bryan faked snores until I went away, sometimes he actually fell asleep mid-lecture, and sometimes he whined about how his nine-year-old sister, Jenny, didn't do chores, and I still paid *her* five dollars every Friday morning.

So, yet again, just after ten p.m. on a Wednesday night, I found myself pulling first one, then the second thirty-gallon garbage can down the driveway, and trying to align the grimy plastic containers near, but not off, the curb. Do *not* get me started on sloppy, lid-flinging, half-trash-dumping garbagemen who are extraordinarily picky about the definition of "curbside pickup."

When huge, hairy hands grabbed my shoulders and heaved me across the street and into Mrs. Ryerson's prized rosebushes, I didn't have time to scream, much less panic. The whatever-it-was leapt upon me and ripped open my neck, snuffling and snarling as it sucked at the bleeding wound.

Good God. What sort of man-creature could hold a grown woman down like a Great Dane and gnaw on her like a favorite chew toy? It slurped and slurped and slurped . . . until the excruciating pain (and, honey, I've suffered through labor *twice*) faded into a feeling of weightlessness. I felt very floaty, like my body had turned into mist, or like that time in college when I took a hit of acid and had the "Tinkerbell" episode. I knew that if I just let go, I'd rise into the night sky and free myself from gravity . . . from responsibility . . . from Bryan and Jenny.

Just thinking about my kids slammed me down to earth. My husband had passed away a little more than a year ago in a car accident. Don't feel too sorry for me, though. I was in the middle of divorcing the son of a bitch.

I couldn't scream. I couldn't lift my arms. I couldn't open my eyes. But I felt my body again, every aching, pain-throbbing inch of it. The heavy, smelly thing pressing my limp body into thorny branches and noisily smacking against my throat grunted and rolled off. Dry grass crunched and leaves rattled as it moved, growling and groaning like a well-fed coyote. I didn't flicker an eyelid for fear it would try for a killing blow, though if the state of my neck wound was as bad as I thought, I was dead anyway. Then I heard the sounds of bare feet slapping against pavement and realized the thing was running away. Fast.

I don't remember how I disentangled my sorry self from the bushes. I have vague memories of the roses' too sweet scent as I crawled across the street and collapsed near my knocked-over garbage cans.

For those who know me, meeting my end amid muttered curses and spilled refuse was not a great shock. But, shock or not, it was still a crappy way to go.

Some people believe that dying ends all possibilities of humiliation.

Not so.

When I awoke, I wasn't standing at the pearly gates of heaven. Well, not unless the religious definition of "pearly gates" was way, *way* off base.

I was latched onto the velvety inside of a muscular male thigh, my teeth embedded in the flesh near his groin, my mouth soaked with warm, very tasty liquid.

No, the man was not wearing pants. Hell, he wasn't wearing underwear. Who am I kidding? The man didn't have on a stitch of clothing.

I wish I could say that the embarrassment of my cheek brushing against his testicles outweighed my need to suck his blood—and yeah, I know, *ew*—but it was like . . . it was like . . . a half-off sale at Pottery Barn. No, better. It was like eating, without gastrointestinal or caloric consequences, a two-pound box of Godiva's champagne truffles. No, no . . . like . . . oh God, like *finally* fitting into that pair of skinny jeans that taunts every woman from the back of her closet.

Uh-huh. *Now* you know the ecstasy I'm talking about.

After another minute or two of sucking on the stranger's thigh, I felt firm, long fingers under my chin.

"That's enough, love," said an Irish-tinted voice. "You're healed now."

With great reluctance, I allowed the fingers cupping my jaw to disengage me from the yummy thigh. I sat up, licking my lips to get every dribble of blood *(ew, again)* smeared on my mouth.

"Where am I? What happened? Where are my kids?"

"Ssshhh. Everything will be explained." He tilted his head, looking me over in a way that caused heat to skitter in my stomach. "Your children are fine. Damian is watchin' them."

Damian? Who the fuck was Damian? Whoa, girl. Deep breath in. Deep breath out. Well, crud. The whole breath thing wasn't working. I didn't even want to think about my lack of heartbeat. I had to stay calm. I focused on the room and realized I could see everything clearly. What the hell? I had been relying on glasses to see past my nose for almost ten years. With this kind of vision, I probably could see all the way to Canada.

"So . . . with all the, uh, blood-sucking, I'm guessing I'm a vampire now." Just saying "I'm" and "vampire" together was so ridiculous, I wanted to giggle.

"Yes. We Irish vampires call ourselves *deamhan fhola.*" He grinned at me. "It means blood demon."

"Oh. Well, that's certainly . . . descriptive." In a bad, yucky, soulless way.

We were in a small white room. It had a long, uncomfortable steel slab sticking out from the wall and we were on it. About six feet from the steel slab on the left side of the room was a door without any visible knob or handle. I looked down at myself. I was in a white hospital gown and I smelled like antiseptic.

I was a vampire.

Jessica Anne Matthews. Vampire.

The stupid giggle erupted and I nearly snorted and snarfed myself into a seizure. "Me. A vampire."

"Yes." The guy who'd been my lifesaving snack was leaning against the wall, his knees drawn up slightly. Raven black hair feathered away from his face, the ends of it curling on his shoulders. He watched me with the strangest eyes I'd ever seen. He looked like Pierce Brosnan in his *Remington Steele* days, except for the color of those eyes. "With eyes like the sea after a storm," I muttered, quoting one of my favorite lines from *The Princess Bride*. Those strange eyes were an ever-changing silver that seemed to eddy and swirl like a fast-rising river.

Given his size, my guess was that he was just about six feet tall. He was muscular and trim like an athlete, rather than bulky like a gym freak, with a light dusting of black hair on his chest and thighs.

I might've been delirious or crazy or dreaming, but I checked out his package. It was impressive, too. From a patch of black hair sprang a large erection. His testicles tightened underneath my blatant scrutiny and I remembered the soft feel of his balls against my cheek as I suckled his flesh just inches from his groin. His gaze dropped to his penis, his lips curving upward as his eyes met mine again. He seemed to ask, "Want a ride, little girl?"

And you know what? I did. *I wanted a ride.* I hadn't had sex in eighteen months. Sessions with the battery-operated boyfriend did not count. The last man I trusted to touch me, to bring me pleasure, had betrayed sixteen years of marriage by doing the same lovely, naughty things to another, younger woman. Then, before I could seek proper revenge, he had gotten killed in a car accident. I always thought it had been a mundane way to go for a man who had ripped out my heart and then stomped it to bloody bits with his cloven hooves.

But I digress.

"Do not have sex with Mr. O'Halloran." The command echoed around the room. Even with my new vision, I couldn't spot the speakers.

The Pierce Brosnan look-alike rolled his eyes. "She fed on me like I was the last Twinkie in the box. A little thanks might be in order."

"If you have sex with Mr. O'Halloran," said the voice, obviously unimpressed, "you will be mated to him for the next hundred years."